BODYGUARD BEAST

GEORGIA LE CARRE

D1313089

ACKNOWLEDGMENTS

Many, many thanks to:

Leanore Elliott
Elizabeth Burns
Nichola Rhead
Kirstine Moran
Tracy Gray

Bodyguard Beast

Copyright © 2020 by Georgia Le Carre

ISBN: 978-1-910575-66-6

CHAPTER 1

ANGELO

https://www.youtube.com/watch?v=YxvBPH4sArQ
-Staying Alive-

*M*y hands and feet were bound by plastic ties as I swam through the silent, blue water, alone and totally at peace with myself. I'd made countless laps up and down the pool. I had about ten minutes left before I finished my full hour. Suddenly, I sensed movement above. It was way past midnight and much too late for any member of the family to be wandering about. It could be Security.

Regardless, it was an annoying interruption to my training.

Silently, I maneuvered myself to the bottom of the pool. Bouncing on the toes of my tied feet, I launched myself upwards until I broke water. The indoor pool space was dark, illuminated only by the distant lamps of the compound coming through the floor length windows. I saw a girl I'd never seen before, making her way towards the lounge chairs. I couldn't see her clearly, because she held her phone in front of her face, but it could only be one person … the boss's daughter, just returned from her education overseas.

Her ears were plugged with air-pods, as she hadn't turned on the lights upon her entrance, so I deduced that like me, she wanted to be alone. I accepted the fact my time in the pool was over and started to swim towards the other end of the pool when she screamed.

The scream was followed by the sound of water splashing.

Through my goggles, I watched her flailing underwater.

She was actually trying to catch her phone, but it evaded her grasp and sank to the bottom. She obviously wasn't a good swimmer because she immediately struggled up to the surface and started clinging to the edge of the pool. "Hey you!" she yelled. "Can you help me please?"

My first thought was to ignore her. I had no time for spoilt little girls, but she was the boss's daughter, and I sure as hell didn't need that kind of trouble. I swam towards her and stopped a wary foot away.

I'd heard the rumors that she was a looker, but it came as a shock to see how insanely beautiful she was. Seeing was indeed believing. The lights in the floor of the pool turned her eyes to an almost unreal green. Like a doll's eyes. They were set wide apart and fringed with long, wet lashes. I wondered how she would look while she was climaxing, then caught myself mid-thought.

What the fuck is wrong with you?

Yes, she was heartbreakingly beautiful, but I wasn't into shallow, selfie-taking, narcissistic, manipulative Cleopatra types who needed a bunch of servants just to get dressed. And even if I was, lusting after the boss's daughter was a bad, bad idea. It usually meant ending up in an unmarked grave in a field somewhere. Nope. Not for me. I turned away from her.

"My phone," she gasped. "Please help me get it back or it's going to be ruined."

I paused. This was the deepest part of the pool and it would be quite a feat to get my face to touch the bottom. To soothe my sour mood, I accepted her request as part of my training for the night, and dove back into the water. With my teeth, I gripped the phone and swam back towards the surface. With a swing of my head, I flung the device out of the pool.

Sucking in a lungful of air, I began to head towards the steps. On the edge was a knife. Retrieving it with my teeth, I dropped it into the water, and dove down after it. A few seconds later, the ties around my wrists and ankles had been cut off and I was free. I pulled myself out of the pool to head towards the changing rooms.

"Hey!" she called out. "Aren't you going to help me?"

I could hear the irritation in the Princess' voice. I didn't bother turning around. She would eventually get herself out of the pool. She was the boss's daughter, after all.

CHAPTER 2

SIENNA

https://www.youtube.com/watch?v=UtvmTu4zAMg
-Mr Vain-

*H*ow rude! How unbelievably rude!

I could hardly believe what that man just did. First, he held my phone between his teeth as if he was some kind of animal, then he flung it out of the water straight onto the tiled floor. If it hadn't been damaged by the water, that would definitely have done it. Even more unbelievable, was the way he callously abandoned me when all I was asking for was a bit of help getting out of the deep end of the pool.

I watched him walk towards the changing rooms, water sluicing down impressive broad shoulders and the gleaming slabs of tight muscles in his back. Water slipped over the skin-tight briefs which left almost nothing to the imagination. The cheeks of his butt were firm and round. The water ran down those muscular, thick thighs as he took long and sure strides. As I watched in a daze of shock, he lifted his powerful hands and raked his fingers through his raven hair.

He looked like a big, wet Greek God, but he had to be one of my father's guards. They frequently used this indoor pool for their training sessions. The outdoor one was designated for leisure and entertainment and used solely by the family, but I hadn't felt like battling mosquitoes, and had headed here. As a result, I'd clearly interrupted his training session, almost given myself a heart attack, and doubtless destroyed my phone.

He'd been so quiet as he swam through the water that I hadn't seen him. When I entered and when he had come into my peripheral vision, I'd mistaken him for a corpse floating on the surface. The shock made me slip off the edge and fall in the water.

It was a sheer miracle I hadn't broken several teeth.

In fact, I had bloodied my elbows and they stung as I clung on to the edge of the pool and made my way back to the shallow end. I could swim, but I'd always avoided the deeper parts. For some inexplicable reason, I had an irrational fear of deep water. When at the shallow end, I could swim like a fish, but I felt an unexplainable terror overwhelm me when my feet couldn't touch the bottom.

Maybe I'd been dropped into deep water and suffered trauma when I was too young to remember, or maybe it was a memory from a past life, but the fear was real. Hanging on the edge of the pool, I treaded water and pulled myself along until I got to the shallow end. As soon as I knew my feet were only about two feet from the bottom, I let go and swam to the steps, then pulled myself out of the water.

I sat on cool tiles as I realized even my air-pods were lost. And it had all been his fault. If he hadn't startled me. If he hadn't treated me like he was pure and I was some infectious disease. Who did he think he was anyway? Asshole. Hell, I could have had a panic attack and died in the water.

Brushing my hair out of my face, I jumped to my feet and marched towards the men's changing room. Without knocking, I barged in. "Hey!" I called out. "Hey!"

No response came.

I stopped to listen and heard water running, so I immediately headed towards it and found him in a stall.

I pounded noisily on the door. "Hey!"

I was fuming, my chest nearly about to explode with anger. "How could you just leave me there? I could have died."

The arrogant brute didn't respond.

"There's something called basic human decency, you know. Like helping someone when they're in need, especially when you're the cause of their almost death in the first freaking place." I kicked at the door to the stall.

The cascade of water ceased and I froze. No doubt, he expected me to run off, but I stood my ground and waited, ready to give him a piece of my mind the moment he came out.

True enough, the door to the stall was pushed open and he appeared.

"You owe me an apology—" I began but the next words, whatever I had planned to say, were snatched out of my head.

6

He stood there naked.

I was a civilized person and I had assumed wrongly that he would be as well - believing he would emerge with a towel wrapped around his waist, but instead - he had deliberately appeared naked.

I pulled my jaw off the floor and shot my shocked gaze up to his face. Wow, without the goggles, he carried the blue-green Caribbean ocean in his eyes.

He stared at me with an irritated expression as if I was a nuisance he could do without. He then took a step towards me.

I instinctively took a few steps backwards.

It gave him the space he needed to turn left and walk away from me.

It took a few seconds before I recovered enough to get my brain working again. A feat, given what I'd just seen.

The man was hung like a damn horse!

I'd followed the tanned muscles of his torso, partitioned into perfectly, proportionate slabs and still glistening with the steam from his shower and down there, shadowed with a dusting of dark hair across the top of his groin was his cock. Half-raised as if in arousal, but it'd probably just been the stimulation from the shower. Not that I would know much about that.

Either way, the slightly paler shaft had been beyond impressive. It made me shiver to think of how it would look … and feel, when fully erect.

He hadn't seemed even a little bit concerned about exposing himself to a complete stranger, and I knew then what his problem was … he was completely shameless. If he thought he could embarrass me into not speaking my mind because he'd flashed me, he had another thing coming. I marched after him.

I found him seated on one of the benches in the locker room.

Thankfully, he was already covered in dark briefs. The arrogant stud didn't even turn around to acknowledge my presence.

"You're one of the bodyguards, aren't you?"

He remained silent as he rose to his feet and began to rummage through his locker.

I went on, "If you are, then you must know who I am. Why didn't you help me?"

Silence.

I didn't want to be that insufferable bitch no one liked, but I had already pursued the matter this far and my pride needed a response. "I can report this," I threatened. "And there's no way it's not going to get you in trouble."

He slammed the locker door shut.

I couldn't help but jump.

"Sure," he finally spoke. "Report that you couldn't do something as basic as get yourself out of the pool. Such incompetency would no doubt make your father proud."

I felt astounded. Robbed of speech, all I could do was stare as he dressed himself. First, came his jeans, then he carelessly pulled a dark tee over his head. He grabbed his bag and without looking at me, he headed out.

I recovered from my daze and jumped in front of him.

He stopped at the sudden ambush, a slight frown tugging at his brows.

Hell, up this close, he was really handsome with an aristocratic Roman nose, sensuous lips, and of course, those eyes. Those wonderful aquamarine eyes. It made me wonder why I hadn't seen him around, and I began to doubt he was even one of the bodyguards who resided in the compound. I couldn't imagine one of my father's employees being so rude to the family. But if he wasn't a bodyguard, who the hell was he?

"Apologize," I said fiercely. "And then I'll let this go."

"Why do I owe you an apology?"

"You should have helped me."

He shrugged those powerful shoulders. "I'm not obligated to do anything without your father's instruction. And I did retrieve your phone."

"Which you broke!" I accused. "You flung it on the tiles."

"I don't have time for this," he said impatiently. "Get out of my way!"

"No, I'm not moving until you apologize."

"Then you're going to be here a very long time," he drawled.

"What's your name?" I demanded, getting exasperated. "Because I'm not going to let this go."

He took a step towards me.

It took everything I had not to move back. I folded my arms defiantly across my chest, suddenly aware I was half-naked before him, and the movements had brought my breasts together to create a not-inconsiderable cleavage.

But his eyes didn't stray. Not one bit. He was totally uninterested in my charms. "Angelo Barone," he replied. "That's my name. Off you go, little brat. Go and do your worst."

I actually felt too shocked to respond.

He stepped around me and walked away.

Speechless, I turned to watch him leave.

What an asshole!!!!

CHAPTER 3

SIENNA

"Gemma, are you familiar with the bodyguards?" I asked.

Gemma had been with our family for so long, there were pictures of her holding me as a one-day old baby. She had come from Sicily to work as a maid when she was eighteen years old. Slowly, she had risen in rank to become housekeeper. Then when she turned forty, my mother hired another housekeeper to take over almost all of her duties and made her head housekeeper, her only job was to oversee. Now she was more family than staff.

"Not really. Bodyguards don't come under my jurisdiction," she replied absently. "Why do you ask?"

"Uh, I was wondering if you knew one of them. A man called Angelo Barone."

"Barone? No, I don't think so. He might be one of the new boys. Why don't you ask your father?" she murmured, wrapping the last section of my hair around the curling iron. A smile remained on her face as she ran her fingers through the wavy mass she had already completed. She exhaled a sigh of satisfaction. "You look like a Princess, Sienna."

"Me, a Princess? I'm a tomboy, remember?" I grinned at the reflection in the mirror at her. She really was more like family than staff.

"Not anymore. You're a beautiful woman now." She released my hair from the iron, and fluffed out the thick soft waves of hair down my back. "I can still remember that time you found a pair of scissors and gave yourself a haircut. Huge chunks gone. In some places, all that was left was buzz. Your mother was furious. 'You look like a boy,' she scolded. 'But that's exactly how I want to look,' you replied, thoroughly pleased with your efforts." She paused, a smile on her face. "Four years old you were then. You were so adorable I could have popped you between two slices of bread and eaten you. Ah, time does fly away so fast."

"You know, I remember that day. The look on your face when you found me in the bathroom shearing away at my hair. You were so horrified."

She nodded. "I was. You could have cut off your ears. The way you were snipping away."

"You took a bit of flak for that, didn't you?"

"Nah, nothing your mother said could have been worse than what I told myself. You were my baby."

I placed my hand over hers on my shoulder, my gaze filled with the deep love and gratitude I felt for her. I wished I could tell her she'd been more of a mother to me than my glamorous socialite mother, but I couldn't betray my mom so I just said, "And you were my second mother, Gemma. Thank you, Gemma. For everything."

"Don't let your mother hear that. It'll make her jealous," she said heartily.

I laughed. "Don't worry. It'll be our secret."

She joined me in laughter before she announced, "Alright, we are finished." She moved away to switch off the curling iron.

"Funny you should bring that incident up, because I've been thinking of cutting my hair," I mentioned, as I went to my bed to pick up the satin, knee length dress I had chosen earlier.

"To what length?" she asked, taking a seat on the stool of the vanity I'd just vacated.

"About here." I placed the tips of my fingers on my shoulders.

Her eyes widened in horror. Then she smacked her thigh and rose dramatically to her feet. "No! Don't do that. Beautiful, thick, waist-length hair is a rarity these days."

"I need a change, Gemma," I said, as I slipped off my robe.

"Moving back home from London is already a very big change. Leave your hair alone. Every time I look at it, I envy you. Just look at mine." She leaned down so I could inspect the thin layer of hair on the crown of her head. "I tell you, there is very little difference left these days between Anderson and I."

The expression on her face and the incongruous idea that there might be very little difference between her dramatic, colorful self - and our terribly stoic and now almost bald English butler - made me laugh so much, I ended up falling on the bed with the dress tangled around my legs. "You're one crazy woman, you know," I gasped, wiping the tears from the corners of my eyes. I never really realized just how much I missed being with someone I completely trusted. Someone who would never betray me no matter how much money was on the table.

"I'm serious," she said, coming to sit on the bed next to me. "As the years go by, I begin to think we're starting to look alike, no?"

When I was younger I'd watched *Remains of the Day* and always imagined Gemma Cannizaro and James Anderson as the characters that played the part of the butler and house-keeper. I'd been sure there was hidden yearning there - but more than two decades later - they were both single and showed no intention of ever leaving my parents' home. To the best of my knowledge, Gemma was still a virgin. Some-times I sensed the sadness in her smile, and always tried my best to behave as if I was the daughter she never had.

"Well, I've got news for you. You look absolutely nothing like James." I rose from the bed and pulled my dress up over my body, thank God, it was one of those materials that never creased.

Gemma stood up. I turned around, and she zipped my dress up for me. Then I turned back to face her. "Do you know I always thought you guys would marry one day."

"So did I."

Her answer surprised me. "So … you *were* in love with him," I whispered in awe.

She smiled, but sadness showed in her eyes. "Yes."

I sat heavily on the bed. "What happened?"

She shrugged. "Nothing. He just wasn't interested in me. It was all on my side."

"You mean you asked him and he said no?" I gasped incredulously.

"Of course not," she replied immediately. "I'm not that bold, but he had his chances. More than a few and he didn't take them. Anyway that was another lifetime ago. We are both old now."

"You're forty-two. That's not old. Haven't you heard, life begins at fifty."

"His pee-pee is probably all wrinkled and soft by now, anyway," she muttered with a scowl.

I giggled. "I could tell you how to get it hard again."

She looked scandalized. "How would you know? Have you been with a boy?"

"No," I admitted, "but I've done some reading and I've watched some movies."

She grinned naughtily. "Ah, dirty movies. I've watched a few of those in my younger days and all I learned is that plumbers have very big pee-pees."

I laughed, but didn't tell her porn was no longer cheesy sketches about plumbers with big pee-pees. It had become an altogether different animal. I moved to put on the pair of blood red Christian Louboutin's I had selected for the evening.

Immediately, Gemma got on her knees to help me.

I caught her hand. "Don't do that," I told her softly, "I can put my own shoes on, Gemma."

"I know that. I just wanted to help you."

"The way you can help me is to sit on the bed and entertain me while I put my own shoes on."

Amused, she sat on my bed and watched me. "Haven't you had any boyfriends at all after these years abroad?"

A bundle of memories instantly came to mind, none of which I particularly wanted to revisit, so I just gave her a summary, "Not really. There was no one that I really clicked with. Somehow, it was never right. I could never imagine any of their pee-pees inside my body."

"You'll find someone. Someone who deserves a beautiful soul like you," she said softly.

When I was done with the shoes, I stood and walked towards the full-length mirror.

Gemma clapped her hands with sheer delight. "I love the cut of that dress," she said.

"It's beautiful," I agreed, turning and looking over my shoulder to inspect the back of the dress. A perfect fit. The cream material had an off-shoulder neckline while cinched at the waist. The skirt was cut to swirl gently around my knees.

I sprayed perfume into the air and walked into it a few times, then turned towards her. "All done," I announced.

"Sei Bellissima, amore mio," she complimented in Italian.

You are very beautiful, my love. It had been a long time since I heard that. I felt my cheeks heat. I walked up to her and kissed her cheek. "You know, I love you, right."

"I know," she whispered.

A brief knock came on the door. We both turned as it was immediately pushed open.

My mom appeared in a stunning, form fitting floor-length black gown. Her dark hair had been pulled into a chignon at the back of her head, and pearl earrings adorned her ear lobes. As beautiful as a movie star, no one could imagine she was my mother. "You're ready," she said. "Finally! Everyone is waiting. They can't wait to meet you. And Gemma, Nonna needs you." She waved her hand in the air. "She was complaining about her stomach. Apparently, only you can help."

"On my way, Senora," Gemma replied and immediately left the room.

My mom came up to me and critically inspected me. "Turn around," she ordered.

Obediently, I twirled for her.

"Gorgeous," she approved. "All eyes will be on you. Let's go."

"I really don't understand why eyes need to be on me," I grumbled.

"Don't be silly," she said as she dragged me along. "These are your friends and family, and they haven't seen you since you were a little girl."

"I'm pretty sure I won't know more than five people down there. They're your friends and family."

She stopped. "Are you going to be grumpy about this?"

"No," I groaned. My mother and I didn't see eye to eye. I would never be able to understand the need for throwing a banquet to welcome a nobody back home.

But since I had returned for good, I couldn't pick a fight and not be haunted by it for weeks because my mom actually could keep a grudge for that long. I always had London to escape back to when my holidays came to an end. But for now, I needed to keep the peace as much as I could.

If I let my mother have her way for now, it wouldn't count as a strike against me in the future. I had a list of difficult requests I wanted granted later. Things she wouldn't like. Things she didn't consider women should be doing.

CHAPTER 4

SIENNA

*T*he party was held in the foyer, an expansive glistening area that could have passed for a mini ballroom. Exquisite marble columns, black and white granite floor, crystal chandeliers, and the grand piano by one corner, made the area a perfect hosting space.

When we reached the top of the stairs, I looked down and the base of the dramatically sweeping staircase was filled with elegantly dressed, chatting people holding flutes of champagne.

Families and friends, I was told they were, although I couldn't pick out a single familiar face. I had been away too long. First boarding school, then college. It had been my father's way of protecting me and keeping me out of the way. Once he realized my mother could bear no more children, I became precious to him. I was just about to descend one side of the dramatic winding staircase, when I realized my mother had halted at the top.

"Aren't you coming?" I asked.

She shook her head. "Go ahead. I want you to make an entrance. All of the spotlight needs to solely be on you."

It took all of the restraint I had not to roll my eyes at her or argue with her. This was exactly the kind of thing I hated. I was no society belle and this kind of attention would probably just make me trip and fall. But the window for protesting had closed as some of the guests had already began to notice me. I let out a sigh of resignation, and with my head held high, I began my careful descent. The prospect of falling and breaking my bones seemed very real.

"Sienna! Darling!" a high shrill voice called.

More people stopped their conversation as heads and eyes turned towards me.

I felt like an animal in a cage. There wasn't anything less necessary in the world than this. My preference would have been to take the elevator on the other side of the house and unobtrusively join the crowd.

The stairs seemed to go on forever, but finally I conquered the last step and felt the solidity of the black and white floor.

Bright, smiling faces closed around me.

I smiled back nervously as compliments and well wishes were showered on me.

"You look gorgeous!"

"Beautiful!"

"Welcome home, darling!"

"How proud your parents must be."

Of course, I didn't voice my feelings, but the extravagance and lavishness of their compliments repelled and horrified me. Was this how it would be from now on? I had thoroughly enjoyed my humble, anonymous existence in England and longed to have it back. More compliments were showered on me. I knew they weren't real. They were just paying homage to my father's power and money.

"You look so beautiful!"

"Welcome back, sweetie. You look amazing."

"You're not going to say hello to your Aunt Aldina?"

This particular Aunt I immediately recognized and I turned blindly towards her. I was pulled into a fleshy bear hug as her strong perfume of jasmine and spices filled my nostrils. Before I could recover, I was pulled away by another family member. Someone introduced me to cousins I hadn't seen in years. "Remember when you guys used to play naked in the pool."

I smiled.

They smiled, but we were all strangers to each other now.

"Next on the agenda is a grand wedding for Sienna," a woman's voice boomed.

I died a little inside, but outwardly, my smile didn't fade.

A waitress dressed in black with a frilly white apron came around with a silver tray full of champagne flutes.

I grabbed one and downed more than half the glass in one gulp. What an incredibly long night I had ahead of me.

A barrage of intrusive questions began. I should explain … Italians have no sense of personal space or privacy. I looked around for my mother to rescue me, but she seemed to have disappeared. I sucked it all up and made my way through the crowd. My eyes were firmly on the arch at the back of the room. As I got closer to escape, I began to move faster.

When I could bear it no more … I broke into a run.

Hurrying down the corridor, I pulled open the door of the kitchen, and stepped into the familiar space. It was bustling with activity. In the stark white of the massive space, I instantly spotted Gemma in her navy blue and white house-keeping uniform. She stood next to the massive island. Platters of food were spread across it.

There were about five waiters surrounding her, listening to her instructions.

I made my way over to her.

She turned and smiled. "What are you doing here?"

"Hiding."

"Come, come now. It's not that bad to be belle of the ball."

"Ugh … I hate it. I don't even know them and they're all obsessed with when I'm getting married."

She laughed. "Smile and they'll forget what they asked. You're *that* beautiful."

I reached for a mini bruschetta and popped it into my mouth. "Yeah, right," I muttered.

"Sienna, what are you doing here?"

My eyes widened as I heard my mother's voice. I picked up another bruschetta and turned. "Nothing. Just came for one of these."

She frowned. "Everyone's asking for you."

"Yeah?"

She took the tiny piece of garlic toast covered in chopped tomatoes and basil away from my hand then pushed me back out to a sea of smiling snakes. I tried to apply the advice Gemma had given me as the outright harassment continued. To my great surprise, it worked. All I had to do was just smile and nod.

"I suppose your father will be grooming you to run the family business now," a sly man I had never met before commented.

My smile slipped.

He stared at me curiously. "No?"

I swallowed audibly. What I wanted to say would have caused a riot in the room.

Thankfully, at that very moment, the attention shifted perceptibly to a different part of the room. The twittering crowd went silent.

My grandmother stood at the edge of the room. She looked as if she had come from a glamorous past long gone, perhaps from the court of one of the ancient ruling houses of Italy.

Although all eyes were on her, hers was solely on me.

I felt my tense body sag with relief. She had come to rescue me. She extended her hands towards me, and immediately the wall of people parted. With my head held high, I walked towards her. From the corner of my eye, I could see my mother scowling furiously, but like a guardian angel Nonna spirited me away from the madding crowd towards her apartment on the ground floor.

As soon as my back was to them, I stared while grinning from ear to ear. Only Nonna could have gotten away with such blatant rudeness.

CHAPTER 5

*M*y angel and I sat in her living room overlooking the rose garden while we played dealer's choice and drank cups of soothing chamomile tea. She had beaten me twice already and was enjoying every moment of her wins. I relished her victory with all of my heart.

"Nonna, every time I play this with you, it seems like you've gotten better."

"I do have a lot of time on my hands," she replied in her elegant voice, "and nothing to do but practice. Did your father ever tell you that he lost this house to me when we were playing in the spring?"

My mouth fell open. "You're joking. Did he really transfer the deed to you?"

"Not yet." She laughed.

"Will you? Accept it from him, I mean."

"Of course not, it was a friendly match. The only perk I'm interested in is the power to lord my ownership of the roof over his head. I do this whenever he gets out of line."

I revered her. No one but Nonna could say such a thing about my fearsome father. I lost any influence over him when I was two. He ruled over our household with an iron hand. Stand means stand. Sit means sit. "Next time you're playing with him, can you please win me his *Performante Spyder*? He's never let me touch it, but yet he doesn't use it himself either. What a waste."

She frowned. "What on earth would you do with that beast of a car?"

I grinned. "Drive it fast somewhere?"

She shook her head disapprovingly. "Young girls nowadays. The things you want to do …"

I raised an eyebrow. "Well?"

"No, I won't."

"Why?"

"Because you'll probably wrap it around a lamppost and kill yourself in the process," she stated, then revealed her cards.

Yet again, I lost! Severely. "Again?" I mock complained, when in actual fact I loved watching the twinkle in her eyes.

She held her chest as she cackled with laughter at my expression.

"Nonna, you're way too scary when you laugh like that."

"Like a hyena?" she asked, her voice filled with amusement.

I made a face. "Exactly."

We put the cards away when one of the maids brought a platter of fruit.

"What are your plans from here onwards?" she asked, picking up a slice of persimmon.

She was the first person to ask me this. Ever since I returned, I had featured inside everyone else's plans, but only she had asked me about *my* plan. About what *I* intended to do.

I leaned forward, and enveloped her in a hug.

"What's this for?" She laughed.

"Thank you," I said, "for all the calls and letters while I was in England. I kept every single letter you wrote."

She patted my back gently. "You're my baby. Why should you be thanking me for something like that? I don't thank you for writing back to me. I expect it. Now tell me what is really bothering you."

I pulled away from her. "I've always danced to everyone else's tunes. I've gone to school, I've gotten the degree, and now it seems I'm going to be pushed down the 'next step'. What I really want to do is try my hand at something I'm passionate about."

"For instance?"

I searched her eyes, for just an instant, I had a fear of being mocked. This would be the first time I told any member of my family about this. But in her eyes, I found only patience and pure love, so I took a deep breath and dove in, "For instance, I've always wanted to try my hand at something related to fashion … well, not fashion exactly, but shoes …

and since we're in LA perhaps even create a brand? Who knows?"

"Don't you have to learn that trade first?"

"I've done that already."

Her eyebrows flew upwards. "I thought you were studying economics and business administration."

"Yes, I was, but I took a course at the London College of Fashion. I paid for it myself and went to class every Saturday for a year. They taught us everything, the different leather, how to design, the machines we need. I've got a certificate, and my teacher said I have real talent for it. She said she would be happy to recommend me to any of the big fashion houses, but I told her I had to come back. I knew Papa would never allow it."

Before she could respond, a knock sounded on the door.

My father suddenly appeared. "Mama, it's time for dinner," he said, in that quiet voice of his.

My father was tall and commanding. Awe-inspiring, in fact. He had very dark, intense eyes, and thin lips often set in a hard, uncompromising line. Tonight, he wore a dark tuxedo, his gaze sharp as he assessed my appearance. He looked utterly aloof and unapproachable. "I heard you've been avoiding everyone," he said.

"Well, I did say hello to everyone," I replied.

"Hmm ... Bring your grandmother out." With a nod at Nonna, he turned around elegantly and exited the room.

Although Nonna was just sixty-nine and definitely did not need my help or assistance in walking, I did cling to her as a form of support. Amused, she allowed it. With her hand tapping a rhythm against mine, we walked out together and headed over to the grand dining room.

It was already filled with the guests.

CHAPTER 6

SIENNA

*S*uch a grand room, the ceilings painted with ancient images from Rome, marble statues, and three massive hanging chandeliers, giving off a warm golden light. To the right were extensive floor to ceiling doors and windows that allowed the scenic view of the estate's fountains, rolling lawns, and the gigantic old trees beyond.

The table, covered in pristine white linen, seemed much longer than I had remembered. It looked amazing with four tall candelabras adding a warm glow to the flower arrangements, crystal glasses, and gleaming silverware.

All around it sat guests, who regarded us curiously.

Nonna's seat was to the right of the head of the table, next to my father. I settled her in, then glanced at my mother who was seated to my father's left.

Her lips curled upwards in an approving smile.

I'd hoped the seat by her side or Nonna's would be left empty for me, but they were occupied by my uncle Piero, who was second in command to my father, and another person I didn't know.

"Take your seat by Fabio, Sienna," my mother said. "We're beginning now."

Fabio? Who the hell is that? Painfully conscious of the at least thirty pairs of eyes on me, I ran my gaze down the table, found the empty seat halfway down the table, and hurried over to it. I settled down and my napkin folded into a formal bishop's hat shape, was whisked open and spread neatly across my lap by a waiter who appeared behind me.

I murmured my thanks, then turned to the vaguely familiar woman on my right and smiled at her politely. "Hello."

"Sienna," she acknowledged with a nod.

I knew the person my mother actually wanted me to sit next to was on my right. Reluctantly, I turned to that person and stopped. His sharp, dark gaze, wide nose and thin lips, all instantly recognizable features of the Siciliana clan, made him seem familiar.

"Hello," I greeted.

He was actually good looking, that was, until his lips curved into a smug smile.

I immediately suspected he and I would not get on. When almost a whole minute passed and he still had not taken his gaze away from me, my prediction was confirmed.

The waiters began moving around, serving the first course, lobster bisque. I waited till mine had been placed in front of me, and when he still hadn't looked away, I squashed my irritation, and said in a light tone, "If you carry on like this, you're going to bore holes into me ..."

"You don't know who I am, do you?"

I turned to face him. "I apologize. I've been away for so long that everyone seems so changed. I'm still trying to familiarize myself with everything."

"You really don't remember me?" he asked incredulously. His voice rose louder than necessary and piqued the interest of the other guests.

I took a deep breath, my gaze on the finely chopped chives in the midst of my creamy soup. Then I turned to him again with a smile plastered across my face. "I do—"

"Then who am I?" he demanded aggressively.

I exhaled my growing anger through a breathy laugh. "If you had allowed me to finish you would have heard me say, I don't remember you, but you look very familiar."

Suddenly, he swung his gaze away from me and towards my mother. "Aunt Marzia," he bellowed.

The entire room's attention was arrested. Even my mother looked startled by his outburst.

I wanted to bury myself in the ground—actually, he was the one I wanted to bury. Arrogant, little prick. I wished I had the freedom to tell him to piss off. That I didn't give a damn who he was, but all I could do was maintain a serene smile. I didn't want to embarrass my parents like the idiot was doing.

"Aunt Marzia, Sienna doesn't know who I am?" he fired off in Italian.

I didn't miss the glance she gave my father before she let out a tinkling laugh and said, "That's your cousin Fabio, Sienna. Don't you remember? He used to come with us to Rosedale vineyard for the summer vacation. You used to ride bicycles together and play in the pool."

"Sienna," one of my other cousins who I actually remembered, spoke up from across the table. "Fabio used to chase you around with frogs from the fish pond."

"Ah," I exclaimed, as the reminder jacked an old forgotten memory to life. Fabio was an arrogant, entitled, idiot even then. I turned towards him with a smile. "I remember now. It's very nice to see you again."

He kept frowning. Apparently, this hadn't been the memory he wanted everyone to remember. "No worries. Henceforth, it'll be impossible to forget me," he boasted.

For a moment I almost asked what he meant by that but I caught myself. *Don't feed the troll, Sienna.* Praying he wouldn't speak to me again that night or preferably *ever*, I returned to my soup and took a spoonful. It tasted wonderfully fiery and smooth in my mouth.

"Fabio just graduated from a university in Edinburgh," my mother said. "Since both of you have similar educational experiences from the United Kingdom, I'm sure you'll have lots to talk about."

"Sure, Aunt Marzia," he replied, "but the rigors of a postgraduate degree are not to be spoken lightly of, or even compared to the minimal effort needed for an undergraduate degree. Even if we were in the same country, I doubt Sienna would be able to fathom the level of stress and demands that I had to endure."

Someone somewhere on the table snickered.

Oh my, what a colossal prick. I clenched my fork tightly. "You're right." I smiled. "We have absolutely nothing to talk about."

"What did you study, anyhow?" he asked.

"Economic and Business," I replied.

"Why did you waste your time and money on that?" he scoffed. "Those degrees are totally useless. Either you are business minded or not. You can't teach anyone to be an entrepreneur."

I hated to admit it, but he was right. My degree was useless. Those Saturday classes were by far more useful to me.

"It's a great thing then," he continued, thankfully his voice had dialed down to normal, "you won't be searching for a job with that dead-duck degree. A comfortable position should be waiting for you at one of our family's companies."

I gritted my teeth and tried to steer him away from the topic of me. "What did you study?"

"I got an MBA," he responded proudly. "It takes much more than common sense to manage the spread of businesses that our families run, so I couldn't just choose blindly."

The waiters came once again to retrieve our bowls and cutlery in preparation for the next course.

The moment the waiters walked away, he continued, "All is not lost though. The most important thing anyway is that you have an education. With that, you should be able to handle yourself in the years to come."

Thanks for that, Fabio. Very magnanimous of you. Seared duck breast with creamy potato dauphinoise and caramelized chicory was placed in front of me. I used the distraction as a valid reason for ignoring him, however he wasn't finished.

As he droned on, I stabbed my fork into the duck breast. I would never know how I sat through the rest of the meal, but by the time dessert arrived, I didn't even want to look at it. Which was a tragedy because the golden opulence sundae with its bean ice cream, gold dragnets, Drambuie soaked cherries, and truffles was absolutely gorgeous. I took a few mouthfuls while he enthused about something else he had accomplished.

As soon as my grandmother rose, I too got to my feet, and escaped from Fabio's braying voice.

CHAPTER 7

SIENNA

I couldn't however completely disappear, since the party was in my honor, so I made my way to the balcony overlooking the gardens. Thankfully, I was the only one there as the rest of our party had moved out of the house and spread out around the pool.

From where I stood, I could take it all in; the gentle breeze of the evening, the fire-eater, and the live Italian music which some of the guests were dancing to.

This was the perfect spot for me. I wasn't in the midst of the action, but at the same time, I wasn't too far away from it either, and this, I had come to realize, was my preference for the most part. I enjoyed solitude in big doses, and I suspected it was because I was an only child. My mother suffered a great deal during her pregnancy. She spent nearly five months in bed. So after I was born, the doctors told her having another child would not be a good idea. My mother wanted to try again because she was afraid my father might stray, but my father wouldn't hear of it. To prove he didn't want another child, he went and got himself a vasectomy.

Perhaps if I had been surrounded by siblings, I would have been a different kind of person.

It made me think of the handful of people I had come to call family back in England. Charlotte, Danny, and Christine. Christine's family also lived in Los Angeles, and she had returned home just as I had. We had both been busy settling in in the last few days, but we had agreed to call each other and plan some sort of meet up.

I'd considered inviting her to this homecoming dinner, but I'd changed my mind at the last minute, preferring to keep this extravagant part of my life a secret a little longer. She knew me as a conservative young lady from an ordinary family. She thought I was like her, my parents had saved up for years to send me for an overseas education.

My peace was interrupted when I sensed someone's approach.

I didn't turn around, hoping whoever it might be was only passing by, but of course, no such luck.

"Princess."

I gritted my teeth. It was once again, the grating, hoarse voice I'd had to listen to for the last hour. We didn't have an audience anymore, so there was no need for me to extend basic human courtesy anymore. I gave him a dry look. "My name is Sienna."

"I know what your name is," he said, a nauseating smile on his face.

"So why are you calling me princess, then?"

He came over to stand in front of me with a tumbler of what I presumed was whisky in his hand. He took a sip, before he fixed his gaze on me. "You're going to be feisty, aren't you? I should warn you I am not turned off at all by that."

I cringed at his words and took a step back from him, certain now something was very wrong with his brain. Never, had I met someone who was so inept at reading another human being. Could he really not tell I felt repulsed by him?

"I do admit though that when I heard you were returning, I didn't know what to expect. You certainly weren't a head turner back then. I didn't expect much to have changed. In fact, I was prepared for the worst but seeing you now … you have indeed come a very long way from the girl with the ugly haircut and buck teeth."

The reminder of my less than glamorous past would have made me smile, if not for the offensiveness of his gaze as it ran down my body. I cocked my head and gave him the same condescending once over. I'd met him seated and then been so upset with him I hadn't noticed his physical build, but now I realized he was solidly built, but he was shorter than me.

Perhaps if I took my heels off, we would be somewhat the same height, but that wasn't exactly good news for him since I was 5 feet and 5 inches tall. I told myself he was deserving of my sympathy. Perhaps his brutish and overbearing nature was him trying to make up for what he lacked in height.

"You're exactly the kind of woman I won't mind having in my bed. Curvy hips, full breasts, that fire in your eyes. You are quite the surprise dearest cousin. I definitely won't have any problems accepting the marriage proposal."

I'd been about to cut him down to size for his comments when his words stopped me. "Marriage proposal? What are you talking about?"

He studied me, surprised at my reaction. 'You're not aware?"

"Aware of what?"

"That we have been betrothed? This banquet was thrown as an unofficial introduction for us. You didn't actually believe that it was just to welcome you, did you?"

My blood stopped flowing through my veins. "You're joking?" I gasped in shock.

He chuckled as he drained his glass. "My darling Sienna," he said. "Our fathers have settled on a marriage between us, and I for one, very much look forward to our union."

His hand lifted and before my frozen body could react, it was already on my shoulder and caressing its way down the bare skin of my arm.

"Don't fucking touch me," I hissed, as I shoved his hand away.

He lost his grip on the glass and it fell to the stone floor, shattering with a loud sound.

It drew some attention from down below.

"Sienna?" I heard my mom call, but I was too furious and confused to respond.

"Sienna!"

"It's okay, Aunt Marzia, we're fine. I dropped my glass," Fabio explained.

"Sienna," my mom called once again.

Finally, I came back to my senses.

"Tell her you're fine," Fabio whispered through gritted teeth.

I could see the annoyance gathering like dark clouds on his face, but I couldn't have cared less. "I'm fine!" I called out angrily, and stormed off the balcony.

CHAPTER 8

SIENNA

"*H*e did what?" Charlotte exclaimed.

"Stood right in front of me. Completely naked," I repeated.

"You're joking!"

"I wish I was," I replied, grateful I was finally able to speak with my closest friend in London. "A lot of crazy things have been happening over here. And I haven't been able to reach you and rant."

"I'm sorry," she apologized. "The time difference is impossible. Plus, I've been trying to find a room to rent in South Ealing."

"You're moving out of your parents' house?"

"Of course, I am. I'm not going back to sharing a room with my bratty sister. Anyway, back to the guard. How could he do that? Is he shameless or just cocky? Pun intended."

I chewed my bottom lip. "I think he's both."

"So …" She paused dramatically.

"So … what?"

"How big is he?"

Closing my eyes, I rolled onto my side. There was a flutter in my tummy. "Uh … big."

"Oh, your poor virgin pussy," she cried gleefully.

"Stop being crude, you," I scolded.

Ignoring me she went on, "You know, this could make a nice little enemies-to-lovers romance for you."

"Are you kidding me? It would make a nice little tragedy. My father will kill me if I cozy up to one of his guards." Even though those words came out of my mouth, and I knew he was strictly off-limits, I hadn't been able to get him out of my mind. Whenever I had a quiet moment, my mind immediately went to him, at least until the nonsense I'd heard from Fabio earlier. I wasn't even going to share that part of my report. As far as I was concerned, it had all been one big joke. And I had been stupid enough to believe it for a little while. As if my parents would arrange a marriage for me. If that had been their intention why send me overseas for an education?

Charlotte and I chatted a bit more about how different everything was from our life in England, before the call came to an end.

I stared at the ceiling and before I could stop myself, I began to think about what Fabio had said. What if it were true? He didn't look like he was lying. A tight ball of anxiety formed in my belly. *Of all people, not Fabio.* I took deep breaths.

It was just a joke, Sienna. Just a stupid joke.

You were being rude and he decided to punish you. He had always been a jerk. Not only did he chase me around with frogs, he once put a green snake in my bed. He thought he would scare me, but I knew green snakes were not poisonous, so I just gently picked the poor thing up and let it out of my window. It was not poisonous. All I had to do was gently let it out of the window.

The arranged marriage was the adult Fabio's green snake.

The best stress reliever was some gentle coaxing of the bud between my legs, and despite my irritation at the guard's arrogance, he was undeniably the best stimulant for my arousal. I shut my eyes and brought the cocky Angelo Barone to mind. It was not difficult.

Almost immediately, I felt my body begin to heat up as I thought of him …

Opening my bedroom door, standing there looking at me with those hostile eyes, then coming into my room. The arrogant bastard does not speak. He just kicks the door shut, strides up to me, rips my panties off, and roughly grabs my ankles. Before I can say or do anything, he opens my legs wide and crouches between them.

I gasp.

"Fuck, you're wet," he growls. He doesn't ask permission. He just lays his velvet tongue flat on my sex and starts licking. Up and down my slit, licking, licking, licking. Sucking. That cocky, rude mouth eats me out without any manners. Like the uncivilized caveman he is.

I want to scream, but I can't. I'm in my parents' home. I grab his thick hair with both hands and grind myself against his mouth. I feel his tongue shoot into me. In and out. In and out. Like a piston. Oh, so good. So good. My back arches off the bed.

He slides two fingers into me and the walls of my sex squeeze them. Exactly how I would tighten around his cock, if it ever gets inside of me.

"You're so fucking tight. I have to fuck you now," he growls, and stands.

He pulls his clothes off and there it is ... his massive cock at full mast. Standing as proud and untamed as its owner. He is a dick, but he is my dick. And that Neanderthal cock there, that is all mine.

Of course, he doesn't wear a condom or ask if I want him to. He just pounces on me like a wild beast.

My legs wrap around his lean hips.

Then he forces that massive cock into my virgin pussy. He doesn't realize it is my first time or more likely the jerk doesn't care. His entry shocks the breath from my body. Then he just starts pounding into me, my hips jerking at the force of his thrusts. I rake my nails down his back and hope he bleeds.

I hate his guts, but it feels soooo good to be under him. To be used this way by him. To have his hard, hot cock drill into me. Again and again. I feel myself begin to quicken. The waves start to come. I welcome them. My core tightens. I already know it is going to be a good, strong climax.

"Angelo," I gasped out his name, as the sweet ecstasy overtook me and I went over the edge. My body writhed against the sheets, my free hand kneading my breasts as I kept the image of the cocky bastard in my fantasy.

When I came back to earth, I felt strangely unsatisfied and greedy for more ... an almost ravenous need to be filled ... by him.

CHAPTER 9

SIENNA

I woke up with the same damn need.

When my hands automatically moved between my legs, I stopped myself. What was I doing? This was not me. Masturbating day and night like some insatiable nymphomaniac. To start with, I felt irritated and antsy with myself for wanting such a brute. And to add insult to injury, the insolent way he had treated me made it clear, this was nothing more than unrequited lust on my part.

With a frustrated sigh, I rose to my feet and headed towards the bathroom. I needed a cold shower. Freezing cold water, yeah, it pushed all thoughts of him out of my mind and got rid of the need, but it was too much torture, so I turned it back to warm.

By the time I returned from my shower and sat down on the stool of my dresser mirror to dry my hair, my thoughts were back to what Fabio said last night. It had to have been his sick idea of a joke. A carry-on from the days he thought putting snakes in my bed was funny. Or he just wanted to rile me up.

Get on my nerves because I did not immediately not recognize him.

Yes, he was an egoistic kid. I must have hurt his pride. Satisfied that I had found the reason for his crazy idea of our family's intention for us to get married, I finished drying my hair. I brought the brush down the silky strands and found a hair tie in the top drawer. I pulled it through my hair when a knock sounded on my door.

"Come in," I called, watching the mirror to see who my visitor was.

The door pushed open and my father appeared.

A strange sense of foreboding filled my belly. My hand dropped into my lap. I didn't want to believe it, but suddenly, I knew. Fabio was not lying. "Papa," I greeted softly.

He came over to stand behind me, a rare smile on his face. He placed a hand on my shoulder.

I watched him in the mirror. "What's going on?" I asked.

"Do you have any plans today?"

I wanted to say I did, but avoiding the difficult was truly not my style. I would rather know, so I could do something about it than bury my head in the sand. "I don't. What do you have in mind?"

"Good. I was thinking about a trip to Rosedale. How would you like that?" he asked, his eyes cold, but his smile benevolent.

This was the moment when I realized I didn't trust my father. I never did. From the time I was a child, I had never felt truly comfortable with him. I didn't move. "With who?" I whispered.

His hand dropped away from my shoulder. "With Fabio."

I swallowed hard. "Papa, I … I—"

"Sienna, you know that after I am gone someone will need to handle the company, right?"

My spirit began to sink. "You're not going anywhere anytime soon, so let's not dwell on that."

"I could die at any time, Sienna," he corrected me. "That is the nature of the world I operate in."

I only had the courage to hold his gaze for a moment before lowering mine. I did know exactly what he meant. Even though most of his businesses were legitimate, there were some that stayed in the darkness and boosted those in the light. And I hated that. It was one of the reasons I wanted to be free and earn my own money.

"I'm very glad you have returned. From now on, I can begin to guide and instruct you on all that you need to know about this business. I'd like to involve you in the part that is not dangerous."

I nodded vaguely. Maybe he didn't intend to marry me off to Fabio. Maybe he just wanted me to help him run his business. In my mind, I saw myself helping him and running my own little shoe enterprise, handmade, small and exclusive. It wasn't a disagreeable image. "I understand, Papa. I promise to work hard and do my very best for the business."

"Good," he approved, "but that is not everything I want from you."

My hands clenched into fists.

In the mirror, our eyes clashed.

"I want you to get married. To someone who is good at business but not cunning enough to cut you out. Someone who will have the best interests of the family, and ensure that things continue to run as smoothly as they should. You will be at the helm of all decisions, while he'll be the hand that you use to take care of things as needed, and as you deem fit."

I jumped up from the stool, putting some distance between us and turned to face him. "And you think Fabio fits that role."

"Yes, Fabio's father and I discussed the matter and came to the conclusion that it will be the best solution for keeping everything in the family. You met him yesterday at the banquet, what did you think?"

I kept my voice respectful. "I don't like him, Papa. In fact, I can't think of a worse choice."

"Well, I have watched him for a little while and I'll grant you that he isn't perfect. He is too loud, he can be irritating, and he has an inflated idea of his own capabilities, but he does have some very commendable qualities, like a strong sense of loyalty to the family, and an unflinching duty to the business. As far as you are concerned, the only thing that's important is you are smarter than him, so you will be able to manipulate him easily and make him do whatever you want in business and in your family life. And I am certain there will be enough between the two of you to guarantee an amiable partnership."

It became very clear to me that although he might have watched Fabio, he knew absolutely nothing about him and his unbearable arrogance. The kind of arrogance that needed to belittle other people so he could feel superior. "I can't marry him, Papa."

"He's been managing Uncle Piero's branch of the business," my father went on as if I hadn't spoken, "and thus far he has done a very impressive job. He showed a keen awareness of what needed to be done for the advancement of the business. I'm convinced with a little guidance from me over the next few years, he will be able to protect and provide for you when I am gone."

"Papa, I don't want to marry him," I said, staring at my father. I could hear the desperation that had crept into my voice.

"I didn't ask you if you wanted to. You are my daughter and you will do as I tell you."

"This is not the nineteenth century. We don't do arranged marriages anymore," I flung at him.

He frowned. "What do you want to do with your life? Go around the nightclubs flaunting yourself like Paris Hilton?"

"No, of course not. I want to start my own little shoe business."

My father's eyes widened, incredulous. "A shoe business? What do you know about shoes?"

"I took a course at the London fashion school."

Just like that, my father changed. "You went behind my back." His eyes narrowed and his voice was deadly quiet.

"I didn't go behind your back, Papa. While everyone else was lounging about in bed on Saturday after partying hard on

Friday night, I went to school and learned a trade. I would have thought you would have been proud of me."

"I never imagined you would turn out to be such a spoilt, selfish brat."

CHAPTER 10

I gaped at him in genuine disbelief. "Me, a spoilt, selfish brat? How can you say that? That is the last thing anyone can say about me. I have never done anything that wasn't in accordance with your wishes. I didn't make a fuss about being sent away to boarding school even though I spent many lonely nights in England crying for Nonna and Gemma. Even when you insisted I continue my education there instead of returning here, I didn't contest your decision. And because you didn't want anyone to know who I was while I was in England, you made me live like a pauper. Never once did I complain or even care."

"You lived like a pauper for your own good. All I have ever done has been for your benefit," he cut in. "To ensure that you thrived and was safe."

"I know that, Papa, and I am incredibly grateful. That is why I have complied with everything you have ever asked of me, but I've always felt discontent … as though I've been living someone else's life. I understand that things can get dangerous in our world and it is crucial to be vigilant, but I don't want to marry a man simply because he will protect me. I have dreams and desires, apart from those you have for me, and I want to explore them and see what joys they bring me."

The scowl across his face was frightening. In that moment, he was no longer my father, but the cold heartless Mafia Don that made grown men cower in their shoes. "And what if my enemies see an opportunity and you get gunned down while you are exploring these … dreams and desires of yours?"

I looked him square in the eye. "Then so be it. I only have one life and I want to live it fully without regrets."

The silence between us dragged for so long that I couldn't take it anymore. "Papa? Say something." My voice was hushed.

"I'm going to pretend we never had this conversation," he said finally. "You'll get married to Fabio as planned," he said, "and immediately resume your responsibilities with the company."

I couldn't believe my ears. My father was actually going to force me to marry a man I detested. "So this is not a request, but a command?"

"Sienna, you have been pampered for a long time—"

"I have not been pampered!" I cried in frustration.

"But it cannot go on any longer," he carried on, completely unmoved by my outburst. "You are an adult now, and you need to act—"

"Okay, just one year," I cut in desperately. "Give me at least one year to do what I want. Afterwards, I will do all that you ask."

"No," he said coldly and started to walk away.

I jumped in front of him and grabbed onto his arm. "Papa!"

He tore his arm away from my grasp and took a step back. I could see the growing annoyance in his eyes. My father expected total obedience from everyone he dealt with. With exception of Nonna, I had never seen anyone dare talk back to him. "You don't know the wars that we are constantly fighting here. You have been shielded from all of it, but that cannot go on any longer. You cannot get a year. I could be killed tomorrow and there is no way in hell I am leaving this world without ensuring that you're settled and in safe hands."

"I could die tomorrow too," I yelled back at him.

He stilled.

"Have you thought of that?" I demanded. "I could die tomorrow and all that you'd have is regrets that you did not grant me the one request I've ever made to you."

He smiled, but it was dark and mocking. "I was mistaken in thinking you are now a woman. You're still a very selfish and immature child."

"With all due respect, Papa, you're the one who is being selfish right now. Why are your desires more important than mine? You do exactly what you want with your life. Why can't I?"

"Because you don't own yourself—"

My jaw dropped. "Who owns me? You? I'm a chattel? Part of your holdings and possessions?" I held his gaze, daring him to respond.

He didn't allow himself to be diverted from his path. "Your betrothal has already been set in place. You will be married to Fabio, and afterwards if you still want to take a year off to do whatever you want, then that will be up to you and your husband. But nothing will change your impending marriage—"

I decided to stop pretending to be civil. I clenched my fists to my sides. "I will *absolutely* not get married to Fabio." I had only asked for a year so I could find a way to either change my fate of being attached to a man like Fabio, buy me time to plan some sort of escape. There was nothing left to do but stand my ground.

"You will," he said and turned away to leave, as my willingness was of no consequence, his decision was all that mattered.

"Have you spent any time with him, Papa?"

He did not stop walking towards the door.

"You're usually a great judge of character," I shouted, "so I refuse to believe that you haven't noticed the absolute rubbish of a human being he is. He is obnoxious, egoistic, loud, and downright rude. Is that the kind of man you want to give me away to? Will your mind truly be at peace? If that's the case, then I don't think you even deserve to be called my father."

He stopped in his tracks then, and turned around to face me.

We glared at each other.

"I will not marry Fabio, Papa," I declared. "And there's nothing you can do about it. Unless you plan to drag me kicking and screaming down the aisle. And even if you do that, are you going to force me to agree to the vows?

Remember that old saying Nonna loves to repeat. 'You can take a horse to the bank, but you can't force it to drink water.' Unless of course, you intend to kill me and marry him to my dead body. If that works for you, then go right ahead."

He walked back to me.

My heart jumped into my throat at the fury in his eyes.

I saw it coming but it happened so fast I couldn't dodge it in time. His hand flew backwards, then forwards, and struck my cheek with such a violent force, I lost my balance as my body tilted backwards. My hand shot out towards the table with the hope of breaking my fall by catching the edge. I caught it, but the table turned over with me. I landed on the floor on my ass, the table nearly hitting me on the head. I looked up at him in shock. He had never hit me before, but I had never disobeyed him before either.

"You dare threaten me?" he fumed.

My cheek felt as if it was on fire and my eyes stung with hurt, but I refused to let him see he had wounded me. I maintained the adamant look on my face. "My condition is one year," I told him. "Give me one year and afterwards, I'll do whatever you want. I know that being born into this family automatically takes away the privileges of a normal life, but this much I demand. You will otherwise get no cooperation from me."

He looked as if he wanted to kill me, but saying nothing … he stormed away.

CHAPTER 11

SIENNA

https://www.youtube.com/watch?v=vx2u5uUu3DE

A taxi took me away from home. I was unsure of where to tell the driver to take me. He didn't mind. He'd seen the house and knew I'd be good for the money. Soon we passed by the Alamo Draft house movie theater downtown, and I told him to stop.

A few minutes later, I stood staring unseeingly at the row of posters advertising the films that were showing. I walked up to the ticket booth and bought a ticket. I had no idea what the movie was about, nor did I care but it promised gun fights and explosions, and those were the only things I could currently stomach.

Taking my bucket of popcorn and soda with me, I headed into the darkened theater to watch the movie. Halfway down the aisle, I suddenly stopped, and turned around. I found myself running out of the room into the corridor and towards the Ladies room. I ran into a stall, locked the door behind me, and started bawling my eyes out. Some kind soul knocked on the door to ask if I was okay and I told her to fuck off. I was that furious with my life.

How could my father expect me to marry a man like Fabio when he could see I hated the man?

Eventually, the sobs stopped, so I unlocked the door and went out. Only one woman was in there and she gave a funny look. And not surprising I looked a mess. I washed my face and stood up straight. The cry had been just what I needed. I gazed at my reddened, swollen eyes in the mirror's reflection. "This is your one life, Sienna," I said to my reflection. "Somehow, someway you will sort it out."

Then I forced a smile to my face, and left the cinema, my head held high. No way would I marry Fabio. I would find a way out, one way or another.

I returned home to find the entire house in a massive uproar. The guards' faces showed relief.

"Come with me. Your family is waiting for you," one of the maids said running up to me.

"What's up?" I asked, as I followed her.

She opened the door of the Japanese room where my family were gathered, and silently backed away. My mother rushed up to me and crushed me in her embrace. I could feel the bones in her thin body press into me.

Apparently, I'd been gone for nearly two hours and had nearly given them all heart attacks.

"Stop mollycoddling her," my father roared.

My mother reluctantly let go of me.

"What a disappointment you're turning out to be!" my father spat. "You know about the risks we constantly face and yet, you run off without telling anyone, without a single care for your safety. And you switched off your phone. Are you that stupid? Didn't you know we would *all* be worried sick about you? Get out of my sight right now, you thoughtless girl!"

I blinked several times, dumbfounded by the outburst. I opened my mouth, ready to give him an equally heated response, but the sad look on Nonna's face as she sat stiffly on the couch by the corner, stopped me. I released a deep breath and reined in my anger. "I'm so very sorry for making you all worry. I have been free for so long in England to go where I want and do as I please, I did not realize I would cause such an uproar. It won't happen again. I promise."

"Damn right it won't," my father muttered. "Go to your room. I'm so furious with you I can't even look at you."

Before I exited the study, I sent an apologetic look in Nonna's direction.

As I climbed the stairs, I felt myself begin to panic, my nerves strung with fear at the world that seemed to be closing in around me. I needed to escape, to find a way out before it was too late, but I did not have the heart to leave Nonna or Gemma.

I was still sitting on my bed wondering what the hell I was going to do half-an-hour later, when a knock came on my door.

"Come in," I called.

Nonna entered. She came to sit on my bed and I clung to her arm. She ran her fingers through my hair as she spoke softly, "It's okay, little one. You made a mistake. Your father will not stay angry for long. If he did not love you he would not be angry."

"Papa wants me to marry Fabio, but I can't do it. He is horrible," I whispered.

Nonna looked at me unsurprised.

"You've heard about the betrothal, haven't you?" I asked, searching her face, feeling a tinge of betrayal that she did not tell me. Was I the only one not consulted about what was going to happen in my life?

"I have," she replied, her kind eyes sad. "You don't like him?"

"I loathe him," I said with a shudder. "And I want absolutely nothing to do with him."

"My goodness, such passion," she said mildly.

My eyes filled with tears. "Please help me, Nonna. I absolutely cannot get married to him."

"Sweetheart, don't you think you are being too hasty? You both have only had one interaction with each other. At least give it some time. Don't dismiss him so easily, based on your perception after one meeting. When you come to know him, you will realize that he is indeed a decent man. I've known and watched him for a long time and—"

"Nonna," I cut her off and stood. I couldn't believe what was happening. "Don't tell me that you're with them on this? You want to barter me off too?"

"Sienna!" her call was sharp. "Your father is very concerned about you, and up till now, I haven't seen any other man that will be able to step up and handle all the—"

"I don't understand why I have to be someone else's responsibility in order for it to be acceptable for me to exist. What is going on? I don't matter? At all? My desires and wishes don't mean a damn thing to anyone? I'm not allowed to even chart the course of my own life?"

"Sienna," she warned.

But I was too hurt to care. Of all the people in the world, I thought Nonna would understand. "What the hell is this? If this was the plan you all had in mind, then why did you tell me to return from England? I was safe and protected there wasn't I? Why the hell am I back here?"

"Sienna, try to understand your father," she said. "He is incredibly worried about—"

"Nonna, I wish he would keep his worry to himself because that unsolicited concern is the guise under which he's going to ruin my life."

With a sigh, she rose to her feet. "You need to rest. It has been a very long day for you. Get some sleep and when you wake up, you will be in a better frame of mind. Perhaps then, we can have a real conversation." She took her leave.

I was left standing in the middle of the room in complete despair. I grabbed my phone and called Christine.

"Hey," she answered on the second ring.

"I need to get away," I told her. "Can I spend the night at your place?"

"Uh, sure," she replied. "Is everything all right?"

"For now," I answered. "I'll tell you the rest when I see you."

"Alright, I'll send the address to you. When will you be here?"

"I'll leave right now."

"You're okay, aren't you?" she asked, in a worried voice.

"Yeah, I'm fine."

"I'll be waiting."

As my phone pinged with Christine's address, I went towards my closet to grab the biggest purse I could find. I dumped the toiletries I would need inside it, included a change of clothes and underwear.

I jumped guiltily when I heard a knock on my door. Stuffing the bag away, I went to open the door.

Gemma stood there holding a tray filled with a pot of tea and a plate of pastries. "I brought these for you," she said.

"I could have come down for these, Gemma," I said, attempting to take the tray from her.

But she shook her head and went past me to put the tray down on the coffee table by the window. Then she straightened and looked at me. "Are you all right?"

I shrugged. "I've seen better days, but yeah, I'm fine."

"Your father wants to see you in his dungeon," she said.

I could see the anxiety in her eyes and this made me sad. I didn't want Gemma to have to choose between loyalty to me and the man who paid her wages. I didn't come back here to cause trouble amongst the people I loved most in this world. I walked up to Gemma and pulled her into my arms. "Don't worry, Gemma. It's going to be okay. Honestly, it's all going to be fine."

"Maybe, the boy has a good heart," she whispered.

I forced a smile. "Maybe."

She nodded. "He will protect you."

If it had been anyone else I would have told them I didn't need an arrogant swine like Fabio to take care of me, but I didn't want to worry Gemma any more than I already had. I nodded. "Yeah, I'm sure it's for the best."

"All right. You better go see your father now. He is waiting."

I didn't want to see Papa right at this moment, but I couldn't disobey him and I needed him to think nothing was wrong until I could find a way to fight back.

Before it was too late.

CHAPTER 12

SIENNA

https://www.youtube.com/watch?v=OMOGaugKpzs

I didn't know what to expect as I walked down the stairs, but to say I wasn't afraid would be a lie. I had given him an ultimatum, and men who had navigated their way in the top of the pile the way my father did never took well to ultimatums. My greatest fear however, was that this would destroy the relationship I had with my family, especially because I felt ready to go the distance for the cause I stood for.

I took a deep breath and knocked on his study door.

"Come," he called.

His curt voice sent a chill down my spine. I squared my shoulders and pushed the door open.

He sat behind his massive oak desk and his face was expressionless and cold.

I didn't make any attempt to move further into the room. Unthinkingly I adopted the defensive stance of folding my arms across my chest.

He made an impatient beckoning expression with his hand.

I walked into the middle of the room, then I noticed another person in the room. He wore a baseball cap and was seated on one of the chairs facing my father, and he was as still as death.

My skin tingled with a warning. Ahead, lay trouble.

First of all, my father's study, or dungeon as everyone else referred to it was his sanctuary. Only two types of people had been allowed in here. It wasn't even a room anyone unfamiliar with the house could access. You could only get to it through a hidden door in the kitchen's pantry, and down a secret stairway all the way to the base of the house. His immediate family, myself, my mother, and grandmother were the only ones allowed to be in here - and his most trusted aides.

But more important than this, I recognized the man's head and the way his raven hair curled around his ears!

"This is Angelo," my father said. "From now on, he will be completely in charge of your safety. You are not to be or go anywhere without him, until I say otherwise."

My heart leapt into my throat.

In a daze, I watched my father as he grabbed his phone, and a bunch of keys from his desk, told Angelo that he was off in Italian, and walked past me without even glancing at me. He was that disgusted with me.

The plans I'd already set in motion to escape later that evening flashed before my eyes as I stood there rooted in shock.

By the time I found the wits to spin around, my father had already reached the door. If he'd assigned someone to follow me around day and night, that would mean his teeth were already sunk into me. I didn't know if it was even possible to escape now, but even though I knew, at the very least, I'd lost this round, I couldn't just let it go. I had to show I wouldn't make it easy. I would fight to my last breath. "Is this your plan?" I demanded furiously. "Because I refuse to marry Fabio, your next course of action is to imprison me?"

Ignoring me, my father continued on his way, and shut the door closed behind him.

I was fuming, my breath coming in harsh painful puffs, but I could do absolutely nothing. I turned around and saw that Angelo had not moved.

Not even turned around to see what went on behind him. He just carried on sitting there like some Roman statue.

"And fuck you too," I spat viciously as I headed towards the door. When I pulled it open, I sensed him rise to follow me. He was to be my shadow, and it made me want to smash my head into the wall. Again, nothing I could do about it, at least not right now, so I just walked as quickly as I could away from him. I considered running, so he would have to run to keep up, but I decided against it. That would be undignified and do nothing to further my real plans.

While I made my way across the kitchen though, I realized I couldn't hear the sound of his footsteps, even though I could sense he still followed me closely. Still, he was as silent as a ghost. I couldn't even pick up on the sound of his breathing. How could a man so big be that silent?

I had reached the staircase and began to climb it when I couldn't take it anymore. I swung around suddenly and faced him.

He stopped only a few feet away. The baseball hat that hung low on his head hindered me from properly seeing his face. He wore a white t-shirt, black leather jacket, and a pair of black jeans that sat snug and low around his lean hips.

My mouth instantly watered at the sight of him, but I gave myself a quick mental slap. I'd never been a fool around a man before, and I certainly would not be starting with him of all people.

He raised his head then and directly met my gaze.

My knees weakened, and I clutched the banister for support, but to my everlasting pride and joy, my voice came out dry and cynical, "Wow! What a turn up for the books. You're now my bodyguard when you left me to drown to my death a couple of days ago?"

He said nothing, just stared at me.

This infuriated me even more. "Did you tell my father what happened at the pool?" I taunted. "He definitely wouldn't have assigned this job to you if he was aware of your rude behavior."

Angelo slipped his hands into his pockets and with a low, long-suffering sigh, looked beyond me up the staircase.

I glared at him. Never in my life had I met someone as arrogant as this man. "You're not going to speak to me? You're going to keep ignoring me?"

"Sienna," he said quietly.

The command in his tone instantly held my attention.

"Let's make this situation bearable for the both of us. My job is to guard you, and I will do just that. Please refrain from any other unnecessary communication."

"Did I do something to offend you, or are you just naturally a dick?"

I saw the anger flare in his gaze and didn't miss the slight fear that tightened my core, but I also couldn't ignore the buzz of arousal seriously agitating my body. It just made me all the more irritated at him. "Maybe I should tell my father about what happened at the pool. I'm sure that'll make him change his mind about replacing you."

He smiled slowly.

Oh my God, I nearly died right there. He was that sexy. If I didn't detest him as much as I did, I would have—God, I don't know what I would have done. Then he opened his mouth and all I wanted to do was stab him in the groin.

"Sure, tell your dad. Tell him how you followed me into the men's changing room and how you couldn't take your eyes off my dick. You stared at it as if you wanted to lick it."

My mouth dropped open in shock. "That's not true," I gasped.

"No?"

"I mean, yes, I followed you into the changing room, but you make it sound as if I chased you there to see you in the nude. I followed you because I was angry. And I certainly did not look at your dick as if I wanted to lick it."

He shrugged carelessly. "Good for you. You like fairytales."

"I don't want you to be my bodyguard, so just leave. I'll speak to my father and demand a replacement."

He touched his cap mockingly. "I'll really appreciate it if you could do that."

With a murderous glare, I turned around and stormed away. When I arrived at my bedroom door, I turned around to see the rude bastard remained behind me. Blatant as you please. Following me. "Didn't you hear what I said?" I raged.

"I take my instructions from your father," he replied calmly. "Want me to stop following you? Get your father to tell me to."

I was on the verge of exploding with anger, but the fact he acted so cool and unaffected made me determined not to show him how upset I was. I took a deep breath and found some semblance of calm. "Fine," I replied sweetly. "But are you going to follow me in here too? I'm going to take my clothes off and lie naked on the bed. Is watching me in that state part of your job description?"

Something flashed in his eyes, but it was gone so quickly, I must have imagined it.

I opened my bedroom door and violently kicked it shut.

Whoa! Stupid decision. The door was a heavy antique and probably weighed as much as a car, and I'd probably broken my toe. Trying my best to muffle my cry of pain at the agony, I hobbled into my room and collapsed on my bed in despair. I curled into a ball and clutched my throbbing toe with both my hands. In the space of twenty-four hours, my life had become unrecognizable.

I tried to understand why he had taken such an instinctive and immediate dislike to me. I had done nothing wrong to him. Perhaps he was so dismissive because I was born into such extravagant wealth and privilege and he had to work hard for everything he had. Maybe he had judged me unworthy of his respect or even courtesy because he had prejudged me and slid me into the category of rich bitch, which of course, I wasn't.

Still, I was well aware of the well-used cliché; any girl born into unfair wealth must be a spoiled little Princess. I scowled. The very thought of anyone thinking of me as a spoilt brat annoyed me.

I'd been able to escape that taint in London, but it seemed I had been firmly and inflexibly returned to my default status of being the *do-little princess* in the tower.

Well, I wasn't going to accept that and neither would I accept the fact that everyone thought they could so easily allocate me a husband and a life they deemed fit. Not from my father and not from Angelo Freaking Barone.

None of this was a joke.

I was a human being, with emotions, desires, aspirations and fears just like everyone, but I was practically fighting for my life here. I could never have imagined it wouldn't be out in the world but within the confines of my own home. Feeling absolutely drained from all of the drama and surprises, my eyes began to sting with tears. It reminded me of how I had felt the first night I climbed all alone into my cold, narrow bed in my new boarding school in England.

CHAPTER 13

SIENNA

"*H*ey, when are you going to be here?" Christina asked.

I tried to swallow the lump in my throat. "I don't know. I don't know anything anymore. I'm so pissed."

"What the hell is going on, Sienna?" she demanded worriedly.

"I've been saddled with a bodyguard?"

"What?"

"Yeah, and just by looking at him, I can tell he wasn't randomly picked by my father. He's going to be damn good at his job. I won't be surprised if he can even hear me breathing right now."

"Is he in front of you?"

"No, but he's probably somewhere near enough to save me from myself."

She laughed, then quickly apologized.

"It's okay. Don't apologize," I said, and pulled my thick duvet over my head to further muffle the sounds from the conversation.

"You're not allowed to leave the house at all?"

"Actually, I am." I threw the cover off my head, and sat up with a widened gaze. "Holy shit, I am!"

"I'm confused. Are you or are you not allowed to leave the house? You just said that there's someone guarding you."

With a stink-eye at the door, I told her, "I *can* leave the house." I lowered my voice as I scurried off to the bathroom and shut the door firmly behind me, "My father didn't explicitly say that I was forbidden to leave, but the guard is required to come with me."

"Um … is this good news?"

"Of course," I said. "Well sort of. It's passable news. Since I *can* leave the house, it means I'll have to find a way to escape from him when I'm in town. It will be much, much easier there than in this cage."

"Okay, so what's the plan?"

We hashed it all out, and I thereafter, rushed to get ready. A few minutes later, I was dressed and ready. I had left almost everything I owned behind, because going out with a big suitcase would be a dead giveaway. All I had was my passport, some money, a change of underwear and some toiletries. Until my father saw reason and understood that I would never marry anyone I didn't even like or respect, Los Angeles would be too small a city to hold the both of us. I intended to return to England and remain just out of his reach until he was ready to treat me like an adult.

I threw the door to my room wide open, and without checking for Angelo, stalked out my head held high. Contrary to what I'd imagined, he wasn't hanging around my door because no one followed me as I headed regally down the stairs. I could hear the sounds of people talking and laughing in the kitchen as I took the elevator alone down to the underground garage.

As the doors swished open, I kinda thought he would be standing outside there, hands folded with a self-satisfied smirk plastered all over his handsome but completely detestable face. But the fluorescent-lit area seemed empty and quiet. I almost couldn't believe it could be this easy.

I hurried towards the matte black Mercedes I received for my 21st birthday. The sound of my shoes echoed around me as I pressed the button on the remote clutched in my sweaty hand. It unlocked the doors with a bleep that sounded too loud. It had been parked here since I test drove it on my birthday and never used all this time but I was good with cars and didn't worry about not being able to remember what to do. I glanced back nervously and to my horror, I saw him arrive out of the side stairs door.

"Hey," he called out.

Wings sprouted from my feet and I ran like the wind. I wrenched the door open, slipped in, and locked the doors, so he wouldn't be able to force his way in. My shaking fingers crashed down on the ignition button and the engine roared to life. A shadow fell over me and I jumped. He tapped on the window and pulled at the handle, but I didn't even look at him. I struck the accelerator and the car jumped away with a screech. I pressed the remote for the garage doors and felt a wild mix of relief and fierce joy as the door slid upwards, just in time for me to zoom out of the gap.

I was free!

God, I actually made it. I looked in the rear-view mirror and saw Angelo appear at the entrance. So he wasn't as sharp as my father thought. For one crazy second I felt a strange sense of loss or disappointment. That it had been so easy to elude him. I'd imagined him to be more resourceful, more lethal, at least better at his job. I congratulated myself.

What the hell is the matter with me? He is nothing to me.

I turned the sweeping bend in the tree-lined driveway and the house disappeared out of sight. No way would he be able to catch up now. By the time he got into a car and came after me, I would already have merged with the traffic.

As I came up to the tall cast iron gates of the house I didn't slow down. I knew the gates were monitored day and night, but before anyone realized they were supposed to stop me, I would be long gone. I pressed the button on the remote that would pull the gates open for me.

One last time, I turned around to make sure he wasn't following me and he was nowhere to be found. It was such a great feeling to know I had outwitted the rude beast.

With a triumphant shout, I pressed down on the accelerator as I swung my gaze back towards the gates. I was ready to shoot through them, but with my heart leaping into my throat, my foot slammed down on the brakes. The car juddered to a stop a few inches from the locked gates.

The gates had not opened.

What the hell is going on?

I grabbed the remote and pounded on the button, but still the gates wouldn't roll away. Shifting the gear into the park mode, I rolled my window down, and pressed the button again. Still— no movement. I glared angrily at the button, the pit of my stomach broiling with annoyance.

I realized what had happened.

The remote's connection to the gate had been disconnected at the house. Damn, the rude beast.

My heart sunk. Just then, I sensed movement at the corner of my eye, and lifted my gaze to the rear view mirror to see that indeed, Angelo was approaching.

He must have run to get this far this quickly, but now he had his hands in his pockets, and strolled leisurely towards me down the driveway as though he had all the time in the word. I felt so infuriated I wanted to stab him in the heart. I could have turned the car around and drove past him back to the house. Actually, for what could have been a whole minute, I seriously considered running him over.

But that would be defeat. Real defeat. No, I would sit right here and confront him.

When he finally arrived before the passenger's door, he knocked on the window.

I knew he wanted me to open the car door and it would be the less humiliating option in the long run. But I couldn't bring myself to open it for him, so I rolled the glass down.

He put his large hands on the base of the window.

I refused to meet his gaze, and instead stared straight ahead in fury, but from my peripheral vision I sensed his large powerful hands resting on the base of the window.

"You're not allowed to go anywhere without me," he said.

I had half expected him to just put his hand into the car, release the latch and get in next to me, but he didn't make any effort to do so. I understood why he was doing it. He wanted me to explicitly ask him to come along, or neither of us were going anywhere.

This was quite the slap to the face, especially since I had ignored him earlier and madly driven out of the garage.

My face burned with embarrassment at his silent message, but I tried not to let the poison infect my mind. He had definitely won this round, but if things went as planned today, then I would never have to see him again. I gave up on the battle of egos between us, and focused on how I could get to Christine's house. Freedom was more important than scoring points with him.

"I have to go see a friend," I told him from between gritted teeth.

"Where?"

"Long Beach."

He straightened and tapped his hand against the door.

I was forced to open it.

First, he carelessly and I might add, rudely, tossed my purse onto the backseat, then his long legs slid in one after the other. All accomplished with the lithe gait of a silky but hostile big cat.

I tried my very best to ignore the masculine energy filling the space inside the car. Or the citrusy smell of his shampoo. The last time I had smelled that—

"Put on your seat belt," he ordered.

"Open the gate," I muttered, infuriated by the fact that he was right, but I didn't want to appear to obey him.

He didn't respond. Actually, he didn't even bother looking at me. He shifted in his seat and rested his head against the headrest like someone who had settled in to enjoy a ride from his personal driver.

What an asshole!

I took in a deep, wholesome breath to rein in my galloping temper. Once that was securely reined in, I swallowed my pride, grabbed the seatbelt from over my shoulder, and clicked it into place—like he had *commanded*.

Calmly, he revealed the remote in his hand and pointed it at the gate without a word. The iron gates rolled away smoothly open.

The incredulousness of the whole situation left me stunned and speechless. All I could do was shift the gear into place and drive.

CHAPTER 14

*L*A was infuriatingly slow.

Back in London, I had relied heavily on the underground tube system which was punctual and reliable, and the buses weren't half bad either. But here, with everyone and their pet owning a vehicle - the traffic at this hour through Lakewood Boulevard south to the San Diego Freeway - was enough to frustrate one to death.

Ordinarily, I wouldn't have been too annoyed by it, but having to sit in abject silence beside the evil mannequin by my side was too much to bear in my current state of mind.

I felt like the universe was testing me to see just how much I could take before I completely lost it and exploded. My finger tapped impatiently against the steering wheel as I stared in annoyance at the standstill traffic.

Although, I tried my best not to, I couldn't help sneaking looks at him. I had thought he wasn't too big compared to all the other gorillas that constantly hung around my father, but his presence right now in the car was almost overwhelming.

It felt too crowded to be in such a confined space with him, especially since I could very vividly remember our encounter at the pool, and the way I had fantasized about him fucking me out of my mind.

With every passing moment, it became increasingly difficult to breathe. Rudely, I turned off the air condition and rolled down the window on my side. I thought of rolling his down too, but decided he did not deserve the kindness. He could very well do it himself if he wanted to. I did feel a slight twinge of guilt. I knew in my heart that he was simply just doing his job as he had been instructed, but did he have to be such a prick about it?

To my surprise, he did nothing. Just sat as still as a statue in the boiling heat.

How could he remain so still? I wondered. His eyes were closed. Had he fallen asleep? He must have. His hat still sat extremely low on his face, so I was sure he wouldn't see me even if he was awake. I grew bolder as I watched him.

His skin looked as smooth as milk, and the thick lashes resting on his tanned flesh made me feel quite envious. They were far thicker and longer than mine. No man should have such showy lashes. It was simply unnecessary. His nose was straight and strong, a full Roman nose. I let my eyes travel down to his jawline. It looked sharp enough to chisel stone. It was what gave him that aura of barely suppressed impatience.

Then I was back to his mouth.

His lower lip looked gloriously plump and sensuous. I could imagine sucking on it. Not that I would in real life. I didn't even want to touch him. As a human being, he was almost worse than Fabio.

The cars around me were beginning to move so I turned away, rolled his window down, and focused on my driving.

Half an hour later, I pulled into Christine's apartment complex in Long Beach and turned off the engine. I eyed him. I knew he was awake, but he didn't stir. Without a word, I pushed my door open, and retrieved my purse from the backseat. It had my passport and credit cards, all the necessities needed to book a flight out of the country in a flash.

He got out of the car and followed me as I headed up the stairs towards her apartment, and soon arrived at her door. I turned around then to face him.

This time around, his gaze met mine.

Something struck my heart.

In the daylight, his eyes were the most stunning ocean blue I've ever seen. I opened my mouth to say what I had wanted to, but I had no recollection whatsoever of what I'd intended to say. Annoyed even further, I lowered my head and tried to restart my brain. *What the hell is wrong with me?* Yes, he was hot, disgustingly so, but he was also a horrible person.

When I could put him back in the box of all the horrible people, I was able to remember what I wanted to be rude to him about. "Are you really going to keep following me like this?" I taunted.

He shrugged. "It's my job."

"So you're actually going to come inside?"

"After the stunt you pulled back at the house, yes."

"Later this evening, I'm going on a date. You're just going to come along for that too?"

79

He didn't even blink. "Yeah."

I held myself together. I wanted to needle him. "My friend and I are going to paint our nails while we gossip about men. Will that be interesting for you to watch?"

He folded his arms across his chest and leaned against the wall beside the door. "No, but I get paid to be bored."

Frustrated, I turned and pounded on Christine's doorbell.

CHAPTER 15

SIENNA

*C*hristine didn't respond, and after a few seconds, I pressed the doorbell again.

"I'm coming. I'm coming," she called from within. As she pulled the door open she shouted over her shoulder, "Sienna's here."

Christine was a curvy blonde and my roommate in London for two years. "Hey," she said as her gaze darted over to Angelo. Her eyes widened at the sight of him, before she hurriedly swung them back to me. Reaching out, she pulled me into her embrace. "Sienna" she breathed, hugging me tight.

A brunette appeared behind her.

She looked somewhat familiar, but I couldn't actually tell if I had really met her or she just looked like someone I knew. "Hi, nice to meet you," I extended my hand for a handshake as Christine let go of me.

To my surprise however, the brunette lightly smacked my hand away. "Don't you remember me?" she asked.

My eyes narrowed as I tried hard to recall her.

Christine chuckled. "Don't you remember Mandy? From fifth grade? The girl from Miss French's class."

I tried my very best to place her face but nothing came to mind

"Uh, she used to stutter."

"Hey!" Mandy smacked Christine on the arm.

At that moment recognition came. "Oh! I do remember. Oh, my God. Hi, it's been forever!"

"It has." She smiled. "And for the record, I don't stutter anymore."

I stared at her in wonder, as a vague picture of the frail ten-year old she had been came to mind.

Her gaze left mine as she noticed the man who silently stood behind me. Her mouth opened to ask the inevitable question.

I didn't want to start explaining who he was in front of him, so I quickly pulled both girls into the house with me … and shut the door in his face.

I leaned against the door, fully expecting Angelo to ring the doorbell, but he did not.

"Is *that* the bodyguard?" Christine whispered.

I nodded.

"He's so freaking hot," Mandy observed.

There was no lie there, but I made a face. "He's horrible."

"In what way?" Mandy asked curiously.

"He's an insufferably rude Neanderthal," I muttered.

"Oh, I love insufferably rude Neanderthals. Especially when they throw you over their shoulders and carry you off to their unmade beds." She grinned wickedly.

"This Neanderthal is more likely to hit you over the head with his club," I said sourly. For some weird reason, I didn't like Mandy lusting after him.

"Right, the moody type. Nothing I can't handle, but can we just take a moment to um … process the fact that you have a bodyguard? I know your parents are loaded, but a body-guard? I thought only the children of billionaires and celebri-ties needed that kind of intense protection?"

I applied my age-old avoidance technique and just smiled sweetly. "Let's move away from the door. I'm sure he can still hear us."

It worked. The conversation was steered away from my parents.

"Shouldn't we let him in? Won't he get lonely out there?" Mandy asked.

"Cut it out, Mandy, this is serious," Christine cut in impa-tiently.

I turned to her. "Did you manage to book me a ticket?"

She nodded and led me over to her open laptop on her small kitchen counter. "Just paid for it. Your flight leaves at 6pm this evening, so you have about three hours to get to LAX. What's the plan?"

"We'll go together to a mall and while we're there, we'll slip into one of the dressing rooms where we'll be able to ditch him. I'll call an Uber and be on my way to the airport before he knows what hit him. Since you paid for my ticket, my tracks will be covered, so they won't be able to stop me in time before I board and return to England. I pressed the home button of my phone to check the time. "I need to get going."

"You do," she said, "but you really think it will be that easy to get rid of Tony Stark out there?"

I was surprised by the comparison. "Is that what he looks like to you?"

"Hell no!" Mandy protested from the couch across the room that she had plopped into. "Your bodyguard's a freaking ten. Isn't Stark that sassy, middle-aged, Iron Man guy?"

"I was referring to his demeanor," Christine explained. "Brooding, arrogant …"

"And creepy?" Mandy added.

That amused me. "I thought you considered him hot?"

"He is," she said nodding sagely, "but he is still creepy in a 'damn you're dangerous and might kill me but I still want to do you' sort of way."

"You're crazy," Christine said with a laugh, before turning to me and adding, "Personally, he looks as sharp as a new knife and I don't think we should underestimate him."

"I think I can give him the slip."

"Okay, if you say so. Anybody want a soda?"

Slipping onto the battered stool in front of her laptop, I nodded. "Me. You got a Coke?"

"Of course," she replied heading towards the open plan kitchen.

I turned my attention to Mandy. "I never thought I'd see you again."

"Yeah, neither did I. How have you been?"

"I've been great," I replied.

"Christine told me about how the two of you met again at college. That's a long way from middle school."

"It is." I laughed. "What're you up to these days? Are you in college or finished?"

"No." She shook her head decisively. "I tried it for the first year but then dropped out. Much too expensive and completely unnecessary for what I want to end up doing."

"Oh, what do you want to do?" I asked.

"I want to be a score composer."

"A score composer?"

"They create original soundtracks for movies and shows ... like John Williams, Hans Zimmer."

"Oh, that's interesting."

"Yup, much better than whiling away countless hours in college learning generic things at best, and earning a degree that is probably not worth much. It made sense to drop out."

I stared at her. How brave she was. I carried on going to classes I detested because I didn't want to annoy my father.

"Anyway, I got a job as a waitress and I'm saving up so I can go backpacking next year across the world. I'm planning to visit fifty countries. Much better than being caged up in a boring classroom."

I completely understood her, and even felt a bit jealous that she could just go ahead to do what she wanted while I was literally in the midst of running away from home like a damn teenager. I took a swig of my drink.

Christine reappeared, fully dressed, with what I assumed were her car keys dangling from her fingers. "You ready to leave?" she asked.

I was suddenly sick to my stomach. I didn't even say goodbye to Gemma or Nonna, but this was not a decision I could waver or negotiate on. One day when my father had forgiven me, I would come back. Even as the thought appeared in my head I knew it was a lie. Even though I was his only child, my father would never forgive me for disobeying him. He would consider my actions as a dishonor to him and his authority. Both my mother and grandmother got married under similar dictatorial circumstances. This wasn't going to happen to me. Not while I had life in my limbs. I set the can of Coke down, my resolve strengthened, rose to my feet and looked Christine square in the eye. My voice came out sure and decisive as I said, "I am."

"All right, let's go. Hang on, I forgot to ask, where are you going to stay when you get back to England? With Charlotte?"

"I guess so," I replied. "I'm sure she'll let me crash on her futon for a couple of days, until I figure out what my next step will be." Even if she wasn't around, I knew my way around London and I could easily get a job as a waitress at the café of one of my friends.

"Good," she said, her gaze sympathetic. "I can't believe you're going through all this barely a week after we got back."

"I can't believe it either." To be honest I didn't feel anything. I was still in a state of shock and would probably start to feel hurt and sad when I got to England.

"Aren't you traveling with any luggage?" Mandy asked.

"Nah," I replied. "A suitcase would kind of give the game away."

Christine crossed her arms. "I really think you should crash here for a couple of days and make better plans. It all sounds so flimsy."

I sighed heavily. "I wish I could, but after my father assigned the beast out there, I've realized that there is no time to waste. I need to fully escape from the country before I am trapped here forever."

"When will you return?" Mandy asked.

I could feel my heart sinking. "I have no idea."

"Hey, you don't mean that, do you?" Christine asked, a deep frown etched on her forehead.

I forced a smile. "I'll come back as soon as they come back to their senses. I love my parents and my grandma, and it's incredibly heartbreaking that this is what things are resorting to. Let's go. We absolutely cannot fail at this. It might be my only chance. If this goes wrong, I will most probably be grounded until the day of the wedding."

"My God, that sounds like something from the 17th century," Mandy said with a shiver.

I exhaled my breath deep and shuddering. "Yeah, and you haven't even seen the man they want me to marry." I rose to my feet. "Let's go."

CHAPTER 16

SIENNA

*T*he sun shone brightly when we filed out of the apartment, but a heavy shadow rested on my heart. I pushed the images of Nonna and Gemma out of my mind.

Angelo stood waiting against the wall, his hands jammed into his pockets, and his head lowered as if he stared at the ground. At the sound of the door opening he turned and looked at me.

"We're going to the mall," I said airily, and began to head over to the car park with my friends.

When we arrived at Christine's red Camry, I got into the backseat without a word. Mandy slid into the passenger's seat while Christine took the wheel. Mandy rolled down the window and gazed at Angelo, who stood glaring at me. His hand lodged between her door and the frame. There was no way she would be able to close it.

"Sienna wants to ride with us," Mandy said with a cheeky smile. "You can follow us behind with her car, right?" She reached out to me with an outstretched hand. I dropped my keys on her palm, and Mandy offered them to him.

"Where are you going?" he asked cupping my keys in his hand.

I leaned into the backseat with my arms across my chest and my face turned away in annoyance. Something about him set my teeth on edge. He always behaved as if I was a bratty child he was minding.

"We're not sure yet," she said. "We're just going to head downtown to do some light shopping and maybe get something to eat. Then we'll come back."

He kept his eyes on me as he listened to her.

I felt like I couldn't breathe … like his gaze was boring holes into my skin. I kept my head turned away. Seconds passed. I could feel the tension coming from him. Crazy, fantastical thoughts galloped through my mind. He would drag me out of the car. If that happened my stellar plan was to scream that he was a molester and pray people would come to our rescue. In the ensuing confusion, I would slip away. Or … maybe he would call my father. Oh God!

Suddenly, he removed his hand from Mandy's door and walked away to the car.

I was shocked. My heart stopped beating.

Both girls released shaky breaths.

"Holy fuck, he's intimidating!" Christine exclaimed, her hand on her chest.

Mandy waved her hand in front of her face. "I swear for a moment there, I thought he was going to pull the door out of its hinges and rescue you. Jesus Christ, that's one hot man."

"Let's go," I muttered, unwilling to waste even a second more.

Christine started the engine and put the car in motion. We drove out of the lot and I glanced behind to see that he was following us. "Damn, is that your car, Sienna?" She turned to me, her face filled with wonder. "What does your father do for a living?"

"He's a Sicilian Mafia don."

She cracked up laughing. "Get out of here."

How I wished that it were a joke.

"Do you know if Angelo is an LA native?" Christine asked.

"No idea, but judging by his accent, I don't think so," I replied.

"Buckle up, girls. You never know. We might be on a bit of a car chase."

"Don't you dare," Mandy said, her voice rising with alarm. "I have plans that don't include getting whiplash."

"Don't worry. I'm a good driver," Christine responded confidently as she glanced into the rearview mirror.

"What happened to our plan of going to the mall and losing him there?" Mandy whined.

Christine shook her head. "Well, now that I've seen his eyes up close, I don't think that plan is going to work. He's too sharp. So we're going to—"

"Going to get into a car chase with the latest, high-performance Mercedes Benz?" Mandy cut in incredulously.

"Have some faith," Christine said calmly as she drove us into the Freeway heading north towards Downtown. "My plan is a lot more diabolical than that."

"I can't wait to hear it," Mandy said sarcastically.

"My plan is not to give any indication of taking one of the upcoming exits, but at the very last moment to swerve into it. It would be impossible for him to stop or change direction at the speed we're doing and he would simply have to remain on the freeway and zoom past us."

"Jesus, Christine. That's one dangerous plan."

I frowned. Mandy was right. It was a highly risky plan and I did not want to put my friends in any danger.

"How about this exit?" Christine asked.

Mandy shook her head. "No, there are too many cars on it. It's way too dangerous. We need one that is somewhat free, and we also need him to speed up, otherwise he could swerve in time with us. Christine, step on it."

"Look you guys, let's not do anything dangerous, okay. I don't want anybody getting hurt on my behalf. Hell, if we are not careful we could cause a multi-car pile-up," I warned.

"I know I can do this," Christine insisted.

"Let's just take the next exit," I suggested. "And see if he's able to follow or not. If he does, we'll find another way."

Christine's hand tightened on the steering wheel as she vigilantly moved her gaze between the side and rearview mirrors. "Don't nobody look behind. We don't want to warn him that we're up to something."

"This next one," Mandy cried suddenly. "14B. It looks empty enough."

I was too afraid to even speak.

"Ready?" Mandy said, her voice high with a mix of excitement and fear.

"Yeah," Christine replied tightly.

"Then step on it," Mandy shouted.

"If I go any faster, he will guess what we are up to," Christine yelled back.

Mandy turned around to look at the traffic. "Okay, now!" she screamed, as we were almost on the exit.

I turned my head and saw a huge truck coming on the right of us. "There's a Mack truck coming up. We won't make it. Don't do it," I screamed.

"Yes, we fucking will make it," Christine said through gritted teeth as she swerved suddenly to the right. The sound of tires screeching on the hot asphalt - Mandy screaming, and the furious truck driver blaring his horn at us - filled the air. We could have caused a fatal accident. I turned to my left and for a split-second I saw into my car, directly at the driver. Our eyes met. And it was as if the world stopped. In that crazy second, something passed between us. A knowing. An inevitability. I knew then I wasn't going to escape him. Then the moment was over.

Our car accelerated away. We were speeding down the exit we had taken.

"Hell, yeah!" Christine shouted victoriously, whirling her head to look behind at me. She kept gripping the steering wheel so hard her knuckles were bone white. "We fucking lost him. For a moment there, I was sure he was going to reverse on the freaking highway and chase us down the exit."

"Oh, my God. That was fucking dangerous. I think I'm about to pass out," Mandy gasped.

I was trembling. I brought my hands to my face and I could see the goosebumps had broken out across my skin. "Let's hurry. I fear he's going to somehow catch up to us."

CHAPTER 17

"*T*he airport's only about twenty-five minutes away," Mandy said. "Christine, why don't we just take her there ourselves?"

"No," Christine said. "He might still be able to find us with this car. It's best if she just gets a taxi. Mandy, order one now. Tell them we'll be at Citibank on Sepulveda Boulevard."

"Uh, I don't think so," Mandy retorted. "It's going to take us a while more to get there."

"We'll be there in about eight minutes," Christine corrected.

"Not with this traffic we won't."

Mandy was right. We pulled up behind a row of cars at a red light, and as far down as we could see, the traffic light wasn't what was causing the delay.

"Don't worry. I know which side roads to take," Christine said and ventured off into the east intersecting road.

From then on, I lost any inkling of where we were headed and had no choice but to completely trust her as she drove through side streets and into neighborhoods I'd never been into and never wanted to.

As we passed a group of young men, who looked like thugs, huddled by a fence, Mandy spoke up nervously, "Christine, where the hell are we? Are you lost? This is so not our route."

"I wanted to avoid the traffic," Christine said. "I've taken these routes before but it was some time ago and I might have taken a wrong turn, but don't worry I'll find my way out again. Maybe I'll recognize the next road …"

"Will we even make it to the airport at this rate?" I asked worriedly.

"Hey, is that car following us?" Mandy observed suddenly.

I swung my head around and saw a nondescript blue Toyota behind us.

"I noticed it a while back," she continued, "because the numbers on the plate are almost the same as my dad's car."

Christine turned into yet another deserted street and suddenly, jammed on the brakes.

It came so sudden I hit my cheek on her headrest.

Mandy was jerked forward violently. "Fuck! Christine," Mandy cursed.

I raised my head and saw a van had stopped at a slant right in front of us. It was blocking the entire street.

"What the hell?" Christine swore.

"Christine, reverse," Mandy said, her voice eerily quiet.

"What?"

"Go back! Right now!" Mandy yelled.

Before she could even begin to act, two men in black balaclavas jumped out of the van.

I stared in disbelief. "Go, Christine!" I called sharply, as I stared at the men in shock.

Christine stepped on the gas pedal and we hurled backwards until we crashed into the blue Toyota. We were thrown violently forward. Fear as thick as fog hung in the air.

"Are you guys all right?" I asked.

"What is going on? "Who are these men?" Mandy cried.

Two more men jumped out of the blue Toyota, their faces covered with masks.

"Sienna, are these your father's bodyguards?" Christine asked, her voice trembling with hope.

I knew there was no way these men came from my father. For one, they wouldn't have to hide themselves from me in this way and for another, they just rammed into our car.

"They're coming over. Oh my God, what do we do now?" Mandy screamed.

"Everything will be fine," I said first to myself, then repeated it to the girls, "Everything will be fine. Don't panic."

All three of us jumped with fear at the thump on Christine's side of the door. Mandy screamed. A masked face appeared next, then one at my window, and another at Mandy's.

"Don't panic," I repeated automatically, even though I didn't believe my own words.

The men pulled on the latch of the locked doors.

"Christine, can't you step on the pedal and blast our way out of here?" Mandy shouted.

"No!" I screamed now more afraid for the sake of the girls whom had tried to help me than myself. "That van will not give way to this little car—"

There was a sudden strike and the window to my right cracked with a thud. While Mandy screamed, the man produced another instrument, which he tapped on the cracked window, and the glass shattered into pieces.

"Get out!" the man yelled. "All of you."

Chaos broke out in the car with all of us screaming.

A gun appeared, and the command that followed was curt and simple, "Shut the fuck up!"

It was effective. Christine's jaws snapped shut, Mandy's hands went to her mouth to seal it in silence, and my mouth was still open but no sound came out.

The man put his hand inside, yanked the latch, and pulled the door open. "Get out now!" he ordered.

We all did as we were told, but the moment Mandy stumbled out, she made the mistake of trying to run for it. The result was an immediate and brutal strike across her face. She fell to the ground with a scream of pain and terror.

"Mandy!" I yelled and turned towards her, but the hard nuzzle of the gun pressing into the back of my head stopped me cold.

"Move another muscle and I'll blow your head off."

Such fear filled my chest I couldn't even breathe properly.

"Tie them up," the one with a gun to the back of my head said. It was clear they were professional, purely by how quickly and efficiently the plastic ties were bound to our wrists.

Mandy was dragged roughly and slammed against the car. "Please don't hurt me," she cried. "Please."

Her quiet sobs broke my heart as I tried to meet her gaze to tell her how sorry I was, but she wouldn't even look in my direction. I couldn't understand what was happening. I had no idea this kind of danger was lurking around me. Now, I desperately wished I hadn't rallied the girls around to help me.

Christine had gone extremely quiet, and was also leaning against the door beside me.

"Who's Siciliana?" he asked, but he stared at me. He knew it was me, but he was making sure.

None of us spoke.

One of the men lifted his arm again. He pointed his gun to the back of Christine's head. "Who the fuck is Siciliana?"

"I am!" I instantly surrendered. "I am. I'm Sienna Siciliana."

The man who had asked the question nodded to his companion with satisfaction.

"We need to get out of here," one of the men said. "Get to it!"

"I'll come with you but please, please let my friends go. They have nothing to do with this."

None of them bothered responding.

Instead they moved into action. "Move," they commanded and they shoved us into walking.

The three of us were herded towards the van ahead.

I kept looking back to catch the gaze of the one pushing me. "Please. Let them go. I'm the only one you need. They have nothing to—"

"For the love of God, will you shut the fuck up?" he snarled.

"Calm the fuck down," another man scolded him in Italian.

A phone began to ring. It had the same ringtone as mine and I froze thinking it was mine. The last thing I needed was to have my phone confiscated.

"Yes," one of the men said gruffly.

I breathed easier at the realization that it wasn't mine.

He listened to whoever had called, then turned his head to look at me with cold, dead eyes. "Are you sure?" he asked.

My heart began to beat like a trapped bird against my chest.

"As you wish," he said and ended the call. He slipped the phone into his pocket and addressed his companions, "Let the other two go. Only she comes with us."

I released a deep breath, my knees almost buckling in relief. At least the immense guilt I felt for dragging them into this mess with me could stop now. My friends, still tied up, were tossed aside like garbage, and I was led to the van.

"Sienna," Christine called out from where she and Mandy had been thrown to the ground.

"Don't worry about me," I assured her. "I'll be fine. Be careful on your way back."

When I arrived at the back of the van one of the men slapped a patch of duct tape over my mouth. He glared at me. "Jesus, preserve me from rich girls." Then he unzipped my purse, took my phone out and threw it with force onto the road. It smashed into pieces. Then he pushed me roughly into the empty van and the door was slammed shut behind me.

I found myself lying on my side in pitch dark. I could still hear the men speaking outside though.

"If either of you say a single word about anything you've seen to anyone, we will hunt you both down and kill you. Do you understand?"

There was no answer from my friends, so I assumed they must have nodded. The van shook slightly as the men got into their seats in the front.

Now I knew what my father had been so frightened about. Why he had felt it necessary to marry me off to a stranger to keep me safe. Was I being kidnapped for money? Somehow, I doubted it. I had no idea what these men wanted from my father. I could only hope that whatever their demands were, it would be something that wouldn't break my father.

I knew now that my decision to run away from Angelo had been the wrong one, but even though I had jumped from the pan into the fire itself, I couldn't bring myself to regret my choice. I had only done what any other girl in my situation would have done if they had been forced to marry a man they detested. No matter what happened ... I would never regret standing up for myself.

I began to wonder if these masked strangers would be the last people I ever saw. I thought of my Nonna and Gemma, and tears filled my eyes as I bent my head in complete and utter dejection.

Suddenly, a gunshot exploded somewhere nearby, and before I could even lift my head, the van careened off to the left and I was thrown off balance, my head banging on the metal side. My heart leapt into my throat.

It swerved once again, and I was thrown along to the other end. This time, it hurt bad, so I quickly tried to spread myself and press myself to the floor of the van, so I'd have more stability. Then multiple shots rang into the air.

We were being attacked.

My first thought was my father's men had come to rescue me. Other than that, we were being attacked by a rival family. All of a sudden, a bullet zinged past my head, and burst its way out of the opposite end of the van. Whoa! No way, could it be my father's men out there. They wouldn't be shooting into the back of the van. We were being attacked.

I'm going to die here!

More gunshots rang out as I pressed myself to the floor as low as possible and prayed my father's men would win out. Suddenly, something rammed violently into the van. The sound was deafening. With a scream muffled by the tape across my mouth, I slid on the floor helplessly and slammed into the side of the van. The vehicle skidded sideways for a few seconds, its tires screeching, before it completely lost its balance and landed on its side. I felt myself fly into the darkness and ram hard against the metal.

"Arhhhh." Pain spread through my entire body.

The moments that followed were surreal, the only sounds I could pick up was a strange hissing sound, probably from the engine of the van. Other than this, it had become an ominous silence.

It was not over.

I tried to move my legs. They were like lead. I tried my very best to rise, but no dice. All I could do was flail them about like two dying fishes. Another gunshot followed and I went still. I held my breath and waited.

CHAPTER 18

SIENNA

*S*uddenly, the door of the van was pulled open.

Somehow, I found the strength to scramble to my elbows and knees to retreat further into the van, quickly moving as far away as possible from danger. I turned around to meet whatever was coming for me, but my eyes wouldn't adjust to the sudden infiltration of light from outside. All I could see was a dark silhouette watching me silently. It was like the straw that broke the camel's back.

I began to sob with sheer terror.

The silhouette stretched out his hand.

"Sienna," the man called, and I knew instantly I was safe, but I couldn't stop sobbing. The tears came from deep inside me. They were fear, terror, fury, confusion, shock.

"Sienna," Angelo called again. "It's okay. You're going to be all right. Come on out."

My heart lurched in my throat. I immediately crawled forward on my elbows and knees. When I reached the edge of the van, I leapt into his strong arms. He caught me and held me against his warm, hard body as I struggled to control the wave of hysteria that had overcome me at his appearance. I'd never felt relief so absolute and overwhelming.

"We need to get out of here," he whispered urgently into my ears.

I immediately nodded.

In the distance came the sound of sirens as they drew nearer and nearer with every passing second.

"Do you have any belongings in the van?" he asked.

I was about to shake my head when I remembered my purse. "My purse."

He dove into the van. A second later, he had retrieved it and was jumping out, landing as lightly as a cat. He grabbed my hands and rapidly moved me down the road. As we hurried along silently, I saw the bloodied bodies on the ground, and the Toyota that had crashed into a streetlamp. There were men inside, but they were unmoving. I noticed people starting to arrive. They looked shocked at the carnage. Then it occurred to me that he had caused all this damage by himself. The sound of police sirens sounded from not too far away.

"Hey," someone called out.

"Don't stop, keep your head down and don't look around," Angelo muttered. He had his face lowered, so his cap covered almost all his face.

I could feel the tension coming from him in waves. I knew then the danger wasn't over. We had to get out of here as soon as possible before the police arrived.

Self-preservation kicked in then, and together we ran, so fast I felt as if I was flying, my feet barely touching the ground. No one followed us. We turned the corner and I saw my car.

We ran towards it. I jumped into the passenger seat and before I could even put my seat belt on, he had put the car in motion. The Benz screeched backwards in a flash, then he spun around as though he were a race car driver and sped off.

His powerful hands were closed around the steering wheel and I could see the veins popping through his skin then disappeared underneath the sleeves of his jacket. He said nothing, but he seemed calm, the rise and fall of his chest even, his gaze laser-focused on the road ahead.

My mind quickly went to thoughts of Christine. I needed to call her straight away, but I had no phone. "I need to use your phone."

He glanced at me. "Why?"

"I'm worried about my friends and I have to check that they are okay. Please?" I was aware it was the first time I'd ever said the word to him.

He reached into his pocket for his phone, unlocked the screen, and passed it to me. "One minute," he said abruptly.

I took it gratefully and nervously dialed Christine. "Christine?" I shouted when she answered.

"Oh my God, Sienna, are you okay?"

"Yes, I'm fine. I'll tell you everything later. I just called to make sure you guys are safe?"

"We're fine, a little shook up, but in a taxi on the way home."

I sagged with relief. "Thank god." I couldn't live with myself if anything had happened to Christine and Mandy due to my family and me. "Ok, I have to go now, but I'll call you when I'm at home." I swiped the phone. "Thank you," I said and held the phone out to him.

He took it without a word or even a look in my direction.

I let my eyes travel to the lustrous hair that fell in soft waves around the base of his neck. Something seemed faintly vulnerable about the way the ends of his hair ended up in those adorable baby curls.

I swallowed hard and returned my gaze to the road. I knew I was in all sorts of trouble and the last thing I should be doing was lusting after him. I wanted to apologize and thank him and ask him how he had found me so quickly, but the words were stuck in my throat. All I could do was stare straight ahead.

He said nothing and we drove home without a single word being exchanged.

By the time we arrived home, I was as mentally prepared as I could be to meet my father. As I walked into the massive foyer, I couldn't believe the relief that washed through me at being able to return, when just a few hours earlier, this was the one place I would have given everything to escape from.

"Sienna!" my mother called.

I turned my gaze towards her and saw all the people waiting for my arrival. There were at least a dozen expressionless men in black suits gathered there too. I looked for Nonna, but when I found her eyes, they were inestimably sad, which surprised me, because I was unhurt. Nothing truly bad had happened. I'd been rescued in the nick of time.

My mother emerged from the midst of the crowd. "Oh baby," she cried and rushed forward to pull me into her arms. "My baby. My poor baby," she crooned.

I didn't want to cry. I had no reason to cry as I was safe and well, but suddenly I felt hot tears begin to burn the backs of my eyes. I tried my best to hold them at bay, but I just couldn't do it. They poured down my cheeks. I guess it was the release of the pent-up fear and shock.

My mother held desperately onto me, crying into my neck as she stroked my hair and back. "They nearly snatched you away from me. My only child. I love you," she told me over and over again. "Thank God, you're safe."

"I'm sorry I frightened you, Mama. I love you too," I sobbed.

Nonna came forward then. "Let the child go," she said quietly.

"I'm sorry, Nonna," I whispered, wringing my hands.

Her eyes moved quickly, assessing the bruises on my arms. "Don't be sorry. You did nothing wrong. You didn't understand how dangerous the outside world is for you. Why your father sent you away for all those years. Why he wants to make sure you are taken care of when he is no longer around."

The men in black suddenly parted and my father walked through. He stopped a few feet in front of me.

I stared at him through my tears. I had expected a scolding severe enough to make the sky fall, and maybe it would come later, but right now, it was clear he simply felt grateful I had survived the kidnapping. He must have thought he could have lost me forever today because I saw the utter relief in his eyes. He said just one word, "Come."

And I flew into his arms. He wound his arms tightly around me to rain kisses on my head and face.

I had never ever felt safer, more loved, or protected than at this moment.

Everything was once again right in my world. I forgot about Fabio waiting in the wings to take away my freedom and imprison me in a loveless marriage in exchange for this lovely safety.

CHAPTER 19

SIENNA

I woke up to the chirping of birds outside my window.

For the longest time, I didn't want to open my eyes, the events of the previous evening playing and replaying in my mind. The blast of gunshots ringing in the air, the dead bodies on the ground. Mandy as she had been struck by them, and the multiple car accidents.

It all felt like a distant dream, but my body still registered the terror. Multiple places in my body ached, but the raging headache I had gone to sleep with thankfully, had dissipated. With a sigh, I picked up my spare phone from the bedside table and texted Christine. I had called both girls last night to confirm that they were not too shaken, but I didn't want to call this early in the morning just in case they were still asleep. I sent a text instead.

Are you up?

Her response was to call me back. "Yeah, but Mandy's still sleeping."

"Are you sure you are alright?" I asked.

"Stop worrying about us. We're fine. As a matter of fact, that was the most exciting thing that has ever happened to me."

"You're kidding, right?"

"No, I'm an adrenaline junkie remember? And that was better than the best rollercoaster ride I've taken."

I shook my head. Nothing about last night had been exciting to me. It was the bars of my prison. I decided not to dwell on those thoughts. "My father has assigned a security detail on you and Mandy. You won't see them, but they will be around you for a little while, so they can monitor things and keep you safe for the time being."

"Oh," she said.

"Don't worry," I told her quickly. "They won't intrude in any way. This is just my father taking precautions and I'm telling you, so you both can be at ease."

"Well, thank your father for me."

I refrained from mentioning that she wouldn't need protection if not for her association with me. I ended the call when a knock came on my door.

"Come in," I called.

My father walked in.

I sat up straighter on the bed. "Good morning, Papa." I wondered if now was the time when my scolding would come. I felt ready and prepared to accept it all. I completely deserved it.

Instead, he came over to my bed, sat beside me, and placed his hand on my cheek … warm and as soft as a woman's hand. "How do you feel this morning?" he asked.

I shrugged and lied. "Great."

He pulled his hand away. "That's good." He opened his mouth to speak when another knock sounded my door. We both looked towards the door. "Come in," I called.

Gemma popped her head in, her smile lighting up the room, then dying somewhat when she spotted my father. "I've brought breakfast, but I can come back later if now is not a good time."

"No, no, bring it in," my father said cordially.

She came into the room then and stood back to allow the maid behind her holding a big tray of food to approach my bed.

I wasn't usually served breakfast in my room. Not that I would have wanted it. I preferred to have my breakfast in the kitchen, but since my foiled kidnapping last night, it was apparent Gemma had decided to pamper me for the next few days.

Once the legs of the tray were securely locked in place and the tray placed in front of me, Gemma and the maid hurriedly took their leave.

I could tell Gemma had wanted to spend some time with me, but my father's presence made that impossible. I didn't blame her. Even I felt intimidated and on edge when I was around him.

My gaze moved across the tray; from the small basket of croissant and muffins, to the stack of mini pancakes, to the bowl of fruit, and to the large plate of scrambled eggs, toast, cheese, fried sausages and bacon. "This is way too much," I mumbled.

"I'll help out," my father offered cheerfully.

I smiled back, but I felt super awkward inside. Dad never came to my room to have breakfast with me. Hell, he hardly ever ate breakfast with any of us.

He picked up a grape and popped it into his mouth. "I have a flight to Florence this morning," he said. "I'll only return in three days, so I wanted to talk with you before I left."

I nodded. "The uh … men from yesterday … do you have any idea what the attack was about? Was it something personal … to you, I mean?"

"It's always personal, Sienna." He picked up one of the croissants and began to lather it with apricot jam. "It's the nature of my world. Trying to keep count of the enemies I have would be like trying to trap water in my hands. What was jarring yesterday, was you getting harassed. I've tried my best for so many years to keep you away from it all and yesterday, those bastards crossed the line, daring to come after you. I have no choice now but to indulge in an awesome act of carnage to show them all that such behavior will never be tolerated."

I dropped my gaze down to the fantastic spread of food. "I'm sorry, Papa."

He set his croissant down on the tray without taking a bite. "Look at me."

I lifted my gaze to his.

He stared into my eyes, his own were like wet black stones. Impenetrable, unknowable. "Don't ever be so reckless again."

I shook my head slowly.

"Promise me you won't."

"I promise, I won't," I replied sincerely, looking into those hypnotic wet black stones.

"Good." He sighed with relief. "I'm sorry you cannot do the things you want to do, but as I have explained before, our family is not typical, little one. At every turn, there are people waiting to take us out of the game, and that is why we constantly have to be vigilant and careful. I'm getting old, and to those that covet my throne that is a weakness." He frowned. "I also don't have a son, which is an even bigger weakness. There are upstarts, killer sharks, constantly attacking the edges of my turf. And we will continue to be their target, unless you get married to another powerhouse. Then our strength will be multiplied ten-fold and these predators will think twice about attacking us. But right now, we're as naked as mad men on the streets."

My heart ached at his words. I wanted to ask him why he needed to be at the top of the predator chain. Why he couldn't just retire and let them take over. Didn't we already have enough? But yesterday's incident had severely humbled me.

I couldn't say a single word.

"Everything I do is to make sure that my family is okay. That you all are protected and lack for nothing. I know that you might not think much of Fabio right now, but give him a chance. He can protect you. Get to know him a bit more. You'll do that for me, won't you?"

I didn't dare lift my head up because my eyes had filled with tears. I tried to hold them back with everything I had, but they rolled down my cheeks.

"I'll leave you to rest," he said and rose to his feet.

"Have a safe trip, Papa," I muttered.

He bent down and kissed the top of my head. Then he took his leave.

When the door closed quietly behind him, I lifted my head and stared at it. Then I wiped the tears away from my face. I simply couldn't believe the turn my life had taken.

CHAPTER 20

ANGELO

https://www.youtube.com/watch?v=hCuMWrfXG4E
-Uptown Girl-

I stood in the corridor by the window where I had a clear view of her bedroom door and her balcony, basically both her exits. Beneath, Pedro, one of the gardeners, was carefully tending to the Japanese garden. He seemed to gently rake the white pebbles so they would look like a piece of art to anyone looking down from these upstairs windows.

Up ahead, one of the security guards was patrolling the grounds with Roman the Rottweiler in tow. The sleek, tightly muscled body of the dog gleamed in the morning sunlight. The guard spotted me at the window and waved.

I nodded in return.

I heard her bedroom door open and turned towards it.

Her father came out and started walking briskly towards me. "As you already know, I am away for three days. Make sure she is never out of your sight."

I nodded.

"Are you sure you don't want a partner? It will make things easier. I think she learned her lesson last night, but she is young, and freedom is a beautiful thing. She might try something again."

"Do as you wish, but I generally work better on my own."

His eyes narrowed. "So your preference is to work alone?"

"Always."

"Why?"

I shrugged. "I like having total control. Never having to worry what the other guy might do in a stressful situation."

"Fine. I don't want to lock her up, so I'm counting on you to keep her safe."

I nodded.

"Right. I'll see you when I get back, but keep me updated every night. You have my number. Call me day or night if anything happens."

I nodded again.

He turned to walk away, then he turned back and smiled. "Thank you for what you did last night. There'll be a nice bonus in your paycheck."

"Have a safe trip," I said.

For a second I saw a flash of anger and surprise that I didn't seem grateful for the 'nice' bonus in my paycheck, then it was gone. "Thank you," he said quietly and walked away.

I went back to watching her empty balcony. An image of her wet, angry and breathtakingly beautiful popped into my head. A fiery burst of lust flared up in my loins. My cock hardened.

I pushed the image out of my head instantly. I hadn't wanted to be assigned to be her bodyguard. I knew exactly what that meant. It meant fucking cold showers every day. And it also meant distraction from my goal. My goal was to train my body to become the best fighter in the world. Already, she had begun to affect my concentration.

I had to find a way to resist the call of her body. It was like a siren. Calling to me. No woman had ever had this effect on me. And as of yet, I'd been unwilling to examine it, but I knew she was big trouble. I had known it from the first moment our eyes met in the pool. But until yesterday, she'd been like an itch. Annoying, but still bearable and I knew not to touch it.

Or I'd end up scratching myself raw.

I told myself she was just a job. I had my dreams and they didn't include any entanglement with the only daughter of a Mafia family. I was no pushover. I could resist one rich, spoilt brat, no matter how beautiful she was …

But when I saw her, tied up and bruised in the van yesterday, my guts twisted and clenched like a hard fist. Hell, I felt so furious with those thugs, death wasn't good enough for them. I wanted to burn them alive and watch their agonized, horrified screams melt their lips. Even now just thinking about it, made my heart beat faster.

Outside, Juan, another gardener, came to join Pedro. He wore a large sombrero. They sat on the grass and shared a cigarette in the sun. They gestured with their hands as they talked. Then they parted ways and Pedro went back to his task of making art with pebbles.

I stood at my post watching Pedro until about fifteen minutes later, when a sound came from near her bedroom door. I turned to watch. Her door opened and she emerged dressed in a pink tracksuit. It hugged her full breasts and flaring hips in the most distracting way possible.

Hips swaying, she sauntered towards me. This was going to be damn hard.

I could feel her gaze on the darkened bruises across my cheekbones. Then she shocked me. She spread her arms, lifted herself on the tip of her toes and embraced me. She smelled of ripe fruit, flowers, and something forbidden. Her voluptuous curves fitted beautifully against my body. My hands itched to grab her and press her scented flesh tighter against me.

She pressed those luscious lips against mine. "Thank you," she whispered. Then she released me and walked away.

I was staggered. Not only by the way she had affected me, but by how much I wanted to carry her to my bed, spread her legs and pound into her. As I watched her walk away, my chest tightened.

Then I took a deep breath and followed those swaying, tantalizing curves.

CHAPTER 21

SIENNA

I walked away almost in a daze, unable to understand what had possessed me to kiss him like that. Even he looked shocked. Well, if nothing else, I had given him the perfect reason to hand in his resignation: reason for quitting, sexual harassment.

Maybe seeing his face made me feel guilty.

I had caused those bruises he sported and probably a bunch of others on his body that couldn't be seen. I had also almost caused the death of my friends, and judging from the still, bloodied bodies I'd seen on the ground as we made our escape from the scene, none of the men who captured me had survived.

Not that I felt sorry for them or anything, but I hated the thought of being directly responsible for someone's death. They must have had wives, lovers, and probably even children who would be mourning today. With a deep sigh, I headed towards the kitchen. I walked in and saw Gemma seated at the big wooden table by the corner perusing through a magazine. A tan dog sat on her lap.

"Mickey?" I squealed in surprise. "Gemma, is that Mickey?"

Gemma grinned. "Yes, it is."

I hurried over. "Oh, my God. Where has he been all these days?"

"At a dog spa in the countryside. He wasn't feeling too well, so your mother sent him over for treatment, rest, and pampering."

"Awww." I stroked his adorable head, but he didn't act like he was too happy to see me. It stung a little since he'd been part of the family for over a decade, but I could hardly blame him. In the last ten years, I could easily count the number of times I'd been allowed to come home for a visit. Still, after what happened last night, I finally understood my father's almost fanatical obsession for keeping me out of the way.

"How are you this morning?" Gemma asked, her eyes sliding over me.

"Great," I said cheerfully. "Mind if I take him for a walk?"

She lifted Mickey and passed him over to me.

Mickey gave my cheek a polite lick and I smiled at him. I went out through the back door to leash Mickey and put him on the ground. The estate was vast and I didn't want him to wander too far. I didn't trust the Rottweilers patrolling the ground. They might mistake him for a tasty snack.

I spotted the large tree I used to sit under when I was younger and hadn't found the chance to visit since I'd returned. Now seemed like the perfect time. Deciding to take the path north of the pool where the scenery was better, I strolled towards it. I was negotiating the narrow steps the gardeners used, when Mickey ran in front of me and in my effort not to step on him and squash him, my ankle twisted and I fell.

A whimper of pain escaped my throat as I hit the ground. "Damn it," I muttered, as I shifted my throbbing ankle out from under me.

Mickey began to run around me in circles, sniffing at my body with concern.

I stroked his fur. "So you do remember me. And you care." Then I turned my focus to my ankle to massage the bruised ligament. I knew it wasn't sprained or anything because I knew exactly what a sprained ankle felt like. I had fallen out of enough trees to know that not only what a sprain felt like, but also a broken bone.

His movements were so silent I heard him speak before his presence even registered, "Are you unable to get up?"

I felt my heart freeze in my chest. Damn it, he was the last person I wanted to see me sprawled inelegantly on the ground. I took a deep breath, but I didn't look up. Actually, I couldn't look up, or even respond for that matter.

I forced myself to gather up my wits and rise to my feet. I felt a strong, warm hand close around my arm. I wanted to protest, but the words wouldn't come out. I felt him hoist me up, as effortlessly as if I was a doll. I swear I couldn't breathe. I didn't know how it happened, but suddenly, my entire body was leaning against his for support.

"Are you all right?" he asked.

I glanced up and my eyes collided with his ocean blue gaze. Jesus! That eye contact felt like being seared with a branding iron. I jumped away from his hold and stood on my own two feet. "Yeah, I'm fine. Thanks," I muttered awkwardly, then looked around for the dog. "Mickey," I called. He came to me and I picked up the handle of his leash.

Angelo said nothing and I couldn't for the life of me think of anything to say, so I limped away. Not towards the house as a normal person who'd been injured would but away from it. It was just pride.

I knew he watched me as I walked and I couldn't recall ever feeling so painfully self-conscious.

But even pride couldn't make me walk on my bruised ankle all the way to the old tree, so I just headed towards my Nonna's pride and joy, her garden. I was surprised to see how much it had grown and matured since my last visit. It was a sight to behold. Filled with a mixture of fruit trees, flowering plants and herbs. The oranges, lemons and kumquats were ready for picking and the blood red roses were also in flower.

I sat on the bench by the pond. I patted my knees.

Mickey jumped up into my lap and curled up in it.

It was very peaceful here with the sound of water running down stacked rocks to empty into the clear pond, where rosy red minnows and koi swam amongst the broad green lily leaves. I watched the fish as they glided in never ending circles.

Eventually, I turned and glanced behind me. I thought he would be out of sight.

No, he was leaning against one of the trees. His hooded gaze unapologetically zeroed in on me.

My lips stretched into a nervous smile. "I want to explain," I said. "About yesterday."

Just as I expected he didn't respond. It was rude and I could feel myself getting irritated, but I removed my gaze from him and continued, "I know I was wrong, for trying to get away, especially for the way that I tried to do it. It put too many people at risk, but I had my reasons."

I heard him sigh.

"Anyway, it won't happen again," I announced. *You weren't wrong in trying to escape,* my heart cried out. But my realization of the real tragedy that could have befallen my friends from my decision to run away still filled me with remorse. Perhaps someday soon, I'd get over it and try again - this time making more elaborate plans and making sure no one else was in harm's way - but for now, I was physically and emotionally spent. I was ready and willing to do all that my father asked, without even the ghost of a complaint. I went on, "A-and I'm sorry about the hug earlier. I was just thankful, and uh … remorseful at seeing your injuries."

He remained rudely silent, which was really beginning to get on my nerves. I turned my attention to stroking the sleeping dog on my lap.

"What about you?" he asked suddenly. "Don't you have injuries from last night?"

I stared over at him in astonishment. Did he care I was hurt? *Don't be silly, Sienna. Of course not. He thinks you're spoiled garbage.* I shook my head. "No, other than a few bruises, I'm fine." I turned my face away then. Mostly because my cheeks were turning red, a sight he especially did not need to see, but also because holding his piercing blue gaze actually made my toes curl.

The silence ruled between us again, but I could no longer contain the desire to speak to him. I turned around to face him.

His gaze seemed to be set into the distance.

It sure sent me a message: having to guard me was possibly the worst thing he wanted to be doing right now, which perversely made me even more curious about him. *Who is he? And how did he become one of the guards in my father's camp?* "Since it seems like we are going to be spending a bit more time together, perhaps it wouldn't be too bad to get to know at least a little bit about each other."

He said nothing.

"I don't think I've seen you around before this trip. How long have you worked for my father?"

I waited for a few seconds, but *nein, nada, zilch*, from him.

I blushed in embarrassment, but unintimidated I kept going, "Well, um … I guess I'll start. I'll formally introduce myself then. I'm Sienna. Um … I turned twenty-three … a few months ago. What about you? How old are you? Where are you from?"

It was like talking to a dead piece of wood, but I just couldn't let it go. Talking to this rude man became the only thing my heart wanted in that moment.

"Fine you don't want to talk about yourself. Let's talk about yesterday," I began, keeping my voice crisp and professional. "How did you find me? We left you so far behind, I had never expected you'd be able to find us again. I'm glad you did though." A nervous laugh escaped my lips.

He turned to look at me and just shook his head.

I didn't know whether it was in amazement at my stupidity or just exasperation that he had to babysit such a pathetic person.

"I want to know," I said, my temper getting the better of me now. I could feel my heart start to thump. "How you found me."

He started glaring at me.

"I don't think it's proper for you to ignore me. You work for me."

This statement he was quick to respond to. "I don't work for you."

CHAPTER 22

SIENNA

*M*y stomach broiled with anger. I grasped Mickey's leash and shot to my feet. "Let's go, Mickey," I said, and began to walk away. However, I was so furious I couldn't let it go. I had to have my say too. How dare he treat me as if I am being childish and foolish just because I wanted there to be some peace and understanding between us if we were going to be on top of each other all the damn time. Well, not exactly on top of one another, but in each other's way.

How could absolutely no one understand me? Understand that even though my method had been risky, the intention behind my escape yesterday was valid. Why was everyone manipulating me into feeling childish and foolish and over entitled?

I felt too undeservedly hurt, so I turned around and went back to him. "I just want to say that you're terrible at your job. Otherwise, I shouldn't even have been taken yesterday. We were literally three girls in a Camry, and we managed to ditch you. Great fucking job." I stormed off, feeling more pathetic and petty than I ever believed possible, and it made me want to shoot someone.

"You're a fine one to talk?" he sneered.

I froze and spun around to face him. "What?"

"There were just four men," he said scornfully, "and yet you allowed yourself to be kidnapped so easily? Your father told me you were better than a dozen men. That you'd been trained in self-defense since you could walk."

I was sure I was mistaken, but he sounded angry. Why? I did not know. "My friends were there," I replied. "I couldn't be careless. They had guns. Self-defense and outrunning a bullet are two different things."

"You actually thought that they were going to shoot you?" he asked.

The abject condescension in his tone was staggering to me. "I had a gun stuck in my ribs," I shouted.

"I refuse to believe that you could be that naïve. Do you know absolutely nothing about the world you live in?"

I stared at him. "What do you mean?"

He raised his voice. "Couldn't you tell that they had been sent to capture you? Killing you would have been the same as taking their own lives."

"No!" I argued miserably. "I could not tell. It all happened so fast. I was in shock. The girls were screaming. How could I possibly tell the only thing they had been instructed to do was to capture me alive?"

"Even so … how could you just go with them? Your father would have done anything to get you back. His entire empire could have crumbled overnight. Surely, you must know, you are all that they need to get to him."

My eyes watered with frustration. "My friends were with me," I repeated. "They put a gun to Christine's head and knocked Mandy to the ground. What did you expect me to do? Let them kill my friends? They sure looked like they would have done it."

He shook his head. "Did you have to go to college in London to get this dumb?"

Hot tears burned their way out of my eyes and ran down my face. I swiped at them angrily. "Go on then. Tell me what I should have done? Sacrificed my friends for my father's business. Is that what I should have done, oh, super smart man who didn't have to go to college in London to become as dumb as me?"

He ignored my tantrum. "Didn't you also notice," he said quietly, "that the men were waiting for you at a particularly strategic location?"

I blinked. "What?"

"Your friend took you there, so that they could get to you."

"Are you out of your mind?" I yelled in disbelief. Christine was my best friend.

"Does it look like I'm out of my mind?" he responded calmly.

I shook my head. It felt as if my head was exploding. "No, no, you're wrong, buster. You don't know anything. If you think my friend set me up you're delusional. I've known that girl for years and I trust her. Far more than I trust *you*!"

He straightened away from the tree. "Why don't you believe you were set up?"

"Because it's impossible."

"Who else apart from your friends knew of your planned escape?"

My heart ... was hurting.

He shook his head mockingly. "I don't want to be rude about your mother, but I'm beginning to doubt you are Siciliano's daughter."

I lost it then. Dragging poor Mickey with me, I marched menacingly towards him.

CHAPTER 23

SIENNA

*H*e didn't move a muscle.

I stopped in front of him so angry I wanted to punch his jaw. "Take that back," I said through gritted teeth.

"Take what back? That I'm beginning to doubt you're your father's daughter? I'm sorry but I don't know how else to explain why you were so utterly clueless yesterday."

The burn in my chest at the abuse and accusation was too much for me to take. Before I could catch myself, I lost it. Blind rage took over and my fist swung towards him. Unfortunately for me he was quicker than a bolt of lightning. He jerked his head back, and effortlessly dodged the blow.

I, on the other hand, had put too much force into my swing. The momentum carried me forward and I stumbled forward, taking me headfirst into the wall of his chest.

He caught me roughly by my arms, and set me away from him.

But my sore ankle twisted under me and I found myself collapsing to the ground. I was shocked when I looked up at him.

Surprise flashed across his face, then his expression settled into confusion ... and pity!

With a scream of fury, I jumped up to my feet, throbbing ankle be damned, and went for him.

I swung my fists ... one strike and then another, and with the momentum of that one yet another one, but he effectively blocked each one, each time fluidly moving out of the way before I could even so much as touch a hair on his body.

Now I felt absolutely embarrassed, because I had trained almost all my life, so how was it possible that I couldn't even hurt him once? I n*eeded* to hurt him, at least once, otherwise I didn't know how I would be able to move on from the embarrassment. How would I ever be able to face him again?

So I kept on fighting, exerting all my energy, ignoring all the aches and pains I'd incurred the previous evening.

Mickey began to yap in terror at the uneven exchange.

"Stop!" Angelo growled. "You're going to fucking hurt yourself."

"Fuck you!" I roared right back at him and lunged ferociously at him.

This time, he caught both my wrists then held me away from him as I kicked, yelled, and swore at him like a wild cat. "Stop it," he snarled.

I swung my leg, aiming for the bulge between his thighs. But of course, he moved, snapping his legs shut and trapping my leg between his thighs before it could attack the vital area. I was left standing precariously on the leg with the bruised ankle, but that gave me the opening that I had truly been hoping for. Using all my strength I smashed my wrists out of his loosened grasp. This time around, I did not miss.

Quick as an arrow, I balled my fist and struck his face. The blow was so hard his head turned and I lost my balance. I fell on top of him. I went down with him, not even minding the fall for a single second. Before I could catch my breath, he had pushed me off him and was sitting up, his thumb pressed against the corner of his lip. It came away with blood. His cap had flown off his head and landed a few feet away and when he turned his gaze on me, I got the full force of those blue eyes. But they were no longer ocean blue.

They were dark. Incredibly dark. Like a stormy sky in December.

I crawled backwards and scrambled to my feet. I quickly recovered from the shock of seeing those eyes and glared back at him. "Still think I'm not a Siciliano?" I panted.

Ignoring me, which completely infuriated me, the bastard rose to his feet and strolled over to where his cap had fallen as if I hadn't just taken him down and drew blood. He bent down to pick his cap up.

I saw my chance … and took it. While his gaze was on the ground and his body open for attack, I flew towards him. My leg was aimed at his stomach ready to inflict the kind of lethal kick that would drain the strength from his legs and make his collapse to the ground in a sorry heap. It was the only end to this quarrel I would accept. In fact, I needed to triumph over him. The need came from the depths of my soul.

As I was inches away from felling him, he whirled around and with his knees still bent, he grabbed onto the leg I had struck out—the perfect recipe for a disastrous fall.

In a split second, the world turned upside down for me.

I started to fall, and he pounced on me. It all happened so fast there wasn't time to think or react, but with his weight crashing down on top of me I knew my landing would be hard. The summer had baked the ground into a hard surface and I expected nothing less than a cracked skull.

To my surprise, it was not to be.

Suddenly, we were both on the ground, although, his body was on top of me - it wasn't crushing me - with no hard knock to the back of my head and I wasn't seeing stars. It took a few seconds to realize why. One of his hands was curved around the back of my head and it had cushioned the impact of my fall, while the other hand held his upper body cleanly away from me.

The sun was beating down on us and I could hear my wild heart pounding like the feet of a herd of zebras being chased by lions. My breath came in fast, short bursts as I stared with wide eyes up at him. Veins were popping out across his forehead and it was startling how close his electric blue eyes were to me. His hot breath tickled my face. The tips of our noses were almost grazing and our lips mere inches away.

For one crazy, insane, totally mindless, shocking, split second, I saw what looked like clawing, desperate lust in his eyes. Then it was gone and all I could feel was the heat coming from his body and the hardness of his cock digging into my belly. As I stared into his electric eyes, I realized this had never been a simple dispute. This was war! Our bodies were at war. As much as we hated each other's guts, our bodies were being pulled irresistibly and disastrously towards the other. Like magnets we rushed to join and stick.

With a frown, he tried to push himself away from me, but without thinking my arms shot out and encircled his waist, gluing his lower body to mine. Like magnets. With the same blind logic, I raised my face and crushed my lips to his.

His entire body froze.

I could feel him fighting with himself as I licked his lips, tasting him. Like a vixen asking for permission to enter. His lips parted and I slipped my tongue into his mouth. God, he tasted delicious.

He tried to resist. Really, he tried, but I tightened my arms around him, swirled my tongue with his, and pulled it into my mouth.

As soon as I started to suck it, I heard a muffled groan and he gave in. He hooked my tongue and sucked it into his mouth. A pleasure so intense struck me and I almost became paralyzed by it. It felt as if I had died and gone to heaven. I could feel my hips begin to rock. The movement instinctive and out of my control. His cock had become as hard as a piece of wood and I wanted it inside me.

It was shocking, but I had become no more than a shameless animal driven by the desire to mate. Out in the open and not caring who saw or heard.

Suddenly, without any warning, he tore his mouth away and stared down at me. His eyes were hooded and astonished.

Frozen underneath him, I did nothing. Just gazed back at him in a daze of need. I wanted that mouth back on mine, but my hands fell away from around him.

"Fuck," he muttered. He shook his head as if to clear it. "Fuck," he repeated. "What the fuck?" Then he vaulted away from me as though he'd been burned. For a few moments, he stood there as if he couldn't understand what had happened. Then he ran his hands through his hair and frowned. "Don't tell your friends what I said or of your plans, until I've investigated and cleared them." His voice sounded thick and hoarse.

"Fine, I won't tell them anything, but you are wrong about them," I said, my voice not much better.

With one last disbelieving glare at me, he walked away.

I lifted myself up on my elbows, and watched him leave, walking away as though both of our worlds had not just been shaken.

Little Mickey came to me then, nuzzling at my body and my face.

I fell back down and allowed the dog to jump all over me since I couldn't get up anyway. That kiss had sucked out every ounce of energy from my system and it could take a while to recover. I closed my eyes and dreamed of the way those cold blue eyes had burst into flames and burned my core. Then I thought of his cock. How big and hard it had been as it pressed into me. I was so wet and hungry for it. But all of it shocked me to the core.

Maybe he could fend me off effortlessly with his fists, but it wasn't me at the end of the day, who had all but run away for dear life. The thought made me smile. When I'd recovered enough, I rose to my feet. Now, in a significantly better mood I went to retrieve Angelo's cap from the ground. I brought it to my nose and inhaled the scent of him. Butterflies started flapping in my belly. I jammed his cap on my head and headed back towards the house. My ankle hurt a bit, but so much adrenaline ramped through my veins I hardly felt it. In fact, I'd become so high on dopamine, I felt as if I was walking on a cloud.

My confidence began to crumble as the house came into view. What I had done had begun to dawn on me. I had kissed my bodyguard. Mickey's leash fell from my hand as my hand flew to my mouth. I had kissed Angelo Barone! Aloof, ferocious, grumpy, unfriendly, arrogant Angelo.

I had lost my mind. There was no doubt about it now—I had completely gone insane.

"Sienna?"

I spun around, my heart slamming painfully against my rib cage. *Oh, my God. My mother. If she knew ...*

"Are you all right?" she asked, taking a step towards me.

Automatically, I took one away from her. "I'm fine."

I could tell from her face she didn't believe me ... and I didn't believe myself either.

CHAPTER 24

ANGELO

https://www.youtube.com/watch?v=UtvmTu4zAMg
-She drives me crazy-

*J*stood at the foot of the stairs and watched as she descended in an electric blue dress that hung off her shoulders. It was long and would have been demure if not for the slit that ran all the way to the middle of her thigh, exposing her silky-smooth skin … that I had touched.

It took everything I had not to stare at the tantalizing picture. For she was as alluring as a siren singing on a rock and I was one of those hapless sailors. No matter how hard I tried, I couldn't stop myself from the lure of her deathly call. It felt as if there were termites in my brain, day and night, eating relentlessly.

A week had passed since the 'incident' by the pond, but it remained as fresh in my mind as if it'd happened yesterday. Every second of it had been branded into my brain. The feel of her sun-warmed skin, the intoxicating taste of her soft mouth. The way she had tightly jerked those delectable curves against my dick.

She wanted it. Hell, did she want it.

She was as desperate to scratch her itch as I was. I knew she was trouble from the first moment I laid eyes on her, but it shocked me how much I wanted to fuck her. It was unbelievable. I forgot where I was, who she was, who I was. Fuck, let's call it what it was—I lost control of myself. If we had been anywhere more private, I couldn't have stopped myself. As it was it took everything I had to pull away. And walk away.

I'd gone through what happened second by second because I just couldn't understand how I'd gotten myself into such a position. Had it just been my annoyance at her inability to defend herself that had spurred a crazed need in me to rile her up, to get her out of her damn shell of helplessness? But when I had poked what I assumed was a cub, a lioness had awakened, attacked me, and showed me she was ready to mate.

Being the spoilt girl she was, she probably thought it was fun to taunt the bodyguard. See how much she could twist him around her little finger. She had no idea what kind of danger she was flirting with. And I wasn't even referring to her father. I wasn't a man for twisting.

Plus, I came with problems. Big problems.

After that episode though, she must have come to her senses enough to realize she'd crossed a very serious line. Clearly, she was aware of my presence but she pretended like I didn't exist. Which was a great relief because I knew now I couldn't completely trust myself to stop if she decided to pull another crazy stunt.

Thankfully, she also hadn't left the house so there was no need for me to escort her as closely as I would have had to, were we not within the safety of the mansion grounds.

Now, as she came closer to the bottom of the stairs, I could feel her eyes on me, so I forced myself to turn away and stare straight ahead at nothing. I couldn't wipe the picture of her in her decently indecent dress out of my mind, but I could ignore it and focus on my job.

Her mother came out of one of the living rooms and called out to her.

After being fussed over by her mother, Sienna moved towards the entrance and I followed closely behind her.

Outside, he was waiting inside his SUV. He jumped down from the driver's seat and came over to her.

I waited to confirm that she got in safely before I would follow them in a different vehicle.

"You look beautiful,'" he murmured, and pulled her into an embrace. She stood stiffly inside his arms while he placed a kiss on either side of her cheek.

I looked away then with my stomach clenching.

"Who is this?" he asked with a sour note in his voice.

I knew instantly he was going to be a pain in the ass.

"My bodyguard," she replied, and began to walk towards the car, but he caught her hand as she headed to the front seat, and led her to the back instead.

I knew exactly what he was up to, but I saw the slight confusion on her face as he pulled the door open and ushered her inside. Before he could shut the door and turn towards me, I was already walking away.

He had obviously fooled Sienna's father, but not me. I'd met men like him before. Many times. Bullies bloated with their own self-importance, but ultimately cowards who would crawl on their bellies to beg for their life.

"Hey!" he called.

I stopped in my tracks and glanced back at him.

He lifted a finger and beckoned me with it. The gesture was meant to aggravate and establish who was boss.

The reason I had taken this job was because of the ability to use the pool at my convenience, late in the night, and for the fact that it would always keep me on my toes, but I had not foreseen this! A constant battle to restrain myself from punching someone's light out. I did nothing, just stared at him, wondering how he would dig himself out of the hole he had dug.

Glowering at me, he closed the distance between us and stood in front of me. He was a good one foot shorter than me and he didn't like that one bit either. "Take that cap off," he ordered sternly. He was all puffed out like an animal that makes itself look bigger to appear more formidable than it is.

If he was hoping to scare me into submission, he was sorely mistaken. "With *respect*, I don't think I will," I said sarcastically.

Although it was already dark, I could see his face redden with embarrassment. Something about me irritated him and he'd tried to dominate me, but had failed. Now his pride was at stake.

Sienna rolled down her windows. "Fabio," she called with a note of desperation in her voice. "We should get going. We're going to be late."

She had given him a nice out, but of course, the jerk couldn't just take it and leave. He scoffed, then tossed his car key into the air. I sidestepped it and it fell to the ground. He glanced at the key fob on the ground then back at me in disbelief. He was livid. "Can't you fucking catch?" he exploded.

"I didn't know I was supposed to, Sir," I said with maddening calmness.

His whole body stiffened with fury. Clearly, no one had ever disrespected him in that way, and in front of his date too. It was more than the spoilt prick could bear. "Pick the key up!" he spat, the tendons in his neck starting to bulge with tension.

I stared curiously at him. He seemed utterly unaware of the fact that I didn't take my orders from him. To be honest, I was quite interested to see what would happen next. How he planned to make me pick up the key when it was blatantly clear he didn't stand a chance in any fight against me.

Fortunately, or perhaps unfortunately, Sienna jumped out of the car and hurried over. "For God's sake," she muttered as she bent down to retrieve the key herself. She smiled tightly at the bastard. "The plan was for Angelo to ride behind us in a separate car, but your idea is actually better. He might as well just come along with us." Then she turned to me and held out the key.

I looked into her eyes.

Don't make a scene, her eyes pleaded.

I took the key without a word and started walking towards the asshole's SUV.

"I don't like him," I heard him mutter to her.

"Well, you don't have to. Papa believes he's the best man for the job of protecting me and after the way he reacted to my attempted kidnapping the other day, I agree with him."

"He needs to be taken down a notch or two," he promised.

Be my guest, asshole. Be my guest. I got into the driver's seat, started the engine, and waited for them to get in.

CHAPTER 25

SIENNA

I sat in a vehicle with two men who sure looked like they wanted to go at each other's throats, and I knew I was the reason. At some primitive, instinctive level, Fabio had understood the threat Angelo represented.

I watched Fabio as he stared out of the window, his hand to his mouth as though he was lost in thought, but his right foot kept tapping rapidly against the floor. He was fuming … and planning his revenge.

Angelo on the other hand drove like he didn't have a care in the world. Focused solely on what he was doing, he seemed oblivious to us and everything else, but I knew this was a lie. He was very in tune to even our slightest movement.

I turned to stare out of the window. It was Nonna who had convinced me to go on this date … to give Fabio a chance. My confidence had taken a severe beating after my previous escape attempt and I hadn't needed much convincing. I knew now how dangerous my situation was. And worse, how much pain I could so easily cause to my whole family. I couldn't just think of myself and what I wanted to do … I had to think for my family. Besides, everyone had tried to convince me that Fabio wasn't as bad as I thought.

I decided to give him another chance.

So here I was, and so far, his actions had done absolutely nothing to sway me over to his side. But when I thought more deeply about what had just happened, I realized I was being unfair to Fabio. What would I have done if I had found myself confronting a girl Angelo was making eyes at? I would have wanted to punch her mouth in too.

At this point, I stopped my train of thought. Where had that come from? What Angelo and I had was just chemistry. We could never be anything other than ships passing in the night. *Nothing* more could ever happen. My father would almost certainly have him killed if he thought anything was going on between us. I turned determinedly away from this subject and glanced at Fabio, but he appeared to be still smoldering with anger.

Nope, no point trying to strike up a conversation there. Might as well allow some time to pass for the steam to evaporate from his head. Hopefully by the time we arrived at the restaurant, he would have calmed down. No matter how hard it would be, I wanted to keep an open mind on the subject of Fabio.

When we arrived at our table however, he gallantly waited until the waiter had seated me before he took a seat himself and became extremely attentive to my needs. I felt surprised.

He found a wine from my father's winery on the menu that he immediately ordered. The wine arrived and we clinked glasses. As I took a sip, our eyes met and he smiled at me. I smiled back. Finally, we both shared something we loved.

For the first time tonight, I began to somewhat look forward to the outing.

"I'm having the lamb shank. I can recommend it," he said opening the menu.

It took me only a few seconds to make my decision. Chargrilled chicken with baby fennel and wild rice.

"Excellent choice," he complimented softly.

I took another sip of my wine and smiled at him. "Dad told me that you've been in charge of some parts of the business since the beginning of the year."

"Yes," he said simply.

"He also told me you've had an impressive record of growth, especially with the recent foray into Asia."

"I have a capable team behind me," he said.

Again, to my surprise, he seemed to act humble. Maybe I had judged him too fast and inaccurately.

Just then, he snapped his fingers to call the attention of the waiter.

I leaned back and wondered if I would ever like him as a person.

The waiter came over to take our order, and once he was gone, I politely inquired about his family.

Eventually, he started talking about his teenage sister, Maria who was about to round up with high school. I had met the girl a couple of times at parties and vaguely remembered her as a sweet little thing with dark curly hair.

"She wants to go to Florence to study design," he said, a smile tugging at his lips as he thought of his baby sister. "But of course, my parents don't want to hear of it."

"Why not?"

"You don't know?" he asked, twirling the stem of his wineglass in his fingers.

I drained my glass. "They are afraid she will be kidnapped?"

He nodded and looked away.

I followed his gaze around the candlelit restaurant. A grand piano on a small stage, and a man sat behind it, delivering tinkling music that further helped soften the ambience of the restaurant. It seemed like the perfect place to fall in love, which made me wonder as I turned to the man sitting before me, if I would ever be able to love him. At the thought, an image of Angelo out at the bar filled my head. Wearing his baseball hat, his face completely expressionless and drinking a glass of Coke.

"You look beautiful tonight," Fabio murmured.

I appreciated the compliment with a soft smile, but it didn't in any way compare to the intense pull I felt when Angelo even looked in my direction. But that— was just lust and it would burn out in a week. Marriage and lust had nothing to do with each other. Fabio was marriage material. Someone who understood the world I lived in and would stick by me to the very end. With great determination, I pushed Angelo out of my mind and replied, "And you look handsome tonight."

It wasn't a lie. He did look good for a change. His hair swept away from his pale face with an elegant look. He wore a crisp white shirt and his blazer was a dark shade of maroon …

complete with a pocket square. As someone interested in design and color arrangements, it wasn't a bad combination at all.

"Maybe our parents know best? Maybe we can pull his thing off," he observed with a twist of his lips.

I sucked in my breath. Instinctively, my body rebelled against the idea. I took a big gulp of wine. Thank God, the waiters chose that moment to deliver our food.

"Your appetizer looks delicious," he commented mildly.

"So does yours," I replied politely.

"Thank you. *Buon appetito.*"

"*Buon appetito* to you too," I murmured.

We began to eat and engage in small talk. To my surprise, we never ran out of things to talk about. I guess we had a lot in common. We shared the same nosy relatives, we shared the same background, we were both interested in the wine and the family business. Soon, I felt so relaxed and comfortable, I even allowed myself to taste some of his lamb off his fork when it arrived. It was good, but not as good as my chicken, which literally melted on my tongue.

The wine was gone and we decided to share a chocolate lava cake. By now, I was laughing at his story of how he'd once tried to tell his kindergarten teacher that he was allergic to peanuts after he'd accidentally eaten one of the other children's cookies.

"The bitch didn't believe me," he said and the incredulous look on his face made me giggle even more. "She thought that I was looking for a reason to consume more soda."

"You were very greedy when you were young," I said on her behalf. "I think I remember your mother telling Gemma to hide all the chocolates whenever you were coming."

He made an impatient face. "I was a growing boy. Of course, I ate a lot."

"What happened with the cookies?" I reminded, licking my spoon.

"My tongue swelled and they had to rush me off to hospital. My mom threw a massive fit and almost even got her fired. She had to apologize to me."

I leaned back. There was too much satisfaction on his face when he said the last line. I'd had a somewhat pleasant time, despite how absolutely unconvinced I'd been earlier that it wouldn't be. But that last line had kinda spoiled it for me though. I remembered him sporting this same expression when he'd chased me with the squirming frog clasped in his meaty hands. Every time I thought he had somewhat redeemed himself and we could move to the next level, he said or did something that made me dislike him all over again.

"I guess we should go," I said softly.

He snapped his fingers again for the waiter.

At his snapping, I cringed inwardly. I'd worked as a waitress in London and I hated it when people did that. It was so unnecessary. Only the most arrogant, most entitled customers did something so rude.

The silence between us had suddenly turned awkward and I turned towards him to thank him for the evening. "Thanks for taking me out, Fabio. I had a great time tonight."

"You're welcome," he said, with a nod.

I tried to ignore the fact that he hadn't responded in kind.

Once the bill was paid, we went towards the bar where Angelo was waiting. Just the thought of seeing him again made a little shiver of excitement run up my spine.

He didn't even look at me. He just slipped off the stool he'd been sitting on and made his way towards the entrance.

The valet brought the car around and Fabio placed his hand on the small of my back to lead me forward. It felt weirdly intimate, and I had to force myself not to pull away. I was committed to doing my best in giving him a fair chance.

Once I got into the car however, the reverence he had shown in the restaurant dissipated. He stared at me with a smile on his face, and although I didn't hate it, I didn't know how to keep responding to it, especially since it was way too prolonged to mean absolutely nothing.

"You truly are a gorgeous woman, Sienna," he murmured.

I tried not to frown. The compliments before had been empty, but it seemed as if he were somewhere with it and I was simply not ready for it. Whatever it was.

Before I could even think of a suitable thing to say he leaned forward and curved his hands around the back of my head. He was going to kiss me! My heart was beating fast in my chest, but it had absolutely nothing to do with excitement. It was sheer dread. First, at the thought of kissing him and second—at the idea of doing it just a few feet away from Angelo. My hands shot out and pushed against his chest.

My smile was nervous, as I met his confused gaze. "Sorry, I'm a little drunk."

"That's perfectly fine to me." He increased the force behind my head.

I had no choice but to let my face be pulled towards his. I smelled the wine we'd just consumed and felt revulsion. Quickly, I snapped my mouth shut and he brushed his thin, cold lips against mine.

I broke away from him and knowing how fragile his ego was and not wanting to provoke a tantrum, I smiled tightly. "Let's wait till we're alone."

"We are alone," he spat. "Ignore that piece of shit in front, he's nobody."

My jaw dropped. I felt so shocked by the unbelievable arrogance of his words that I was too slow to even shut my mouth when he lunged forward and slipped his tongue into my mouth. My entire being shuddered with anger. I jerked my head back. "Fabio," I tried to pull out of his grasp but his hold just tightened around me.

He refused to let me go, drawing even closer until I was cornered against the door and his body completely covering mine.

"Fabio!" I called, my voice growing sterner.

"Come on ..." he growled.

Then to my utter surprise, his hand was on my breast. I reacted like a cut snake. I twisted and shoved hard at his shoulders.

The impact of the blow shocked him and he fell backwards, his eyes widening at the unexpected attack.

I threw a glance at Angelo and picked up the tense muscles in his shoulders, and his hands gripping the steering wheel so hard, his knuckles showed white.

I didn't need a showdown. I needed to diffuse the situation. And right now. "I'm sorry, Fabio. I'm just not ready yet."

But he didn't listen to me. His dark eyes were on my hips. Suddenly, his hand closed around my thighs and I was pulled across the seat towards him. He slanted his head once again to plant sloppy kisses down my neck.

I knew what this was about. I didn't have much experience with men, but I could tell this didn't come from a place of lust or passion. This was all about Angelo. He was proving himself to Angelo!

I took a deep breath. We had made such progress at dinner ... why oh, why was he allowing his narcissistic pissing contest with Angelo to ruin the night? "Fabio," I warned.

But instead of stopping, his hands slipped up my thighs.

Jesus Christ! It felt like a rodent had crawled up my skin. "I said stop!" I yelled, and was about to shove him off me, when the car suddenly swerved.

He was thrown away from me against his door, and I just about managed to grab onto the handle of the door to stop myself from crashing into him. The car was now back on its straight, smooth course after that jarring swerve.

For what seemed like forever, an excruciating silence filled the space.

"My apologies," Angelo said cheerfully. "I thought I saw a skunk on the road."

I couldn't breathe.

Fabio glared at the back of his head like he had made up his mind to kill him. He knew there had been absolutely nothing coincidental about that interruption.

This whole thing made my face burn with abject humiliation. My breath shuddered as I turned away from Fabio, and curved towards my door. As I stared out of the window, my eyes stung with tears.

CHAPTER 26

ANGELO

https://www.youtube.com/watch?v=129kuDCQtHs

I tried to let it go, but I couldn't.

I needed to know, so despite every fiber of my being telling me I was making the wrong decision, a little while after I had dropped her off, I headed back towards her room. I hesitated outside her door, but my hand raised of its own accord and rapped on the wood.

Seconds later, she opened the door.

Her eyes widened with surprise to see me, but I didn't fail to notice how all the glorious light in them had dimmed. From the reddened rims, it was obvious she had been crying.

"What is it?" she asked, immediately alarmed. Her worried gaze darted past me into the corridor. "Are my parents okay?"

Without a word, I marched into the room.

"What the ... hey!"

At her sharp call, I turned and noted she had also come into the room and automatically shut the door behind her.

"I want to know something," I growled. "Can you truly not defend yourself, or is this 'I'm a delicate little hothouse flower shit' some kind of strategic ploy to make you appear helpless?"

The despair fled from her eyes. Burning anger and disbelief replaced it and that weirdly brought me a sense of relief.

"Is *that* why you're here?" she asked furiously.

"Why else?"

"I can't believe you came here in the dead of night to ask me this?"

"I wouldn't call 10:30pm the dead of night, however ... this is a question that needs answering. Your father told me that you have all the skills needed to protect yourself, so why can't you fend off even one man attempting to assault you?"

She scoffed. "That one man is the man that has been chosen for me to marry. The one that I tried to escape from. The escape that I was branded an idiot for attempting. Have you forgotten all that so quickly?"

I took a step towards her. "That is none of my business. Quite frankly, I don't believe that you're a damsel in distress, but for some reason you're trying to appear so. Please clearly lay out to me the instances where you will need my interference, because the next time that dog assaults you the way that he did today, one of us is going to end up dead. And it won't be me."

"Why do you care?" she asked.

I began to storm away, but her whisper stopped me in my tracks. Every muscle in my body responded to those words. And not in a good way. I hated how she had such a hold over me. Why did I care? Why had her being harassed hurt me so much I wanted to bury a bullet in the dog's head? I felt like a cornered animal.

"For the past week you've been acting like I don't exist. So why do you care now whether I'm assaulted or not?"

"Because it's my job." I turned around and snarled.

She knew she had me then. She folded her arms over her chest. "Is it also your job to storm into my bedroom in the middle of the night, under the pretense of questioning me about my fighting skills?"

I had long mastered the ability to keep my face expressionless but I could feel a muscle in my jaw twitching. She was right. I had absolutely no business being here. I was losing my damn mind. What was it to me if she was harassed by her fiancé? Maybe she liked that sort of thing. After all, she hadn't called out to me to intervene. The truth was none of it was any of my business. "You're right," I said slowly. "It's none of my business." Then I turned around and carried on towards the door.

Before I could get to it, she dashed over and stood in front of it.

I stared at her, and she stared back, her arms folded across her chest. It took all of my will power not to stare at how her breasts swelled up over her hands.

"I could have handled him," she said. "But having the man I'd promised my parents I would give a chance to, return with a black eye wouldn't have sat too well with them."

I nodded. "Do as you see fit." I took another step forward expecting her to move away, but she didn't.

"The last time," she said. "I wasn't in my best state. I was feeling emotionally and physically fragile and you took advantage of that."

I frowned. "What?"

"I want a rematch," she said. "Right here. Right now. You're right, I am well able to defend myself, against a majority of people anyway. But against a self-defense expert like you, perhaps I am lacking so I need to see how my skills compare to yours. Also, this will be a good way for you to gauge if I am able to handle myself in your absence, or if it is necessary for me to take the lessons needed to improve." Her hand suddenly shot out then.

So did mine. I seized her slender wrist in the air.

Her response was a wicked smile. "You're good," she observed, "but then I don't think I'm that bad either." In a flash, she twisted out of my grasp, and the next thing I saw was the back of her head. The next thing I felt, was her elbow as it was driven solidly into the side of my face.

CHAPTER 27

ANGELO

https://www.youtube.com/watch?v=ERT_7u5L0dc

I was completely surprised at just how quick she had been. Once again, she had burst the side of my lip. My thumb came up to staunch the blood flow, but I couldn't take my eyes off her. She was so fucking beautiful.

"How's that for a start?" she asked.

"Not bad," I replied. "But can you get another strike in, especially now that I am fully aware of you?"

She slipped the robe off her shoulders and once again, I was so fascinated by the way the silky material slid down her arms to reveal her glistening pale skin that all I could do was stare, hypnotized.

Before I knew what was happening another blow was struck, but this time it was directly on my chest, and it made me stagger. Before I could recover, she struck me again, but this time one or two of my brain cells had rebooted and started working.

I blocked her clenched fist mid-air with my open hand, but my strength sent her flying towards the door. My heart leapt into my throat as she hit it with a dull thud and gave a cry of pain. I really didn't want to hurt her even though my face and chest throbbed as though I had been hit with a bat.

I managed to keep my face expressionless, but I couldn't let her continue on with this madness. For one thing, she was having a really bad effect on me. I could hardly look at her now since she was indecently exposed in a black baby doll nightie. She had no bra on. I could see the outline of her nipples. They were hard as pebbles. Her full breasts rose and fell with every gasping breath she took. I could already see myself sucking those breasts. There was a bed behind us.

Hell, what was I thinking of?

"Forget it," I said, without looking at her. Not when I was on the verge of losing my mind and taking her right here and now. I reached the door and placed my hand on the handle. "Move!"

To my surprise, she slid between me and the door, her gaze boring up into mine. "Who says we're done? I want to carry on the fight."

"That was not a fight," I said as evenly as I could. I wanted to fuck her so bad my dick hurt, but I'd be damned if I let her in on it. "It's obvious you need urgent and intensive training. Either the person who taught and assessed you as capable of handling yourself was an incompetent fool, or you've forgotten all that you've learned, which I don't know how it's possible. Or worse still, you used the same er … techniques on your instructor you're using on me into giving you a pass."

Her eyes widened and as her pupils enlarged too. "Wow. That's the most I've ever heard you say," she murmured.

An irreversible accident would absolutely happen if I remained here any longer. "Move!" I growled and tried to grab her arm.

She twisted out of my reach and knocked the edge of her hand against the vital brachial plexus pressure point in my neck.

Pain reverberated through my body as the strength instantly drained from my knees. "Fuck!" I hissed. In a flash, I was the one who was grabbed, and pushed against the door.

Her strength was definitely speed … and distraction. It was too easy for me to constantly let down my guard around her and she took advantage of it every single time.

She had a hand held across my chest, pinning me to the door and her eyes … were sparkling. "I got you," she said.

My breath hitched in my throat and for very different reasons. I pulled my gaze away, now at the very edge of my limit. "Let go," I said, the pain beginning to dissipate and other more urgent calls taking its place. I should never have come to her room.

"Will you admit it now? That I can take care of myself?"

I grabbed her wrist to pull her away, but then she shocked me again. She leaned forwards and pressed her entire body against mine. Her breasts were pushed tight against my chest and my cock dug into her stomach.

"You're hard," she pointed out. Her gaze was mocking. "And this isn't the first time, is it? You're attracted to me."

It wasn't a question, but the downright establishment of an incontrovertible fact.

I pushed her away and she staggered backwards. Then I turned around to leave. It was time to request a transfer. There was absolutely no way I could keep working with her now.

Just as I pulled the door open, she said, "Kiss me."

I froze. I knew I should leave—no, not knew I should leave, but every intuitive cell in my body screamed for me to fucking leave right away, but I was frozen. I couldn't move a muscle.

Seconds passed between us. Then I heard a sound behind me. A whisper. Silk on skin.

She really knew how to play dirty. I couldn't help myself. Like a condemned man who stares out of his cell window at the noose he will wear in the morning, I turned around and —watched as the straps to her night gown slipped down her arm. The material shimmied down along her torso and her breasts were fully revealed.

My heart slammed into my chest.

Her breasts were much, much more beautiful than I could have imagined. I gazed, completely stunned at those full heavy mounds and the pale pink nipples. My cock swelled, my fingers itched to feel them, and my mouth begged to taste them. Without thinking, I shut the door and said the stupidest thing I'd ever uttered, "That's out of line."

Supremely confident, she cocked her head to the side, and stepped towards me.

I couldn't move. I felt as though I'd been drugged.

"Are you saying that to me or yourself?" she asked, and then her hands covered her breasts.

I watched, mesmerized as her fingers caressed the soft fleshy mounds. Whatever I'd been about to say fled from my mind. She closed the distance between us and I stood frozen and utterly powerless.

"All I'm asking for is a kiss," she whispered breathlessly, as her bare breasts pressed against me.

Heat washed through me.

She lifted her hand, slowly and carefully, rightly aware she was now before a lit fuse. I'd never in my life been so turned on by a woman, and the realization astonished me. I felt more excitement in these unbearably long moments of anticipation than when I'd been ramming hard into a woman.

She placed her splayed palm over my heart. When she felt its rapid, erratic rhythm, she smiled and licked her lips. With her gaze fully locked on me her hand began to tease its way down my torso.

I almost couldn't bear the way she watched me, as though daring me to put a stop to this madness, especially as she seemed well aware the keys to my body were in her possession.

When her hand reached the front of my jeans and closed around the rock-hard bulge, my eyes briefly fluttered shut. Then she grabbed me, boldly, shamelessly, and I felt the currents of electric pleasure shoot through my veins.

"Angelo," she called.

The music of my name on her lips almost completely buckled me right then.

"Are you still sure you don't want to kiss me?"

CHAPTER 28

ANGELO

https://www.youtube.com/watch?v=tt2k8PGm-TI

I opened my eyes reluctantly. I could have stood there with my eyes closed and let her do anything she wanted, but she wanted me to take full responsibility for my actions.

Her gaze roved across my face as she continued to tease and taunt the front of my jeans.

I had just one last chance … to put a stop to this terrible temptation.

I would have taken it. I knew I would have been strong enough to take it, but she reacted first. She slanted her head and licked my lip. It was like a lick of blue fire. It seared.

I lost it.

My hand curved around the back of her head, and pulled her even closer to me. I sucked her juicy bottom lip into my mouth. God, I'd been wanting to do that ever since I saw her at the pool. She tasted like heaven, even sweeter than I remembered, and I savored every moment of it.

She held onto the collars of my jacket, just as struck as I was by the sheer intensity of the pleasure burning between us. She moaned, the sound rumbling from the very depths of her body. I didn't think I could have been any more turned on if she'd taken my cock in her mouth.

This woman affected me in ways that I just could not understand.

My arms wrapped around her waist.

"Did you think of me?" she asked, pulling her mouth away, her eyes burning with a feverish intensity.

With my hands around her thighs, I lifted her up into the air, and she curved her legs around my waist. My blood was boiling with such excitement at the proximity of her gorgeous breasts to my face, that it felt like I might pass out.

"I thought of you. Day and night." She planted a soft kiss on my forehead and then continued the feverish assault down my nose. "I came … calling your name," she said. "Several times."

My head felt like it was going to explode, as images of her playing with herself took very vivid forms in my mind. My mouth closed around one nipple and gave it a hard, brutal suck.

"Aaaaa." She shuddered against me.

"What did you use?" I rasped out, close to losing my mind. "How did you touch yourself?"

"Just my inadequate fingers," she breathed.

My lips moved to her other nipple.

She writhed wildly against me at the attention that my lips tongue and teeth gave to the pale swollen buds. She grabbed onto my hair and panted. "Oh, fuck," she swore.

I pulled away to once again drown myself in the taste of her lips. Molten, searing desire slid down my throat as our mouths intertwined, nearly becoming one as we breathed through each other's mouths. I couldn't wait to be inside her. I carried her across the room until my legs connected with the frame of her bed.

I dropped her on the bed and she squealed softly with excitement, I leaned forward and pressed a finger to her lips. This was a dangerous game we were playing. It could mean a bullet in my head. I glanced at the door, then I walked over, and turned the lock.

When I came back to the bed, I just stood over her. Savoring the sight of her almost naked body.

Her nightie was bunched around her hips. As I watched she shimmied it further down her body. At that moment, the only thing I wanted in the entire world, possibly even more than my own life, was to push myself into her wetness.

She flung the silk material aside. All that was left was a lacy thong.

I caught her ankles in my hands and opened her legs. The way the string of her thong was caught between her wet pussy lips was so indecently erotic, my mouth watered to lick that wet beauty, but before I could drop to my knees and feast on her sweetness, her hands rushed to cover her sex.

"Don't look at me like that," she whispered.

My eyes met hers, and my voice was hoarse and thick. "Like what?"

"Like you want to ... eat me."

I frowned. Could it be? No, of course not. That would be impossible. She was not exactly a shy little thing. I pulled my gun out of my holster and put it on the bedside table. Climbing on the bed, I began to trace heated kisses down her neck. I felt the burn of each kiss as though I was the one being teased, and felt my heart leap in my chest when I dipped my tongue into her belly button and her body jerked with the intensity of the sensation.

I couldn't help but tease her again.

"Stop," she muttered, her head moving restlessly.

I lifted my head from my position on her abdomen and looked at her. Part of me couldn't believe I was about to have her. There was no two ways about it. She was a goddess! Her cheeks were flushed, her lips swollen from my sucking, and her eyelids heavy with passion. Between the slits, her eyes were brilliantly green, as if set on fire from inside, as her hair lay spread out around her head in a captivating cascade of lustrous silk.

I felt my heart thud violently in my chest and the words came out before I could stop them, "You're breathtaking."

She stilled at my words. "And you're fucking gorgeous."

I felt the appreciation in her touch as she stroked her fingers in my hair.

She blushed, the color running from her chest all the way to her cheeks. "I've been watching you around me, and getting more and more pissed that you weren't …" she paused and licked her lips, "fucking my brains out."

I cocked my head. "You can stop being pissed right now." I broke the string of her lacy thong and wrenched the material away from her hips. Her sex was spread open before me. She immediately grew self-conscious and tried to close her legs, but I grabbed her thighs and pushed even further apart. All the way back, and allowed my eyes to fully take her in.

CHAPTER 29

ANGELO

https://www.youtube.com/watch?v=bpOR_HuHRNs

*H*er pussy was utterly and completely beautiful. Completely clean-shaven, it was like a little heart, pulsing, alive, and greedy for my attention. Her creamy arousal drenched the swollen protruding bud at the center of the delicate, pink folds of flesh. Then there was the little hole, throbbing— begging silently. Excitement gripped me and I didn't waste a moment longer.

I bent my head and beginning at the base of wet flesh, gave her a long, hard lick.

She jerked violently at the contact, her grip on my hair tightening. She whimpered, her body shuddering as I lifted her hips off the bed, and held her in my cupped hands.

I had just begun.

Her musky heated release swirled around in my mouth. Delicious. I went back for more. I lapped her up like a starving man, my tongue digging into that secret begging hole for more, and then sliding upwards to finally meet her swollen clit. I closed my lips around the throbbing bud and sucked hard.

She gave a little scream and almost flew off the bed.

I raised my head. "Shhh," I cautioned.

But she was long past coherence with her body writhing at the pleasure overwhelming every nook and cranny, as her head kept thrashing from side to side.

Her parents' wing was on the other side of the mansion, but as a precaution, I stuffed her nightie into her mouth. Then I returned my mouth to her pussy. I circled the trembling entrance to her body, before once again thrusting my tongue inside her. Desire flowed out of her opening, soaking my mouth with its wetness and I lapped her clean. Two fingers replaced my tongue and I marveled at the slick reception.

A third finger eventually joined the onslaught as I curved and stroked her sensitive inner walls.

Her muffled cries and moans filled my ears. Even I could no longer regulate the harshness of my breathing, or my arousal as I let my finger keep plunging deeper into her depths.

Soon, she began to convulse. "No, Angelo … stop," she cried, trying to pull away.

I ignored her, maintaining the hard, steady momentum of my thrusts in and out of her.

Her release burst through her, spraying me with a sweet shower, as she fought to free herself from my hold.

I let her go. Rising to my feet, I shrugged my jacket off my shoulders as I watched her seal a hand over her mouth in a belated effort to contain her screams. She sounded tormented and it absolutely enthralled me. There were tears of pure bliss in her eyes and I couldn't wait to see them roll down her cheeks.

"Holy hell," she shuddered, as she pressed her hand to her clit, trying to soothe the delicious ache from the orgasm. By the time she recovered enough to gather her wits, my jeans were around my knees and my cock was free.

She gasped as she took in the size of my manhood. "Fuck," she breathed, her eyes wide. She gazed greedily at it, licking her lips and her hands reaching out as though she wanted to touch it. "That's … big. Are you sure it's going to fit?"

If I had been in a different mood, I would have laughed at the astonished, dazed expression on her face. "Don't worry, I'll make it fit," I promised.

She giggled nervously.

I pulled out a condom from the pocket of my jeans. I rolled it on, and moved towards her once again.

When my knees sank into the bed she reached up, encircled her arms around me, and caught my lips in a deep almost desperate kiss. It was as though she was silently requesting I go easy on her, but couldn't voice it out loud because she wanted nothing to interfere with the intensity of pleasure she knew was coming her way.

I brushed her hair out of her face and assured her I wouldn't hurt her.

Then I laid her back on the bed, and held her gaze as I slipped my cock between her folds. I stroked the wet, thick head up and down her little pussy and she arched her back in appreciation and readied herself for what was to follow. I positioned the crest at her entrance, and slid a few inches into her.

"Ahhh," I groaned, the thud of my heart ringing in my ears. She was so slick with arousal her opening immediately accepted me, but then further in, it gripped me so unbelievably tightly that I almost came right then. "Ready?" I asked, but couldn't even hold myself back enough to receive a response.

"It's my first time," she cried out, but it was too late. I had already slammed into her.

All the blood drained out of my brain. "Fuck," I cursed, freezing inside her with shock, and tightening my grip on her hips.

Her eyes were wide and full of wonder. "Wow, it feels amazing to have you inside me. Don't stop."

I swallowed. "You're sure?"

She nodded cheekily. "I'm technically a virgin, but I have finger-fucked myself. Countless times. The last time, you played the starring role."

I trembled or perhaps it was her … it didn't matter. We were both overcome, and overwhelmed at the violent explosion of pleasure that had torn through us. Even now, being joined like this—it was pure ecstasy. I knew she could feel it just as much as I could. Without a shadow of a doubt, my body had been crafted for hers. For my length to fit unbelievably perfectly within her depth.

Her legs lifted up and wrapped themselves around my waist. Being lodged inside of her was pure magic, her walls sheathed me like a second skin, squeezing every ounce of pleasure out of my cock.

"Fuck, you're so damn tight," I groaned. I knew I might just lose my mind if I didn't start moving.

"That's because you're so damn big," she retorted, but her voice shook.

Slowly, I pulled out of her, and the friction of my rock-hard length against her walls sent me reeling. Outside her tight welcoming heat, it was unbearable. I plunged back in. This time around, the force of the thrust made the bed jerk.

"God, you're deep," she gasped in my ear, "… so, so, so deep."

I pulled out and rammed back into her. Again, and again, and again, until I felt the side of my face dampen. I didn't need to look to know it was her tears.

"Mmh… nngh… ahhh, holy helllllll," she moaned incoherently underneath me.

She sounded like a wounded animal. I understood. It was all I could do to keep my own groans muffled. All my dreams. All those nights when I had fought and suppressed the longing for her body, came in torrents that were too violent for me to process.

But I felt it all, amplified by a thousand times. I felt the silk of her skin, the smell of her arousal, the taste of her on my tongue, the sweat beading across my forehead, neck, and running down my spine. The bulge of veins in my arms from holding my weight off her. My hard cock inside her wet pussy. Never had I felt such bliss in the arms of a woman.

The strong walls inside her milked me over and over until I felt her begin to quicken. I was already hovering on the

173

brink, so I pulled out all the stops and fucked us both over the edge.

When her orgasm came, it triggered mine. I came hard, but in a flash of clarity, I knew to cover her mouth with mine. A scream rippled through her. I swallowed the harsh sound and made it mine as she thrashed wildly beneath me.

As her body quaked, I kept thrusting into her. Until we were both completely spent. I knew at the back of my mind that I was supposed to slide out of her. To pull my pants back on and walk out immediately … before we both ran out of luck. But I couldn't move. Or perhaps I didn't want to move.

I remained deeply buried inside her until it registered even she couldn't let me go.

Her arms and legs were locked around me as she moaned softly into my neck.

I understood how she felt. This was what sex was made to be.

When I rolled away from her, she grabbed me tightly and rolled right on top of me.

I looked into her eyes and her pupils were so enlarged, her emerald eyes were almost black. "Now it's my turn to be on top," she whispered, and carefully, keeping me inside her, she sat up on me. Her body glistened with a sheen of sweat. She looked like a proud goddess. She touched her breasts and played with her nipples.

We were both too spent, too raw, too connected, but I felt my cock stir inside her again.

This had never happened before either.

CHAPTER 30

SIENNA

I knew I'd slept way past the early hours when I usually rose. The world beyond bright and alive with activity, but I didn't want to move. I needed a bit more time to replay the fantasy that came true last night … before I opened my eyes and… it all became ashes.

I had fallen asleep curled up against Angelo, but I knew he was no longer by my side. Nothing had changed. If my sex did not feel so hot and shockingly swollen between my legs that I had to keep them apart I could even believe that it had all been a dream.

I needed to feel that way again.

Sliding my hands underneath the covers, I stroked my already slick folds. Never in my life had I ever felt them this way. They were almost foreign, twice their normal size. I remembered how he had ravished me the previous evening. Eating me out, making me come again and again, until I felt certain I was losing my mind.

I recalled the brutal thrusts, how urgent and commanding they had been, and all over again it felt like I was once again underneath him. The bliss had been so complete, so total that the whole night had the quality of a long, unbelievable dream. I clenched my eyes tightly, and transported myself back to last night.

The pad of my middle finger went to my protruding clit, and began to tease the turgid bud in gentle circles. Once in a while, I would move my fingers down my wetness and they would slide effortlessly into me, and I would recall how he had done exactly the same, but with his rough, much larger fingers.

I writhed and moaned as quietly as I could, my heart thundering in my chest, as my body began to ready itself of my impending release. My core tightened at the sweet, mounting tension and although, I already knew it would be nothing close to what he had done the previous night, I needed the reminder of what he had done to me.

My right hand stroked and dipped between my folds, while my left cupped my breasts, molding the tender mounds, and pinching my nipples, pretending to myself it was his mouth sucking hard on them.

I was panting, softly calling out his name, so close, when a heavy knock suddenly sounded on my door. My heart nearly jumped out of my throat. I immediately sat up, my hands flying away from my sex and pulling the covers up to my chin to cover my naked body.

It was only after the knock came again, when I was able to pull myself together enough to respond. "I'm coming," I shouted, and jumped out of bed. I found my silk nightie on the floor, and my eyes darted around in an effort to find my gown. A fruitless exercise. Angelo had flung it away from me and it must have fallen behind something.

I quickly grabbed my bathrobe from behind the bathroom door, tightened it around my waist, and rushed to the door. If I delayed any longer, it would cause unnecessary alarm. No doubt it was either my mother or Gemma wondering why I was still in bed. Unless … I had been heard last night.

Fear struck me!

With a click, I pulled the door slightly open and gave a quick peek outside. Nothing however could have prepared me to see him.

"Get dressed," Angelo said to me. "We're going to the gym."

THE RIDE over to the gym was painfully silent.

Angelo didn't say a single word to me, but after practically throwing myself at him last night, okay, not practically, but actually physically throwing myself at him last night, I felt too embarrassed to even sneak a look at him in the bright light of day.

Slowly, but surely, it began to dawn on me that he just didn't want to speak to me. I was just a body he had fucked last night. Someone who'd forced herself upon him and provoked him so much he had unwillingly taken her.

I felt hurt.

And then I became upset.

By the time we arrived at the private gym downtown that existed solely for my father's men, my guard against him had been rebuilt high and firm. *Fuck him. I didn't need him.*

I got out of the SUV without a word, and slammed the door shut behind me then marched towards the entrance. I stopped when I got through the front door, slightly taken aback. It was filled with men, most of them bare-chested or close enough— all of them showing off glistening sweat slicked abs and thick biceps.

Some were grunting at the strain of lifting impossibly heavy weights. Others were breathing hard as they worked the machines -while the remaining few were gathered around to watch a match inside the elevated boxing ring.

At my entrance, more and more heads were beginning to turn to stare at me.

The maleness all around me was intimidating to say the least. I turned awkwardly towards the door and wished I hadn't been so hasty about coming in here.

Thankfully, Angelo came in then, his bag slung across his shoulder.

"Hey, Boston!" some of the men greeted him.

He sent a nod their way. Without a word he moved past me, and disappeared into an inner room. For another second I hesitated, aware of all the curious eyes on me, then I brushed my pride aside, straightened my spine, and quickly followed Angelo. It was either I dealt with him, or remained under the scrutiny of the men who were obviously wondering why the hell I was in their gym.

"Why am I here?" I demanded as soon as I caught up with Angelo inside the locker room.

He stopped before one of the metal lockers, jerking it open with a hard pull. "Isn't it obvious?"

"Not to me," I muttered.

"To train," he replied shortly.

I jerked my head towards the main hall. "This is an only men's gym, right? In fact, it seems to be an only bodyguard's gym. I don't think I'm even allowed to be here."

"So where do you suggest we go?" he asked.

A response worked its way up to my lips, but when he raised his arms to pull his shirt from his head, my brain stopped working.

Before me was the olive toned, ripped torso that had been on top of me the previous night. Hell, it was even more glorious than I remembered. And broad. And hard. I felt completely dwarfed by all those muscles. My hands itched to touch them, but I balled them into fists and dragged my gaze back up to his.

He was watching me. His eyes were hooded, but completely arresting. There was a hint of something wild and beautiful, but at the same time threatening and dangerous.

Once again, my panties were instantly soaked. I wanted nothing more at that moment than to dig my fingers into his hair and to pull his face to mine for a kiss. Even better, I wanted my back against these lockers and his cock ramming ruthlessly into me.

Just like he had last night. I craved it.

"I had a choice," he said evenly. "Either train you back at the house where there isn't much equipment or bring you with me. It made better sense to bring you here."

179

I chewed my bottom lip. That did make sense, but this place was filled with tough, gruff men who I suspected wouldn't welcome my presence.

"We're going to have a proper round in the ring, so that I can correctly assess your abilities. Then I'll make a report on the ways you need to improve and submit it to whomever will be taking over from me."

I was listening to what he was saying, but at the last statement my head shot up. "What? Taking over from you? What do you mean?"

He sat down on the bench and pulled out a pair of sneakers from the locker to change into. "We can't be together any longer, Sienna," he said tersely. "Last night … last night we crossed a very serious line. I cannot let that happen again."

I finally understood what his entire aloofness on the ride over had been about. "Ah," I said. "Now that you've had me, your appetite has been sated, and therefore you don't need to do it again?"

His gaze shot up to mine, a strange expression in them.

I went on, bruised beyond feeling. "Well, I'm not done with you yet. Fuck me a couple more times and then you can go wherever the hell you want."

"Fuck you a few more times?" He looked amazed.

CHAPTER 31

SIENNA

*O*h, my God. I couldn't believe what I was doing. I was begging him to have sex with me. Thoroughly humiliated, I turned to walk away, but he caught my hand. I struggled to release myself from his grasp, but when he wouldn't budge I turned around to meet his gaze.

"What?" I barked.

"You're engaged," he said softly.

I stared up into his eyes. All kinds of wild emotions coursed through my body.

"Are you that woman who cheats on the man that she's going to get married to?"

I took a deep breath, and shuddered at its release. How in the hell was I supposed to fault his reasoning? "It hasn't been confirmed," I mumbled, "that I'm going to get married to him."

Angelo stared at me in disbelief.

I couldn't blame him. Even I wasn't fully convinced at my words, so why would he be? Especially since he was fully aware of the complete power my father held over me.

He let go of me.

I missed the warmth of his hand and rubbed the place where he had held it. "Well, you don't have to quit because of me. We can stop sleeping together. Problem solved."

"That's easier said than done."

My heart skipped several beats. "Why?"

He took a step closer to me. "Have you forgotten what happened yesterday?" he asked. "How it was between us?"

I was glued to the spot and I realized then, that although Angelo seemed complicated, he really was a straightforward kind of guy. What you saw was what you got. When he felt disgust, it showed, when he felt concern it also showed, and when he was angry, he let it all out. Right now, he was being honest. More honest than I was being about how I felt. He wasn't leaving as a ploy to keep some distance between us or due to a lack of interest. He wanted to leave because he couldn't trust himself not to touch me again.

My heart felt like it was melting in my chest.

I found the courage, lifted my hand, and placed it on his chest, just over his heart.

He leaned into me, as though he couldn't help himself.

I heard the sharp intake of his breath. "Well, let's keep on going then," I whispered.

His eyebrows drew together and he stepped away. "I can't do that. What's mine is mine. It would kill me to see you with him."

"Angelo, I'm not engaged," I argued. "They may think the engagement is settled, but I haven't accepted it yet."

He returned his gaze to me, and I knew he was well aware, possibly even more than I was, of the inner workings of my family. I had less power than an ant when it came to altering my father's decisions.

"Until it's official," I insisted stubbornly. "Until I accept we're not together. I don't owe him loyalty and neither does he owe me any. I won't be surprised or care if he's seeing someone right now." I swallowed hard. "So we can keep going."

"That's not the main reason why I can't be your bodyguard anymore," he said. "Being intimate with you blurs the professional line that should be between us, and sometimes the vigilance from that professionalism can be the difference between life and death."

I did not have an argument to that. "Let's talk about this some other time," I said. "After we're done with training."

"I've made up my mind," he said.

Panic gripped my heart. I couldn't let him go. Not yet. "Then let's just do it one last time."

He slammed the locker shut and began to walk away.

I could see the tenseness in his shoulder muscles. "Angelo," I called.

Although it looked as if he would continue to ignore me, he stopped just as he reached the door.

The words that came out of my mouth then were incredibly difficult. "Fine. Let's keep things professional then. You don't have to quit."

He turned and stared at me.

My eyes stung with the urge to tear up so I quickly turned away and sat on the bench. "I need to change," I said. "Please leave."

Less than a moment later, the door swung shut behind him.

I put everything I had into our round in the ring, and it was mostly because I was fuming. I felt angry with no one in particular but at my world and the inhumane sacrifice my parents were asking of me. Safety at the expense of my happiness. I wished I could run back to England … with Angelo. Going back to England without him would be even more painful than being here and unable to have him.

I swung my fists, covered with thick wraps and gloves, repeatedly at him.

I knew he restrained himself, but I didn't hold back. I managed a couple of body blows and I was even able to make him stagger once. I cheated, by lifting my t-shirt up to wipe my forehead and distracting him with a view of my bare stomach, but a blow was a blow and he should have known after last night that I fight dirty.

The rest of the men seemed to be absolutely captivated by the fight. I no longer cared about being self-conscious at the many eyes on me, or anything else for that matter. All I could think about was that I needed to fight because if I didn't, then I was certain I would just suffocate to death.

CHAPTER 32

SIENNA

*I*t was a difficult week. Angelo wouldn't even look me in the eyes. I felt glad Charlotte would be arriving from England that day for a week's trip. I badly needed someone I could talk to, but I was certain all the phones in the house were bugged so I had suffered in silence.

I almost cried when I saw her at the airport. Both of us spotted each other at the same time. We ran towards each other like long, lost souls. She threw her knapsack to the group and flew into my arms. It felt so good to hug her again.

When we parted, she pushed her wavy dark bangs from her forehead distractedly and said, "Who in heaven is that?"

I already knew who she was referring to, but turned around anyway. Angelo stood only a few feet away from us. His hands rested at the sides of his body, giving the impression of normality and casualness, but his gaze was eagle sharp on us. Coupled with his dark clothes, and his intimidating stance, he truly did seem to be something that fell from heaven … or rose up from hell. But his was definitely the kind of darkness you wanted in your bed.

"Is that the bodyguard you've been talking about?" she asked.

I moved my hand to cover her mouth. "He can hear you, you moron!"

"'Don't be silly. He's not near enough to hear anything in this din."

"Believe me, he can hear things that most people might be too distracted to pick up."

Her mouth rounded into a "oh," and then with a nod, she gave me a thumb's up signal. She didn't stop there. She licked her lips to send the very clear message to me that she thought he was incredibly, sexually delicious.

I wanted to die. "He's also not blind."

"And your point?"

I glared at her. "'We were just talking about him, which he heard, and then you go and do that. What's he supposed to think?'

She slapped her hand across my arm. "I didn't come here for you to harass me. I can do whatever I want and ogle whoever I want. I'll be gone in a week. So be nice to me."

I grinned and grabbed her knapsack off the floor. "I'm always nice."

"That's more like it." Then she grabbed my hand and with a big smile pulled me towards Angelo.

I shook my head. Something told me she would be causing more trouble than I anticipated. Charlotte always was trouble.

"So you're Angelo," she said. "I'm Charlotte."

Angelo gave a curt nod. "We should go."

As we walked, Angelo kept running his eyes around the massive arrivals hall, scanning the hordes of people milling about.

I could almost sense the impatience he felt for us to be out of this space, and I could completely understand it. Being in such a crowded place reduced his ability to keep me safe.

Soon we were on our way, with him in the driver's seat of the SUV. Charlotte and I seated in the back.

"I want a burger from In-N-Out!" Charlotte announced.

"I'll Google it later for you and we can go this evening," I said.

"Wait, you don't know where the closest In-N-Out is? Are you even from LA?"

"I am," I admitted. "But considering the years I've spent in London, I'm almost British. I even have an accent."

"No, you don't," she retorted. "Your accent is a mix of American and British, and sometimes I hear a pinch of Italian when you're pissed." She threw her head backwards for a laugh. "I die every time."

I rolled my eyes at her.

"Can't we stop for one now?"

I looked at her curiously. "Why do you want an In-N-Out so badly?"

"Well, it's all I hear about from everyone who lives in LA."

"I can guarantee you our cook can whip up burgers and fries better than anything In-N-Out can even dream of doing."

"Wait, you have a bodyguard and now you have a cook?"

"Yeah."

"How rich are your parents, Sienna?"

I sighed.

"No, I seriously want to know. You lived like a church mouse in England and yet, you come from all this wealth."

"I'll explain everything later."

"Fine. About my In-N-Out burger. I've been fantasizing about it for years. Can we please get one now?"

"We'll go later in the evening," I promised.

"Deal. But I'll still have your cook make me a burger for now, and there better be tears in my eyes when I take a bite out of it because that's what I expected from In-N-Out."

"Trust me, their burgers are not that great. Completely overrate—"

Her gasp cut me off.

"What?" I asked startled.

"You live here?"

We had stopped outside the gates of my home.

"Wow!" She looked around us with widened eyes as we drove into the grounds. "Your parents are seriously rich, aren't they?" She gasped again when the house came into view.

Part of me felt sad Charlotte was so awed and taken with the house and grounds. I didn't want her to be so impressed she changed the way she felt about me. I liked it better when we were both poor and she treated me as her equal. "Stop gasping," I said mildly.

"What are you talking about, gasping is my thing! But let's get back to all of this unbelievable wealth and lavishness that you managed to completely hide while you were in London. For Pete's sake, you wore one jacket for the whole winter and you had all this ... Whoa."

"I'm humble," I said, as we drew up to the house.

"Humble my ass! I expect a full explanation, young lady," she replied sternly.

We got down and I quickly ushered her up to my room.

She threw her knapsack on the floor, kicked off her shoes, sat cross-legged on my bed, and patted the space in front of her. "Right. Before we do anything else I want my explanation. Why did you hide the fact that you are so rich? And I want to know about the bodyguard too. I know you're sleeping with him."

I walked to the bed, kicked off my sandals, and joined her. "How do you know I'm sleeping with him?" I asked curiously.

She grinned. "I didn't, but I do now."

I smiled at her. "I've missed you, Charlotte."

"Yeah, me too. A lot. Now, quick. Tell me about all this money and why you didn't want anyone to know you're rich."

I explained as much as I could about everything, even about my impending arranged marriage.

She gasped again. "Wow. That's incredible. I can't believe arranged marriages still exist. It sounds so eighteenth century."

I wriggled my bare feet. "I don't know what to do."

"What does the bodyguard think?"

"Well, I only slept with him for one night."

"I knew it. The good-looking ones are always lousy in bed."

"No, he's not lousy in bed. Actually, he's amazing. I came five times that night."

Her eyes widened. "Nooooo …"

I nodded. "Yeah, it was a really great night, but he says he can't carry on sleeping with me because he would lose the professionalism he needs in order to guard me properly."

"What an idiot. So why did he sleep with you in the first place?"

"I kinda of threw myself at him," I admitted.

She began to laugh. "No way. Not you!"

"Yes, me."

"Do you know the guys used to secretly call you Miss Touch Me Not?"

"They did? Why didn't you tell me?"

She shrugged. "It wasn't an insult and it was true, so no point taking them to task or telling you about it. What are you going to do about him?"

It was my turn to shrug. "It's seems there's nothing I can do. He's already told me if anything more happens between us, he won't be able to be my bodyguard anymore and I just can't give him up … at least not yet." My voice sounded sad and dejected.

"There is something you can do. You can go out with me tonight and we'll get drunk together. Your boyfriend can come along with us and have a couple of drinks too. He sounds like he needs a few."

"He doesn't drink while he's working," I said morosely.

"Really? We'll see about that." She arched a wicked brow at me.

CHAPTER 33

ANGELO

I picked the bar.

One I was quite familiar with from my nights out alone. It was never too crowded on weekdays. So, I was somewhat assured of its level of security since I knew the head of security and all the bouncers.

The two girls sat at the bar, while I settled down in a dark corner close by. From where I sat, I could keep my eyes fully on them, but was still able to monitor the rest of the room. More times than not however, I found myself solely watching her.

I thought of how shocked I'd been when I found out she was a virgin. Everything I'd thought about her went flying out of my head. I had been so wrong about her. From day one, I thought she was a good time girl, wanting to have a bit of fun with the hired help, but she was as pure as the driven snow.

I realized she had a special kind of grace about her. I hadn't noticed it properly before, especially since I was determined to think of her only in terms of a bratty Princess, but now that her friend was by her side, the difference was stark. Where her friend was unrestrained - once Sienna had to hold her back so she wouldn't fall out of her chair from laughter and completely unaware of her surroundings - Sienna was watchful. She kept her eyes on the people around her. And once in a while, she even allowed herself to throw me a glance.

I could fully understand her now.

I had grown up that way ... with the need to be vigilant at all times. You could never let your guard down. The threats of attacks were endless. One second of carelessness and you could be dead forever.

Two men came up to them, smiling warmly.

I instantly sat up.

Both women turned their heads towards them. They listened to them before her friend waved her hand to indicate the men could take the seats beside them, a man on either side of them.

Something dark and hot began to burn in the pit of my stomach.

I watched them carefully, and since there was no sign of alarm from Sienna's court, I knew they were safe. However, I noticed her friend had begun to over-consume alcohol in her excitement. I kept count of the glasses of cocktails she kept pouring down her throat, and I knew it would soon become a problem.

The man slipped off his stool and helped her off hers. She staggered into him and giggled.

"Charlotte," Sienna called, but her friend patted her on her back in a reassuring way before she headed off with the man.

Sienna glanced in my direction.

I immediately rose to my feet and headed over to her.

As soon as I arrived at her side, she turned to me. "Could you help me keep an eye on Charlotte?"

"I'm not paid to guard her," I responded.

"I know," she said, "but I didn't stop her because usually she can hold her drink better than me, but I think the jetlag got to her and I'm worried."

I glanced darkly at the man by her side. "Let's leave then."

She almost jumped off the stool in her haste. "Got to go, but thanks for the great conversation," she informed the man who looked stunned.

We found her friend in a corridor.

She had a tongue down her throat, but one word from me and the man jerked away in fright.

Her friend was so shit-faced with the man holding her up, she just slid down the floor in a heap. She would definitely have one hell of a hangover in the morning. "Hey," she protested, looking around her blankly.

"Fuck off," I told the man. He was one of these new breed of metro men. I could smell the gel he had worked into his hair.

First, his eyes widened, then he scurried away without a word or a backward glance.

"What happened to Mike?" she mumbled.

Sienna knelt down behind her friend. "Can you stand?"

"Of course, I can stand. What happened to Mike?"

I bent down and pulled her up.

"What the hell!" Then her gaze focused on me. "Ah, the body-guard," she slurred. "I've heard you're very good in bed, but I need to have a word with you."

I glanced at Sienna.

She looked as if she wished the ground would open up and swallow her.

I slipped my arm around the back of her friend's waist and began walking her out of the bar.

Sienna walked next to me.

The drunk woman's head rested on my shoulder, with her ranting on about forbidden love and how I needed to man up and steal Sienna away from her fate of a loveless arranged marriage. Outside, I knew we were more vulnerable with her hanging on to me, but the coast looked clear and we made it to the car without incident. It was a relief to stuff her into the back of the car. Drunk women were not my thing. I grew up in a family where women were dignified and never drank to excess.

Sienna slipped in beside her, and I got into the driver's seat and started on the journey back.

Once in a while, I snuck a glance at Sienna and every single time she would turn and meet my gaze through the reflection of the windscreen. I would then quickly return my eyes to the road. Not a single word was exchanged between us.

Her friend's semi-conscious complaints however began to grow louder, then her arms began to flail in abject rest-lessness.

"Charlotte ..." Sienna called. "We're almost home. Calm down."

"I need to pee," she muttered.

I kept my eyes on the road and left Sienna to deal with her.

"Just hang on. We'll be back home in a while."

"'I can't wait. I need to pee now," she cried.

"Come on, Charlotte. You can hold it for a bit more."

"I can't I tell you. If you don't stop, I'm going to pee in here," her friend cried.

"Angelo?" Sienna said anxiously. "Can we stop somewhere for a few minutes? I'm so sorry about this."

I didn't want to stop on the side of the road and become sitting ducks to our enemies, but I didn't want her friend using the car as a toilet. Even as I said the words I already knew this was a bad idea, but the words poured out and there wasn't much I could do about them. "If she can hold on for five minutes my apartment is around the corner."

"I don't know if I can wait that long," her friend screeched.

I stepped on the gas.

CHAPTER 34

SIENNA

*I*n the elevator, I'd been careful not to meet his eyes or show my astonishment that he was taking us to his place, but I was also glad. He'd acted so protective of his privacy I knew almost nothing about him. And I wanted to know more. Heck, I wanted to know everything about him.

The only thing I'd ever had from him was his lust. It should have been enough. We were just ships passing in the night— but it wasn't enough. I hungered for him. Every night, I touched myself to get off, and it always left me feeling empty, haunted by the very vivid memory of what it'd felt like to be filled up by him.

His apartment seemed small and strangely bare. There were no pictures, photos, or little in the way of ornaments. Things people usually gathered to decorate their living spaces.

We rushed Charlotte to the bathroom. Angelo actually put her on the toilet before leaving and closing the door behind him.

"He's a gentleman, he is," Charlotte said as pee gushed out of her. "You couldn't do better than him. If I were you, I would seduce him. Oh, what a relief it is to relieve yourself. Where are we anyway?"

"We're in Angelo's apartment."

"Right. Do you mind if I just had a little nap here? Just for a bit," she said. Before I could do anything, she slipped down to the floor, closed her eyes and promptly fell asleep.

I tried to pull her to her feet, but asleep, she was a dead weight. Eventually, I gave up and went out to find Angelo.

He sat on his couch with the news on, but I suspected he wasn't paying much attention to it.

"Angelo," I called softly. I loved calling out his name, and I did it in a way that sounded breathy, hoping it would torment him even a little.

He turned and looked at me, his face deliberately expressionless.

"I need a little help with Charlotte. I can't get her off the floor."

He got up and we went to the bathroom in silence. Effortlessly, he picked her up and threw her over his shoulder. "Got all your things?" he asked.

My eyebrows rose when I realized he planned to go straight to the car and take us back home. "Can we just let her rest for a few minutes on your bed before we return?" I asked.

His eyes narrowed. "Why?"

I threw my hands up. "Because I want to talk to you for five minutes."

"Talk?" he repeated.

"Yes, for five freaking minutes."

"It's a bad idea."

"What's your point?"

"I know you think it's fun and everything to keep having sex with me, but you have no idea how dangerous a game you are playing."

"Stop being so damn big-headed. I don't want to have sex with you." Okay, I was lying about not wanting to have sex with him, but I really did just want to spend some time with him, away from my house where I had to always pretend he was just another bodyguard. Even if nothing more could happen between us, I just wanted to bask in his presence a bit instead of being so afraid to even meet his eyes for the fear that someone would notice.

"Could have fooled me," he muttered as he walked away from the bathroom.

To my relief, he went into his bedroom and lay Charlotte on the bed. The room was lit only by the light pouring in from the corridor, but I could see it was just as bare as the rest of the apartment. A bed, a nightstand. A cupboard.

He straightened and turned to me. "All right. Talk."

Somehow, standing in his bedroom made my stomach tighten.

He had taken his jacket off and had on a fitted black tee-shirt and dark slacks.

The man made me drool. "Can we talk in the living room?"

It was dark, but I'm sure he shrugged.

Without a word, I turned around and led the way to the living room. I could hear him following behind me. When I reached the middle of the open plan space, I turned back.

He stood lounging against the doorway.

"I'm sorry for the inconvenience," I apologized.

He shrugged. "That's not necessary."

I forced a smile. It was clear he intended to make this as difficult as possible. I never was good at squeezing blood from stone. I took a deep breath. "'Do you have anything I can eat? I'm a little hungry."

"Don't have much in my fridge, but I can make you a grilled cheese sandwich. The bread might be a bit stale though."

I'd never heard better words. I grinned from ear to ear. "That would be fantastic. I love stale bread and grilled cheese."

He gave me a disbelieving look and headed towards the kitchen area.

He moved in a quick sure way around his kitchen. A few minutes later, he was moving the bread around in the pan, his hair brushing softly against his shoulders.

I watched the way the broadness of his torso flowed into the leanest of hips. He was driving me crazy. I wanted to be on my knees ... sucking him off. I knew he would never make the first move, but I also knew he wouldn't reject me. So I shut my pride off and walked towards him.

His shoulders tensed as he turned the stove off and moved the pan out of the way to one of the back burners.

I almost smiled. Of course, he knew I was approaching and he knew the kind of trouble I was bringing too. I circled my arms around his lean waist.

His entire body froze. "Sienna," he warned.

"Is sucking you off crossing the line?" I whispered.

He inhaled sharply. "What you're doing now is already crossing the line." He grabbed my wrists, and despite my resistance, pulled away my arms from around him. Then he turned around and faced me. "No," he said, his eyes glittering and his voice thick.

I hugged myself. "I want you to quit. Having you around me and not being able to touch you will end up making me lose my mind. So just quit."

Something dark and dangerous flashed in his eyes. "Okay," he agreed.

My lips stretched into an equally dark smile. We both knew the game I was playing. "Now that we have that out of the way, I want you to fuck me. Right now. I'll take it as a parting gift."

He stared at me, his eyes carefully veiled.

"You can't refuse me." my voice rose with frustration. "If you have a conscience, you won't refuse me. You started this ... you were the one who came to my room and crossed the line."

That got him. "*You* started this. By kissing me in that garden. You crossed a line that wasn't even supposed to exist."

He was completely right, but that was his problem not mine. I dropped to my knees and grabbed at the button of his slacks. I had never been so glad that he wasn't wearing a belt, because in seconds, his button had come undone.

He grabbed my arms and pulled me to my feet. "Sienna!" he growled.

He might as well not have bothered. I forced myself even closer and captured his lips with mine.

He shuddered. With his last remaining strand of willpower, he tightened and tried to pull me away, but every Delilah knows her Samson's weakness. I threw my arms around his neck and took the kiss to another level. The level of tongue.

The feel of my tongue in his mouth broke him.

CHAPTER 35

SIENNA

I felt his hold on me tighten painfully, and this time around it wasn't to pull me away.

He kissed me like a starved man, long, hard, and deep. His hot tongue danced passionately with mine, while his hands slid down the outline of my body to grab my ass. He pressed me hard against him … grinding my crotch into his rock hard one.

My heart was fluttering so hard it seemed as though it wanted to fly away from my chest. I loved the feel of my breasts crushed against his torso. Tender, heavy, and the molten pleasure flowing through my veins at the utter possessiveness with which, he wrapped his hands around me, unwilling for even a hair's breadth of space to exist between us.

I had missed this … his touch and his warmth … I had missed it so freaking much.

He briefly broke the kiss to allow us to catch our breaths, and the sound of our pants was maddeningly erotic. "Fuck," he breathed into my mouth.

I completely understood the wonder in his voice. He was screwed, just as I was. Before he could come to his senses and get ideas about right and wrong, I loosened his hold around me and dropped down to my knees. With shaking hands, I unzipped his slacks and relished the sight of him above as he tried to fight himself.

"Sienna," he groaned, his hand gripping my shoulder.

Before he could push me away, I pulled his massive cock out of his dark briefs and wrapped my hand around it. That was it for him. The fight was over. Shamelessly, I licked the pale skin. It felt as smooth as silk, thick veins coursing its length. The head flushed deep red and already glistening with pre-cum. "Your cock is beautiful, Angelo," I breathed. Liquid lust flowed in my veins.

I loved how he smelled and tasted, clean and musky all at once. It was a scent I wanted all over me. The bud between my legs was throbbing so hard I felt as if I could have orgasmed right there. I had never felt so aroused in my entire life. Well, apart from the last time he touched me. Then, all of it had been quick and urgent, but this time around, I swore I would take my time with him. Especially since it could be the last time we would have together.

I gently ran my hands down the thick rod, stretched my lips, and sucked the thick mushroom into my mouth. His reaction was to rush his hands up to the back of his neck as he could barely bear the pleasure of my mouth on him. I licked him thoroughly, taking my tongue from tip to root, and then going even lower to suck his balls into my mouth, one after the other.

Sucking the head of his cock into my mouth, I pumped his thick shaft with my hand.

Then when he least expected it, I did the thing Charlotte had taught me to do on a condom covered banana: I took him all the way to the back of my throat. He staggered, but I didn't let go of him even for a second. I moved closer as his back connected with the edge of the counter. At my eye level of his big, powerful hands. They were clenched into tight fists. My heart melted at the sight.

"Jesus, whoa …" he groaned, the sound long and guttural. "Sienna, what the fuck!"

My dedication doubled as I pulled out then hollowed my cheeks and once again drew him all the way back into my throat. With both of my hands clasped tightly around the root, I milked him, sucking hard on the sensitive head as I urged the creamy flow of ecstasy out of him.

His hand slammed against the counter and gripped hard to support his frame as his head fell back. "Oh God," he breathed. "Sienna. Fuck!"

My hands and mouth collaborated in an urgent frequency that brought him closer and closer to the edge of his sanity. His face was contorted into a picture of delicious torment as his hands found their way to my hair, and as if he had lost his mind to everything beyond the violent release he was on the edge of, he thrust himself into my mouth.

I let him fuck my mouth. I was incredibly proud to have orchestrated this moment when he completely lost control. I watched him, memorizing everything. The feel of his smooth cock pumping frantically into me, the taste of him, the look of him. The sounds of his urgent breathing. Even the smell of the grilled cheese from the pan.

And then he came.

A roar tore through him. His body twisted and quaked as his climax overwhelmed him.

Thick, hot semen burst into my mouth and shot straight down my throat. I swallowed it all, then grabbed him once again to lick his cock clean of every last drop of his cum. I was so turned on I suspected one touch to my clit was all it would take for me to explode right there and then.

His eyes fluttered open, and my gaze met his as I continued to suck on the head of his cock, needing to milk him of whatever bit of arousal was left inside of him. He bit his bottom lip as he stared down at me and the action was so fucking erotic my heart momentarily stopped in my chest.

Roughly, he pulled me to my feet, his eyes boring into mine. "How do you do that?" he asked, one hand cradling my face. "How the fuck can you make me lose my mind like that?"

My response was to lick my lips.

With a groan, he crushed his lips to mine, and whatever strength I had drained out of my body.

I hung limply inside the arm he had hooked around my waist, aware without his support, I would have melted to a puddle on the floor. The other arm slid beneath my ass and I was lifted off my feet.

He placed me on the counter and spread my legs wide open. Then he settled his body between them. "I've been breaking all my rules for you, Sienna," he growled. "Every single fucking one of them."

I fisted his shirt in my hands, and said through gritted teeth, "I'm worth it."

"Yes, you damn well are," he said. "More than you can imagine." He pulled the t-shirt over his head and violently flung it away.

My blouse was next, and he ripped it open. Buttons went flying everywhere as he pulled the material apart, exposing the fullness of my breasts encased in the dark lacy bra. Vaguely, in the back of my brain, I worried about how I would return in torn clothes, but it was like a hazy thought, without urgency or weight. His arms reached behind me and he buried his face in my neck.

I heard the lace of my bra rip from behind me. Obviously, it must have proved too hard for him to unfasten it in the one second where he'd allowed himself that task. The material was scraped down my arms, as my breasts, swollen and heavy, fell into his tough, rough hands.

"It's been too long," he breathed.

I could feel his body shuddering with anticipation. I was already soaking wet.

"You have no idea how hard it is for me to keep my hands off you. Wanting you is like those damn parasites that get into its host and change it from the inside and cause it to behave in ways that are detrimental to it. I'm doing things I know are a disaster for me, but I can't help myself. The hunger for you just grows and fucking grows." It almost sounded like he was angry with me, but even more so at himself for allowing himself to want me.

It was insulting in a way, but in another part of me that knew no shame, I relished how urgent the need to have me made him—almost brutal. His skin was on fire, waves and waves of heat came off him, washing over me. I gladly drowned in his warmth.

Cupping my breasts in his hands, he bent his head and ravished them. He sucked hard on my nipples, making me squirm uncontrollably from the bolts of arousal shooting through me. The sight of his full head of hair as he moved like a starved man from one breast to the other enthralling me.

His teeth relentlessly teased the sensitive buds as he marked every inch of my chest with kisses before moving across my shoulder blades. He scorched my skin as he worked his way up to my neck.

My head fell back in response and my legs wound desperately around his waist, my arms encircling his shoulders as I tried to hang on to sanity. "Fuck me." I trembled, unable to endure the torment any longer. "Angelo. Take me!"

He bit softly on my bottom lip, and then slipped his tongue into my mouth, engulfing me with his wonderful taste.

Frantically, I began to pull at my underwear, desperate to get the scrap of fabric off me so he could have full access to where I needed him to be. He moved back slightly to help me, and in moments the barrier was dealt with. I was fully and indecently exposed before him, but there was not even an ounce of shyness in my being.

I spread my legs as wide as they would go, my sex pulsing and desperate for his attention.

I thought he would ram his cock inside of me, but instead he lowered down to his knees and threw my legs across his shoulders. Then his mouth covered my sex.

"Angelo," I cried.

He lapped at my arousal like he wanted to devour me. Then he sucked my whole pussy into his mouth.

A small scream went off in my mind and whether it sounded or not—I couldn't tell. My back arched, my hand reaching out to sink my fingers into his hair. I held on tight and moaned as his tongue shot in and out of me. It was beautiful and crazy at the same time.

When I thought I'd lost my mind, he let go and his lips closed around my clit, sucking on the swollen sensitive bud in a hard, ruthless rhythm.

"Oh, God," I cried out.

At that point, his fingers joined the assault on my senses. He plunged three digits inside me, curved them at the perfect angle, and began to relentlessly pump in and out of me.

So there I was— speared, stroked, sucked, and relentlessly finger-fucked. I rode that crest of pure unadulterated ecstasy until the moment he bit my clit …

With a scream, I exploded into his mouth.

He didn't let go. In the violent madness of my climax, I fought him away even as I slammed my sex against his mouth. My eyes rolled into the back of my head and my body rocked as if I was riding his face. I would have fallen off the counter if he hadn't held me in place. When I somewhat recovered enough to open my eyes, I saw the satisfied smile across his face.

"That was the hottest thing I've ever seen," he said. "You lost control of your body. I made you lose control of your body."

"You bastard," I muttered.

He chuckled.

I kinda hated him for it.

"I just wanted to let you feel a tiny fraction of what I feel every day when I look at you," he explained.

"I got the message," I said, and pulled his face down to mine. "Loud and clear." I kissed him hard and desperately. Every fiber of my being perked up to attention, my body throbbing in anticipation of his cock. I was in such a haze of lust I did not even notice that he had found himself a condom and sheathed himself.

He grabbed the massive shaft that seemed to have tripled in size then rubbed it up and down my cleft.

I moaned at the stimulating tease. The flushed head spread my slickness up and down my opening. "Put it in," I begged, unable to wait any longer. My eyes clenched shut and held my breath as I felt the head of his cock slip into my opening. Greedy and desperate for him, my sex instantly sucked him in.

"You are so fucking tight," he growled and his body shuddered at the shallow entrance. But when I tried to thrust my hips forward to pull all of him inside me, he held me in place, his biceps clenching hard under my fingers. "Slow down," he said. "I want to savor this … I want to feel all of you." He breathed harshly into the crook of my neck.

I felt like I would lose my mind. I wrapped my arms around his sweat slicked back when he moved and started sinking deeper into me. Deliberately, I clenched my convulsing sex even more tightly around him.

His breath hitched. "Jesus," he muttered shakily, as his hands curved around my hips. Lifting my ass slightly off the counter and with a smooth, hard thrust, he slammed the rest of his length into me.

I swear my heart nearly failed from excitement.

"Fuckkkk," he swore, as my walls sheathed him like a clenched fist.

I whimpered as he began to pull away, his cock running along the sensitive walls of my sex. The hot friction was maddening and unspeakably delicious. My hips arched to meet the brutal thrust I knew was coming, but I couldn't have prepared for it. I cried out as he slammed back into me.

He had gone so deeply inside of me, it felt as if he had reached a depth that I didn't even think was possible. Every nerve in my body was abuzz with pleasure. He pulled out of me once again, and when he rammed back in, he rolled his hips so his cock entered at an angle inside of me that made me completely lose it.

"Ange—oh God—aah."

It was too much and … not enough. I puffed and panted and clung to him.

My cries settled on a rhythm to match his thrusts.

At first, he kept it leisurely, as he took his time, milking me of every bit of my sanity, then when he too began to lose it, his pace increased and with every second that passed, he grew almost frantic for his own release.

The tension rose and grew between us, working up momentum like a tornado, ready to destroy us both. My nails were clawing down his back, my hips bucking and gyrating violently to meet the force of his thrusts. His tempo was merciless as he drove us both towards the edge, his hands digging into my ass.

Our sounds filled the room ... the slap of our wet flesh, our grunts, our pants.

I had never understood the term *he fucked me to within an inch of my life*. Now, I did. The head of his cock rubbed at the secret spot inside of me that to my shock, suddenly shattered me into tiny fragments. I was gone, driven mad by a different type of orgasm.

Then his hand moved towards my clit. I grabbed his wrist to try to stop him because it had become too much. I felt like I would pass right out. I actually experienced panic at that point. But he was too powerful, he pushed my hand away, and took control of me.

I became a slave to his onslaught as he rubbed around my clit in hard, rapid circles, coaxing the center of my pleasure into total submission. I was completely and utterly possessed.

Another climax started and I came with what must have been a blood-curdling scream. He followed right after. His roar rolled into my scream and we clung tightly to each other as our bodies convulsed and shuddered. The orgasm rocked through my body, soaking every cell and buzzing through my veins like a drug. I bit down on his shoulder to contain myself, while I listened to his heart thundering against my chest.

"Mmmm," he groaned as he continued to pound his hips into mine.

I could feel my consciousness slipping away. He had tortured me in the most devastatingly sweetest way, and my body couldn't take a second more. *Angelo* … I tried to call out his name but my mouth opened and closed as no sounds came out.

I don't know if I passed out, or perhaps I didn't, but a period of time passed by without my brain registering it. The next time I came to, I was in Angelo's arms and he was moving me to the sofa. He cradled me to his chest. I felt disappointed he was no longer lodged inside me, but I couldn't find the strength to complain.

I inhaled his scent as I clung to his neck, allowing his warmth to completely overwhelm me. I tried to remain awake, but couldn't. I slipped away into a dreamless exhaustion.

CHAPTER 36

*T*he apartment was deadly quiet except for Sienna's soft even breathing. I let myself drift off with her weight on my chest. It should have been strange, I never went to sleep with a sleeping woman in my arms, but it wasn't. It felt right. I was a light sleeper and I planned to wake up in a couple of hours.

But less than an hour later, her soft mumblings roused me.

My eyes snapped open, and immediately registered and recognized the woman in my arms. Through the illumination of the streetlights filtering into the room from the windows I watched her. It was astounding, but in sleep, she was like an angel. Vulnerable, peaceful, ethereally beautiful, and with a gentle aura that was almost otherworldly. A far cry from the spitfire, bundle of trouble, total headache she was in real life.

Her arms were still loosely wrapped around me, but her lids were shut. I did not want to wake her up. I just wanted to watch her … forever. Other than her skirt gathered around her waist, she was naked and her hair looked disheveled. Very gently, I brushed some stray hairs away from her face.

I could have sworn she was smiling in her sleep. Maybe that was the same spirit of contentment that was also all over my face.

Heat engulfed my chest as my eyes ran down her body to the curve of her breast. It was pressed down on my chest. I wanted to feel that breast in my mouth again, but I didn't want to wake her. Having her like this was precious. As I stared down at her, the woman I'd done everything over the past several weeks to keep out of my mind and distance from. She used to terrify me. The pull she had on me made me feel weak and vulnerable, but now finally I understood— there would be no running away from her. The further I ran away from her, the nearer I got to her.

I was just punishing us both.

She'd said I could quit in the morning, but I could never leave now. At the thought a chill settled in my chest. Having her would not be easy—a lot was at stake. One, was her father and his cherished dream of keeping the family business in the family. I would also have to give up my childhood dream of being a champion fighter … just when I was so close too. But I knew in my heart, my dream would be nothing without Sienna. If I could not have her, then nothing would be worth it.

She was my dream now.

Without warning, the woman in my thoughts fluttered her eyelids open. There was no moment of confusion for her. Her eyes zeroed in on mine. For the longest time, she simply held my gaze.

I stared into those beautiful emeralds and the world fell away. There was nothing left except us. I felt as if eons were passing by. Then she slid up along my body to kiss me. The feel of her hand as it rested on the side of my face was warm and sweet. My eyes closed to savor just how much such a simple touch did to me. It sent waves and waves of bitter-sweet, fiery sensations through my body that chased off the cold worries in my chest.

"Can we take a shower together?" she asked. "Our time's not over yet."

Her suggestion was perfect and exactly what I wanted to do. I slid out from under her and pulled the skirt down her legs. Then I stood over her and looked down. God, she was a beauty.

"Come on then. It's cold without your warmth," she coaxed.

I scooped her into my arms. Her arms encircled my neck and she buried her face in my chest.

When we arrived in the shower stall, I didn't put her down, but changed her position so she was hanging off me like a little monkey.

"Aren't you going to put me down?" she asked with a giggle.

"Nope," I said and turned on the faucet. A warm cascade of water poured down on us. A smile tugged at the corners of my lips. "You look like a drowned mermaid," I observed.

"Or rat," she muttered.

"Well, you're the best-looking rat I ever saw."

"If you keep holding me glued to you like this, I'm going to want to fuck you all over again."

"That was part of the plan."

She rubbed her wet crotch against my lower belly.

A storm began to brew inside of me. The water poured down on us as I slammed her against the tiles and fucked her hard. No condom. No thought of a condom. There could be nothing between us again. Not even the thinnest piece of rubber.

She was mine. All mine. And God help anybody who tried to get in my way.

I buried my seed deep within her body and I hoped it would grow.

She cried into my neck and clawed vicious marks down the skin of my back, and when we finally parted, she asked me a question in a small voice. "Is this truly our last time together?" She couldn't meet my gaze.

I wanted to tell her everything would be okay, but there was much to be done before I could say this. Let her think nothing had changed. It would be safer for her that way. I told her the only truth I could. "I don't know."

CHAPTER 37

"*I* heard everything."

I looked up from the bagel I'd been mindlessly lathering with cream cheese, and met Charlotte's eyes.

She was watching me with a naughty smile on her face.

At first, I tried to brazen it out. "It would have been strange if you hadn't." I said, returning my attention to my bagel. "We were pretty loud." Then I turned an accusing glare on her. "'Were you even drunk? I keep thinking that whole drunken drama you pulled yesterday wasn't very real."

"Drunken drama? It was … kind of. I was drunk, but not as brain dead as I made out. I don't know, I thought he would stop at the hotel we were about to pass. I could pretend to be so out of it, we would need a hotel room, but it worked out much better when we ended up in his place."

I shook my head. "I can't believe you."

"What? You can't believe me? You should be thanking me. I woke up to you screaming like someone was batting you with a pole."

I couldn't help the smile that slipped onto my face at her expression.

She leaned back on her chair, her gaze assessing. "Was it seriously that good? Tell me, but dial it down, so I don't feel too jealous."

My smile turned into a grin.

Charlotte then shouted, "Son of a bitch!"

"Keep your voice down," I whispered, looking around the empty breakfast room. True, no one was within earshot, but that wonderful girly moment of sharing with Charlotte was replaced with sadness. He would always have to be a secret. On our way out of Angelo's apartment, he had grabbed me and kissed me. Hard.

I didn't need to ask what the kiss was for.

It was goodbye.

I'd nearly choked on the bile rising up to my throat. I had to quickly pull my thin coat over my torn blouse and hurried away before he could see how hurt I was.

Because I was hurt. So hurt. I resented him for not fighting for me, but I decided on the drive back to the house I wasn't going to give up. No matter what, I wanted to keep him in my life. Even if he didn't want anything beyond the explosive physical connection we had ... I would accept it. Perhaps it was better for him to quit, that way he would be under no obligation to my father. Perhaps, then we would have a chance.

"Stop being so paranoid. There's no one else here?" Charlotte asked.

I had to be paranoid. I knew what kind of security existed in our home. Very little could remain hidden. I took a bite out of my bagel and lifted my fruit tea to my lips before returning my attention to her.

"Seriously," she said. "I don't think I've ever heard anyone have sex the way you two did last night. I swear, I was this close …" She held her finger and her thumb an inch apart. "… to barging in and demanding to join the party."

My expression was probably part horror, part shock. "Doesn't what you just said creep you out?"

"It does, but no one's ever made me lose my shit like that. I was drunk and I wanted that for myself too." She sighed as she pushed what was left of her scrambled eggs around the plate. "But I wasn't drunk enough to know there would be no point in trying to join. You were the only one he wanted to be with."

Poor Charlotte was just looking for love. Real love. Not that I had found it yet, but I'd always been too busy with my fashion classes to bother looking, so I'd never felt the disappointment of not finding it. But she looked for it every weekend, and every Monday she put on a brave face and went out into the world again. But it clearly was her secret sadness. I felt so bad for Charlotte I wanted to hug her, but I also knew she wouldn't want pity from me. I reached out a hand and touched hers. "Remember that inspirational video we both used to watch all the time."

She nodded. Then we both yelled in unison, the way the guy in the video used to shout, "I will never give up … until I win."

"You're beautiful, Charlotte, and you will find the right man."

"Maybe, but you never even tried and you've already found the right man. It seems almost unfair."

I dropped my voice to a whisper. "Charlotte, have you heard anything I've said to you? My father will kill him if he even suspects we're together. My father is a smiling sociopath with an army of psychopaths to do his dirty work for him, and Angelo is just a bodyguard. He has no chance against my father. Unless I find a magic genie that can slip me into a parallel universe, I can see no way I could ever have a future with him. Worse, if I don't fight really hard, I will find myself married to a man I detest."

Now it was her turn to look at me with pity. She grasped my hand in hers and squeezed it. "Run away from here, Sienna. Come and live with me," she whispered. "I'd love that. I've really missed you."

"I tried to run away and come to you a few days ago, and it was a complete and utter disaster." I chewed my bottom lip. "If I find I can't talk my father out of marrying me off to Fabio and I do attempt another escape, I will have to plan it much better. No matter what, I can't compromise my family's safety."

Suddenly, the air in the room seemed to change.

I froze.

Charlotte's eyes darted towards the doorway.

Slowly, I turned my head in the direction of her gaze.

Angelo stood in the doorway and watched me quietly. With a curt nod at Charlotte, he made his way into the room and halted a few feet away from me.

"Uh, I think I need to use the bathroom," Charlotte mumbled, and scurried away faster than I could blink.

Before Angelo could speak, I did. "I know—you said you'd be done, after—after. Uh, last night, but could you please wait until Charlotte returns to the UK? She'll be leaving at the end of the week, and I don't think I'll be able to completely trust her safety in anyone else's hands."

His gaze remained unblinking, and completely void of emotion—the stark difference between this stranger and the abandoned, pleasure-crazed man from last night and earlier this morning, was staggering.

"I've brought a message from Fabio Mancini," he spat the last two words as if they disgusted him.

Angelo, I realized then, was not devoid of emotion, he was freaking furious, but he was holding the rage so tightly in check, his whole body clenched as tight as his fists. Inside, he was ticking like a bomb. One wrong move …

I stared at him with confusion. "What? Why is he in contact with you?"

"He has returned from his trip to Italy, and wants to have dinner with you tonight. He will send a car over for you. He also mentioned that you should dress casually as you will be dining in his apartment."

I was speechless. I knew exactly what was going on. Fabio wanted to humiliate Angelo. He had not moved on from the petty competition he had started with Angelo, and he was out to make things as hard as he possibly could for him. What I couldn't understand was how he couldn't see that his attack on Angelo would also make things difficult and unbearable for me.

The answer was simple. He didn't care. All he was capable of thinking of, was his narcissistic self.

I knew I had to go, but I also knew I had to act fast. While I was dreaming of being with Angelo, people around me were making plans for me. Ruinous plans.

I stood and faced Angelo. My voice calm as I spoke. "Please thank Fabio for his invitation, but tell him, I will make my own way there as I'm taking Charlotte on a shopping trip this afternoon, and it will be easier to simply go direct from there." I paused. "As you are in charge of guarding me, I should also inform you that I will be taking Charlotte with me to dinner."

A glimmer of wild joy passed through Angelo's eyes, but it was gone so quickly, I could have just imagined it.

"I will convey your message," he said formally, before walking away.

The strength drained away from my legs then, and I sank back into the chair.

Charlotte must have been waiting around the corner, because she hurried in seconds after Angelo left. "You look like you've seen a ghost. What's wrong?" she asked worriedly.

I told her what Angelo had come to say and she was incredulous. "Why the hell did he send the message through *your* bodyguard? He doesn't have your phone number?"

"He does," I replied, reaching for the glass of water on the table. I saw my hands trembling. In fact, I felt so angry it was painful to breathe.

"You were right," Charlotte muttered. "He's a dick."

"Yeah, and you're coming with me to the dinner."

She wrinkled her nose. "Do you even have to go? Just ignore the invitation."

"I can't," I replied. "I have a plan. I need to show the elders that I at least gave him a chance."

"Oooo ... a plan. I could get on board with that. This holiday is going to turn out far more exciting than I'd hoped it would."

I sighed and hoped Angelo would be able to ignore him. Fabio wanted to show Angelo that he had it all. The money, the power, and the heiress he could summon at will.

Well, I had a few lessons of my own to teach him tonight.

CHAPTER 38

SIENNA

Fabio's luxury condo was located downtown at the century city.

All through the ride there, I was careful not to meet Angelo's eyes, and he seemed to have adopted the same method of defense, keeping his distance from me and avoiding any communication between us. It turned the atmosphere in the car so tense even Charlotte hadn't said a single word.

The ride in the elevator was even worse. I met Charlotte's eyes once in the polished doors.

She widened her eyes and made a strangling gesture with her hand around her throat.

When he got to the door, I glanced away quickly. "Thank you," I said.

"I'll be right here," he replied quietly.

I nodded and rang the bell.

Almost immediately, a man answered the door. Dressed in a navy blue suit, a deep-red waistcoat, a pristine white shirt, and a flamboyantly checkered tie with the Gucci logo printed all over it. Like one of those gay, completely fun guys who would always be the life and soul of any party he was invited to, but he had his professional demeanor on now. He glanced at Charlotte with an unsurprised expression before turning his attention back to me. "*Signorina Siciliano,*" he welcomed politely.

"Yes, that's me," I answered brightly. "I've brought a friend with me."

"Of course," he said, stepping aside, so we could come in. "I'm Frederick, Mr. Fabio's personal assistant. He sends his apologies that he is not here himself to greet you, but he had some urgent calls to handle in his study, so he'll be a little while longer. Would you like to follow me to the living room?"

I sighed. What else had I been expecting? That he would honor the appointment he had set and extend the courtesy of actually being punctual? That would be like asking a tortoise to fly.

We followed Frederick through the foyer into the vast, high-ceilinged space. It was impressive to say the least with a sweeping staircase leading to the second floor. A massive chandelier hung from the ceiling. I guess it was befitting of his inherited status of stupendous wealth.

"Fancy," Charlotte gasped at the grandeur all around her. "I've seen apartments like this only in documentaries about billionaires."

"Well, he's not a billionaire," I whispered back.

Finally, we were led into the open-plan living area and kitchen with a patio beyond, that showed off breathtaking views from downtown all the way to the blue ocean beyond.

"My apartment back home looks like a shoe box in comparison," she muttered.

I smiled at the exaggeration, despite the tension still sitting in the pit of my stomach as it had all day.

"Wow!" she exclaimed as she walked out onto the patio to watch the city spreading below her like a carpet of lights. It was beautiful and the skyline looked almost close enough to touch.

Frederick addressed me. "What would you like to drink, *Signorina?*"

"Any Merlot will do," I replied. "For my friend, a white burgundy please."

"I'll see if I can find a good Merlot," he said and walked away.

I sank onto a black leather sofa. It looked so pristine like it had never been sat on. I focused my gaze on the muted massive television set to the sports channel on one wall and tried to calm my nerves.

Charlotte joined me on the sofa. She squeezed my hand. "Hey, it's going to be okay. I promise. One way or another, it's going to be fine."

I nodded. Then we both waited together for his majesty to appear.

Almost forty-five minutes later, after two glasses of wine on an empty stomach, he did. He wore a three-quarter length silky dressing gown over a white t-shirt. I hoped he'd worn shorts under that because what stuck out was a pair of surprisingly skinny and hairy legs. When he said casual, he really meant casual!

"I heard you brought a friend along," he drawled, as he made his entrance, a tumbler of golden liquor in hand.

As he came forward, I noticed his face looked slightly flushed and his eyes were glittering. I rose to my feet, and so did Charlotte. "Fabio, this is Charlotte. She's a good friend from Eng—"

"Any friend of yours is a friend of mine," he interrupted expansively as he pulled her into his embrace, placing two noisy kisses on both of her cheeks. Then he released her and turned to me with the intention of kissing me on the mouth.

I jerked back. "Sorry, Fabio," I said with an apologetic smile. "I detest the taste of whiskey."

His lips widened with a smile, but he couldn't hide how immensely irritated he felt at how I'd dared to block him. His cheeks were flushed dark red with embarrassment as his gaze darted to Charlotte. "This is a whiskey glass …" He held the crystal tumbler up, and the golden liquid swirling within. "But it isn't whiskey. It's cognac, black pearl. Aged over a hundred and fifty years."

"Ah, well. Never mind, you kept us waiting for so long we're now starving," I said with my sweetest smile.

He smiled tightly and drained his one hundred and fifty-year old cognac in one gulp.

I heard Charlotte suck in her breath.

"So, what's for dinner?" I asked cheerfully.

He was so irritated with me he handed his glass to Charlotte.

In surprise, she accepted it.

"Follow me," he said.

Both Charlotte and I looked at each other. I tried to rein in my temper, but Charlotte winked at me. Then she simply opened her hand and the glass rushed towards the hand-cut Italian marble floor. The noise of the glass smashing into tiny fragments made me flinch. No doubt there would be a mark there.

"Oops," she said, and we both turned to look at Fabio.

He had stopped walking and whirled around in alarm. Maybe he thought it was a gunshot or something. Who knows, but for a moment there, the mighty Fabio had been afraid. "What the fuck?" he swore.

I managed to keep a straight face at his expression.

"What happened?" he demanded, clearly barely able to hold on to his temper.

Charlotte slightly raised her hands. "Sweaty palms, I guess," she said. "Your glass slipped."

CHAPTER 39

"Y ou've caused thousands of dollars' worth of damage," he fumed, as he glared at her.

"Sorry," she offered. "But maybe you shouldn't have given it to me."

He turned to look at me. "She has a point," I said mildly.

He waved his hand vaguely towards a door. "There's a broom in one of the closets in there. Perhaps you'd like to clean up the mess you made," he said through gritted teeth.

"Fabio, you're being rude to my friend," I said. He was incredible.

He headed over to the fridge to retrieve ingredients. "Oh," he said. "How so?"

"There's a broom in one of the closets over there? You're expecting her to clean up?"

"Well, I don't have my housekeeper or the maid in the house right now. I sent them all away for the night since I incorrectly assumed this was going to be an evening with just the two of us and you might like some privacy."

Charlotte pretended to gasp in horror. "I'm not welcome?"

He took a deep breath and forced a smile. "You know what? We obviously started on the wrong foot. Let's start again. As I said before, any friend of Sienna's is a friend of mine. So of course, you're welcome, but you can't blame me for not feeling disappointed that I do not have Sienna all to myself, but I console myself with the thought that there will be many, many years for us to be together."

He smiled again, this time it was broader and slightly more genuine.

"Today, I'm going to prepare my mother's favorite spaghetti dish for both of you. I promise you are going to absolutely love it. Come with me to the kitchen and you can sit and watch while I prepare my masterpiece."

I rolled my eyes at Charlotte as we headed over to sit on the stools around his massive granite white and grey island.

All the ingredients he needed were already laid neatly on the counter, presumably by his housekeeper. There was freshly made fettuccine covered with a towel, tomatoes, olive oil, ground beef, a bulb of garlic, a chunk of parmesan, and a bunch of parsley in a jar of water."

"My mother has only ever used this recipe for our family over the years. Trust me, it tastes like a miracle has exploded in your mouth. Sienna … you and your friend are going to love it."

"Can't wait," I said, and watched him as he began to look around possibly, for pans.

He seemed quite clueless as to where everything was and it made me feel slightly guilty for leaving him to his own devices. Anyway, I was sure my reluctance to help would somehow translate into a joke in future family gatherings of how useless I was in a kitchen. I slid off the stool and rounded the counter. "Do you need any help?"

"Perhaps just chop those tomatoes, and peel the garlic for me. I hate the smell of garlic on my fingers."

"Sure," I replied and got to work, even though I hated the way he seemed to be getting me to do the work he didn't want to do.

"What about you, Charlotte? Would you like to help too?"

Even I had to stop and blink. I turned to see Charlotte had the same astounded look on her face.

She looked at me with an expression that said, *we've got a live one over here*, then she jumped off her stool. "Why not? What do you want me to do?"

"You can fill up that pan with water and put it on the stove, then you can grate some parmesan."

Giving me another look, Charlotte went to fill the pan he had indicated with water and put it on the stove to boil. Then returned to the counter and began to grate the cheese.

Fabio folded his hands and addressed Charlotte. "So … what do your parents do?"

"My parents are academics. My mom is a secondary school teacher and my father is a contemporary art professor at UCL."

"You mean UCLA," he corrected.

"No, I'm referring to the University College in UK, not the University of California."

"Ah," Fabio said. "Interesting."

"What is?" she asked.

He laughed. "Nothing really, but it seems that means that you are middle class and I would have expected you to be more familiar with doing chores. You seemed so surprised earlier when I suggested you clean up the shattered tumbler. And it *is* just myself and Sienna currently slaving away to get dinner ready."

A heavy silence struck the room, and even I didn't know what to say.

Charlotte smiled and then nonchalantly shrugged her shoulders, completely unbothered. "Well, I don't know how it works in America, but in England we value our guests. We would be mortified if they came around and started to do chores for us."

"Hmmmp." He came over to me then and said, "I cannot believe you consider a woman like this your friend. I'm going to get myself another glass of Cognac. Anybody else want a drink?"

"Not me," I said.

"Thanks, but no thanks," Charlotte sang.

When all the ingredients were prepared, he came back. He put the saucepan on the stove, browned the garlic, dropped the tomatoes and beef in. When the beef was cooked, he poured in the sauce that had apparently been already prepared by someone else and let it simmer.

The water in the big pan was boiling, so I dropped in the fettuccine and in few seconds later, the food was ready.

Fabio waved towards some plates and I put them out on the counter. Then he started dishing out the food onto the plates. "Shall we light some candles and eat on the patio?" he asked.

I shook my head quickly. The last thing I wanted was any kind of romantic atmosphere. "No, let's eat here. I like it here."

We took our positions around the island.

Fabio tasted one forkful of his dish and slammed his hand down on the marble. "I told you, Sienna, miracle in your mouth."

I put the food into my mouth and it was edible, but it was definitely far from the 'miracle in your mouth' that he'd been professing it to be. No one in our family dared to tell him his mother was not known for her cooking skills.

He dove at his meal, slurping the fettuccine with the most grating sounds I had ever heard. Perhaps the sounds he made weren't so bad, but at this point, I felt so irritated by him that even his breathing seemed like that of a bull's in my ear.

He didn't bother asking us any questions, but he sure had a lot to say about his recent trip to Milan. He bragged and boasted about everything and made derogatory comments about everyone and to him, none of it seemed rude. From the private jet he had to take because he couldn't stand the filth of the people on commercial flights, to the exquisite hotel suite he'd insisted was given to him since it was the most expensive available and even that was a dump.

I zoned out, and didn't even bother pretending to nod my head or smile. Only a fool would not have noticed how uninterested I was in him or his boasting and preening.

Suddenly, he jumped up. "Actually," he declared. "I've brought back something very special that I want to share with you, Sienna." He headed into another part of the house, presumably his study or something.

Charlotte turned to me and whispered, "I can't believe he's still alive. Why hasn't someone shot him?"

I stopped laughing just as he returned with a bottle of red wine in hand. He had turned the label towards me and I could see it was very, very old.

CHAPTER 40

SIENNA

"*I* present to you Château Lafite Grand Cru. Aged more than two hundred years, and rumored to have once belonged to Thomas Jefferson. I got this at a secret auction in Milan for three hundred thousand dollars. Believe me these types of bottles are worth every penny. You absolutely need to have a taste of this. I opened it just as you arrived to let it breathe and it is ready for consumption now." He half-filled his own glass first before he looked at me questioningly.

For once, I was intrigued with what he was talking about, and pushed my glass over to him.

He proceeded to fill my glass.

I noticed he filled it with less than he did his own.

He took a sip from his glass, then kissed his fingertips. "You will be astounded," he promised. "No offense to our family's vineyard, but I have never tasted anything as exquisite as this in all of my life."

Charlotte had also pushed her glass out, but he had pretended not to notice and placed the bottle by his side. Charlotte received the message loud and clear then she just shrugged.

I couldn't believe the shade he had thrown at her. "Aren't you going to offer any to Charlotte?" I asked.

He glanced to her, and then to me, and then he sucked in his breath. "I'm sorry but, I have also promised a few of my friends a taste and there is only so much in this bottle." He turned towards Charlotte. "I can open another bottle of Merlot for you if you like. It is from Sienna's father's vine-yard and it is one of the best wines in my collection."

Charlotte blinked hard, and so did I.

"Well," she rose to her feet. "You and your bottle can go fuck yourselves. Thanks for dinner." She turned towards me. "I'll go wait with Angelo for you." She threw down her cloth napkin and started to walk away.

"Good. Let her go," Fabio said.

"Fabio," I said calmly. "You're such a jerk." I wanted to grab his precious two hundred and fifty-year old bottle of wine and pour it all over his head. It would serve him right. But I didn't. Instead, I stood up and followed Charlotte.

Fabio jumped out of his chair. "What the hell?" He came after me and roughly grabbed my arm, his eyes ablaze with anger. "Have you lost your damn mind?"

I remained calm. "Fabio, let go of me."

"You know what, Sienna, you are a rude fucking bitch. I invite you over to dinner at my house and without asking, you bring along the most uncivilized person I have ever met in my life. And I'm still polite and feed her. Why should I let her drink the wine that I have paid hundreds of thousands for? She is nothing to me."

"Fine. Save your wine for you and your friends. If it's too good for my friend then it's too good for me too. Now, let go of my hand."

Instead of letting go, he tightened his grip. "No, I want you to stay and drink the wine."

"I don't want the wine, Fabio. Now, let go!" I warned through gritted teeth.

His eyes flashed and it reminded me of him as a boy. He always was a petulant child who used to throw tantrums when he couldn't have what he wanted. He smiled nastily. "I wonder what your parents will say if I told them how you behaved today. Shall I tell them you don't want to marry me because you want to fuck your bodyguard."

I froze.

"You thought I didn't know. Now get back to the table and drink the fucking wine," he ordered.

"Let her go!" the command suddenly came ... low and menacing.

It actually sent a shiver down my spine.

We both swiveled our heads to see Angelo strolling over to us with unhurried, even strides.

Charlotte followed behind him, alarm flaring in her eyes at the sight of Fabio's grip around my arm. "Sienna, are you all right?" she asked.

"I'm fine," I replied.

"Let her go," Angelo repeated. "And if I have to say it again, I'm going to break your hand." His voice was quiet, but no one, not even Fabio missed the absolute intent in the threat.

Fabio's grip around my arm loosened.

Charlotte immediately came to my side and started pulling me away from him.

"All of you," Fabio shook with anger. "Get out of my apartment!"

He didn't need to say it twice.

CHAPTER 41

ANGELO

"What a dick!" her friend exclaimed again as I drove them home. "God!"

Sienna remained quiet, her gaze once again focused on the window as we zoomed along the freeway.

"Sienna, you *cannot* marry that asshole. He's sick in the head. I have never met a bigger asshole than him in my entire life and I've met some major assholes!"

"Charlotte," Sienna said quietly, and then stole a glance at me.

I caught it through the rearview mirror, but she quickly averted her eyes.

I felt sick to my stomach. When I saw him grabbing her I wanted to kill that low life. I didn't even want her to go to him, but I knew I couldn't stop her until I had all my plans laid out. But I let her go because I knew Charlotte would be there. I nearly died when she came out of the apartment without her. I knew now, there was no more time to waste. I had to swallow my pride and do whatever it took to make Sienna mine.

My disturbed, jumbled thoughts came to an abrupt stop when we arrived back at the compound to a flurry of panic going on. Right at the entrance were the flashing sirens of an ambulance, and three paramedics in uniforms.

"Oh, my God," Sienna cried out in fear.

"What's going on?" Charlotte asked, alarmed.

I had hardly brought the SUV to a halt when Sienna jumped out of the car. I didn't know what danger lay in front of her, so I threw open my door and sprinted after her. I caught up to her before she could get too close to the scene and grabbed her hand.

"Let me go!" she cried and tore at my grip. "Angelo."

"Calm down," I said, as I let my eyes quickly scan the scene. Only after confirming the presence of the other guards ... Alessandro, Mateo, and the others was it clear things were somewhat under control.

I was about to let her go when a gurney was rolled out of the house with her father strapped onto it. Her mother and a couple of paramedics following closely. Relief flooded through me when I saw that his face wasn't covered with a white cloth. Instead, an oxygen mask had been fitted over his mouth as his unconscious body lay still.

I let go of Sienna.

"Papa," she screamed, and began to run towards him.

Her mother immediately rushed to her side and appeared to be trying to explain what was going on.

Her grandmother came out. She looked old and lost.

After her father was lifted and placed in the ambulance, Sienna ran towards her grandmother and hugged her. Supporting her, she turned towards me. "Angelo!" she called.

But I already knew what needed to be done. I lifted my hand to acknowledge her and ran towards the car. I drove it towards the house and helped her grandmother into the vehicle. Then we were off and keeping pace behind the ambulance.

CHAPTER 42

SIENNA

https://www.youtube.com/watch?v=aJOTlE1K90k
-Girls like you-

*M*y father had suffered a pulmonary edema.

The attack on his lungs had nearly cut off his air supply. One moment, he had been speaking to my grandmother in his study and in the next, he had collapsed to the floor, wheezing and struggling to breathe.

My mother had been beside herself with panic, but luckily they were able to stabilize him in the hospital and things were soon brought under control.

My grandmother had left the room to have a bowl of soup that Gemma brought for her, so it was just my mother and I by my father's side.

He was connected to a frightening network of tubes and machines, but the doctor had assured us he was no longer on

the verge of death and they were working to return him back to normal.

I still felt so shaken that I could hardly speak. The sight of my all-powerful father lying so weak and helpless on the bed too difficult to take in. He had always seemed so formidable, so untouchable that the possibility of him ever being reduced to this state had seemed a reality far too distant to have to worry about. Maybe when he was eighty. Not now.

But here he was right before my eyes, with my mother holding tightly to his hand her head resting lightly against it. Her mouth was moving soundlessly and I knew she was praying. The scene seemed so intimate and private, it made me feel like an intruder.

I rose to my feet and quietly left the room. Outside, I felt dizzy. My whole world had just tilted to one side. All my plans of running away were in tatters. I could never go anywhere now. I had a responsibility. Now when my father was weak and vulnerable to his enemies, I had to stand by him. I leaned against the wall and waited for the strength to return to my limbs. Slowly, I felt the power that had run in the blood of my ancestors begin to seep into mine. I was strong. I could overcome this setback. My plan was no longer to run away, but to stay and fight for me and my family.

When I straightened from the wall, I spotted a vending machine at the end of the quiet hallway.

It was only when I arrived in front of it did I realize I didn't have a single dime on me to purchase a can of Coke. I almost laughed. Such an apt description of my life … Access to all the money in the world but unable to buy the one thing I wanted. Suddenly, I felt a presence behind me. I didn't need to turn around to see who it was. No one else moved so softly. The hairs on my hands were standing.

"Which one do you want?" he asked.

I cleared my throat. "A Coke."

His large hands curled around my arms. Then he turned me towards the sitting area. "Go take a seat over there. I'll bring it to you."

It felt good to have his strong, sure hands on my body. It made me feel like I would not be fighting this fight on my own. I nodded and went to perch at the end of a blue chair. I watched him walk over, his movements lithe and graceful. He handed over the opened can of coke and I lifted the can to my lips. He took a seat beside me.

I consumed half of it before stopping. The flow of the cold, fizzy liquid through my system was just the wake-up I needed. I held the can in my hand and stared straight ahead just saying, "Thank you."

He took his cap off and glanced at me. "For what?"

I turned to look at him and lifted the coke towards him. "For this, for calming me down, for saving my life, for being there, for protecting me, for … everything."

He didn't say anything and I turned away from his beautiful face.

Many seconds passed before he spoke again. "Your father will be fine."

I nodded, willing myself to believe those words with every fiber of my being. "He has to be. Otherwise, we're all screwed. Now I realize what everyone's been trying to tell me."

"Stay strong. Everything is going to be fine."

I turned to him again. "How did you end up here? Where's your family?"

I felt sure he wouldn't respond. Every time I had tried to ask him anything personal, he had clammed up faster than I could blink.

He ran his fingers through his hair. "Boston," he replied.

"Ah, that is why the men at the gym were calling you Boston."

He nodded. "I left my family and came to LA when I was nineteen."

I was taken aback. "Haven't you been back ever since?"

"No," he replied.

I stared at him curiously. "Don't you miss them?"

He turned to me then and stared into my eyes.

The attention felt way too intense for me to hold onto for long. I averted his gaze and pretended I needed another sip from my drink.

"I do," he said. "But I couldn't stay."

I was filled with curiosity, but I didn't want to push it. He would tell me what he felt comfortable revealing.

Then surprisingly, he kept speaking. "I had to or I would have been sucked into a life not of my choosing."

I stilled—exactly my situation. He had left, but I couldn't.

"I wanted to follow a different path from the one they envisioned for me," he went on. "I wanted to be a champion boxer, they wanted me to take over the family's business. It was not an easy decision, but it was my life. I don't tell anybody what to do and I don't want anybody telling me what to do either. Unfortunately, my father is a bit like yours. It was always his way or the highway." His smile was sad. "I had two options. Get back on the path, or cut off all contact and get the hell out. I chose the latter."

I stared at him, astounded. "I can't believe it. Your story is the same as mine. We're both being pressured by our families to conform. Why didn't you tell me?"

"I never talk about them, Sienna. To anybody," he stated softly.

My heart began to swell as I regarded the man in front of me. It felt almost like I was truly seeing him, for the very first time. Before I could stop myself, my hand lifted and cradled the side of his face.

He immediately reached up to grab my wrist, intending to stop me, but then he couldn't pull it away. I stared into his eyes, and before I could talk myself out of it, I leaned forward and kissed him. This melding of our lips together was heart wrenching. I savored his taste as it seeped into me, sweet and heated, and just like that I became completely lost. I forgot we were in the hospital, and my father's wellbeing was at stake. I forgot that at any point we could be discovered and that would bring even more troubles to both of us.

Suddenly, there was a thud and in the dull silence of the waiting room it felt too loud. We both jerked apart and looked down to see the can I had completely forgotten I'd been holding had fallen from my grasp and spilled out across the floor. A gasp left my throat as we hastily moved our legs away. I lifted my gaze to Angelo's to see him staring at me with his eyes hooded and glittering.

"I'll get it cleaned up," he said, rising to his feet. Then he froze.

A sick feeling rose in my stomach, as my head whirled around, and my gaze rushed to see what he was staring at.

We had an audience ... my grandmother and Charlotte.

I instantly shot to my feet. Time seemed to slow down as a strange fear washed through me. Not for me, but for Angelo. My father was incapacitated now, but what would happen when he again became the lion he was before?

In the deadly silence, Nonna gazed at me, then at Angelo, then she continued on without a word towards my father's room.

Charlotte made a face at me. "Don't worry, she saw nothing."

I sagged with relief. Then I turned to Angelo. "It's okay. She didn't see anything."

CHAPTER 43

SIENNA

That weekend, my family was hosting another banquet to commemorate the winery's twentieth anniversary. My father insisted he was well enough to attend and the celebration must go on.

The event was held in the barrel room, with its high curved ceiling, the aromas of wine barrels stacked up. Glass doors opened up to the panoramic view of the vineyard and mountains beyond.

There were people I knew and many I didn't. They treated me differently. It was as if they knew after my father's health scare that I would soon be the new boss. I didn't like it one bit. I didn't want to be the new *capo del capo*. I wanted my own little artisan business making exquisite shoes. I'd retreated to the food bar and stared at the vast display of food.

Charlotte would have had a blast here, but she had returned to London and left me here to battle the demons of my life on my own.

I picked up what was labeled a sea urchin taco appetizer. I slipped the tiny taco into my mouth - as my eyes scanned the room filled with guests, decked out in tuxedoes and evening gowns - for the one man who'd refused to give up his baseball cap.

Ever since that night at the hospital, things had suddenly changed between us. Angelo seemed to become withdrawn. It almost seemed as if he had completely lost interest in me. I had avoided my grandmother at all costs, the last thing I wanted to deal with was a confrontation of any kind about what she had seen. Even if she hadn't seen the kiss, my grandmother had sharp eyes. She would have noticed something.

Suddenly, I lost my appetite. I took a napkin to the corners of my lips and wondered for the umpteenth time what I was going to do. Ever since my father's illness everything had changed.

Yes, he was better, but the incident had imprinted the very jarring reminder of his mortality in my mind. The alliance with Fabio still hung over me, but after that night, maybe he would have changed his mind. I prayed he would have some pride and would give up the idea of marriage to me.

My thoughts were interrupted by the clinking of a cutlery against glass.

All eyes turned to my father. He put down his knife and glass then stood at the mic to address the audience. He talked about his grandfather's extremely humble beginnings as the son of an immigrant mother who'd fled a difficult life in Sicily. He acknowledged the contributions of the people invited to the gathering.

My mother stood to extend her gratitude as well. Then she mentioned me.

Every eye in the room turned towards me.

She beckoned me with her hand. "Come here, Sienna."

Reluctantly, I walked up while she told the audience how glad she was that I had returned home.

I didn't think it was the time nor the place, nor the right audience for that matter because although the gathering did appear somewhat intimate, we were all aware it was more official than anything else.

They applauded like they truly cared.

It was time to leave, however my father grabbed my hand and stayed me. "Wait a bit, Sienna," he said.

At that moment, someone else emerged from the crowd. *Oh God, no!*

Fabio walked towards me. "I have something to announce," he said, "to this special woman here."

I wanted to run away. I wanted the ground to open up and swallow me. I turned towards my father and what I saw in his eyes made my blood run cold. I couldn't move.

Fabio took the mic. "I've known this beautiful woman here for so many years. We spent our childhood together, running through the fields of this very vineyard, stuffing ourselves with the grapes, and then complaining that our stomachs hurt."

The audience tittered politely, and so did my parents.

He moved his focus from me and focused on his own parents in the audience. "Dad, Mom, I've shared with you how this beautiful woman here, found her way into my heart a long time ago, and no matter how far she goes, there is not a day that goes by when I do not think of her."

My stomach turned. Ugh ... What a liar. There wasn't an ounce of passion in his body for me. Even the time when he'd attacked me in the car, I did not feel real need or even want.

He turned to me.

I felt sick to my stomach. I knew what was coming.

"Sienna," he said smugly. "I've watched you grow and blossom into the intelligent, and captivating woman you are right now, and to be honest, I don't think I can wait another moment without being able to call you mine ... and only mine"

The crowd erupted into applause.

I couldn't even bring the corners of my lips upwards in feigned politeness.

He grabbed the mic out of its stand and started walking towards me with his deadened, dark gaze on mine.

I stared back in amazement. Was this the same guy who called me a bitch and kicked me out of his apartment?

He took my hand, and it took all of my self-restraint not to wrench it from his grasp. Then ... the man dropped to one knee, while my heart dropped into my stomach. I stared down at him. Too shocked by his drama to really comprehend what was going on.

I wanted to scream at him to get up and put an end to his sick act. With an enamored smile, he placed the microphone on the floor and pulled out a velvet ring box from his pocket. He opened it and inside was a blindingly massive diamond ring. "Sienna Siciliano, will you marry me?"

The crowd erupted into a deafening roar of excitement and applause. There were awws and ohhhs.

Fabio savored the attention, flashing his grin conspiratorially at them as they offered their congratulations to him.

I just stood there frozen to the spot like a statue. I was filled with the horror that there was absolutely nothing I could do to stop this. Like being tied to train tracks and watching an oncoming train. I just didn't know what I could do to stop it. When I turned my face to my mother, I saw the delight she exuded. I looked at my father and he was beaming with happiness.

Fabio pulled the ring out of the box.

A strange thing happened then.

I felt as though I had abandoned my body and was hovering in the air, watching the scene unfold.

He grabbed my unresisting hand and slipped the diamond onto my finger.

No one seemed to even notice that I hadn't said yes.

The ring felt like a band of fire. It burned my finger. I wanted to take it off and fling it away from me, but I couldn't.

Fabio rose to his feet and pulled me into an embrace. With his hand stroking my back, he turned to face the cheering audience. They were all so pleased for us.

I turned my gaze then and began to search for *him*, my gaze running across the room in desperation. It felt like I would crumble but something made me believe that if I saw him, even if it was just for a second, then I would feel better—everything would be okay.

But he was nowhere to be found. I felt so alone I wanted to cry. My eyes filled with tears. Through the haze of tears, I saw him. He stood at one of the side entrances. I had to blink several times to focus my eyes.

I whimpered as my gaze locked on him. I moved to take a step away from Fabio.

Angelo shook his head at me.

I froze. I didn't need any special interpretation to understand what he was saying.

Fabio linked his fingers with mine and turned me towards him. "You've made me the happiest man on earth today," he shouted loudly.

And you've made me the saddest woman on earth today.

CHAPTER 44

SIENNA

"What the hell was that all about?" Somehow, my mouth stretched into a smile, I had managed to pull Fabio out of the hall with me into one of the tasting rooms, and now we stood facing each other. I was panting with anger.

He looked at me innocently. "That was a proposal that you have agreed to since you're wearing my ring on your third finger, dearest fiancée."

"I don't care about you," I said, trying to understand him. "And you are aware of that. So why would you do this?"

"Sienna," he said. "What do you think this is? Do you think that our parents paired us together because they give a fuck about how we feel about each other? When the hell are you going to grow up? Use your damn brain and open your eyes."

I straightened. "Fabio, I'm already grown, which is why I'm not going to marry you. I'd rather die." I grabbed at the ring on my finger and pulled it off.

"Oh, you will," he said. "The moment your father does." He moved towards me until there wasn't even an inch of space left between us. "All the vultures that have been circling him for the last thirty years are going to swarm in, and if you are lucky your bodyguard will keep you alive, but it is no longer like the old days. Women and children were out of bounds. Everyone you love will be killed ... one by one ... brutally to teach you a lesson ... and it will all be on your head. Suicide will come quite naturally to you then. It will be as sweet as fuck." He stepped back to turn and walk away.

"I'm in love with someone else," I said. "Will you be all right with it then, if I continue to see him even after we're married?"

He stopped, and turned to face me, an amused smile across his face. "And who is it?"

Fear gripped my heart. "It's someone back in England. We met during my time there."

"What a little liar you are. It's that thick as two planks body-guard of yours, isn't it?"

I lifted my head. "It's none of your business who it is."

He shrugged. "To be honest, you can continue to see whoever the hell you want as long as you're discreet about it. In fact, I'll get you an apartment nearby where you can go to get your kicks."

I stared at him. "You really don't care, do you?"

"I have my own needs that you cannot meet. You remember Frederick? He answered the door when you came over? Well, he's one of several men that I enjoy."

My jaw dropped. He was gay! Suddenly, the image of him in his dressing gown, his cheeks flushed, and his eyes glittering, flashed into my mind. "Oh! my God. You were fucking him while I was waiting for you in your apartment, weren't you?"

"Yes," he admitted, his voice a strange mixture of smug and petulance. "I was angry you brought that stupid friend of yours." He looked at me earnestly. "I want this alliance between us, Sienna. I really do. It brings benefit to both our families."

"So," I said slowly, "your plan is for us to have a completely sterile arrangement while we fuck other people. What about children? Won't our families be expecting a few bouncing babies. Are you okay with us passing another man's children off as yours?"

"No," he said clearly, "I will want the children you produce to be mine. It'll be my duty and privilege to give my family heirs. We'll need a couple of sons to carry on the legacy and it's up to you how we have them. We fuck during the times of the month that you are most fertile until you get pregnant, or we can have it all done professionally at a fertility clinic. The second option would be my preferred method, but it is up to you. However, I will need a DNA test of any child you give birth too."

"You've got it all figured out, haven't you?"

"Yes, I have. I thought long and hard about this. Now, come back in and stand by my side. When people come to congratulate us, smile, and act like I've just made you the happiest woman on earth. Unless you want to see your father collapse once again in front of you, then by all means, do whatever you want. I'm doing my duty, so you at least do yours and we can chase after whatever consolation we'll need along the way."

With that, he turned around, and sauntered away.

I stood in the dim room a long time. The world outside this small tasting room felt hostile and dangerous. Then I squared my shoulders. Somehow, somehow, I would be victorious. The moment I returned to the event, my father had called out to me, and at the frail expression on his face, I felt my stomach clench.

As I reached him, Fabio came over then. He didn't try to touch me and we had stuck together for the rest of the night, receiving the congratulatory messages and well wishes as one, as the world expected.

When I finally arrived back in my room, I closed my door, my purse fell to the ground and my legs gave way. I slid to the floor in a heap.

I would never know for how long I sat there, my thoughts running in circles. No matter which way I went, always I came back to the same solution. I was Fabio's brood mare. I thought of how Angelo had run from the obligation his family had tried to trap him with and I envied him his freedom to do as he pleased. I wanted to run too, but I couldn't. I could never leave now. Not with my father looking as frail as he did.

I thought of Angelo, his bright blue eyes, the way his body melted into mine, and the life that I so desperately wished I could have with him, and it pained me to think I would have to give all that up. Given his comments in the past about wanting me to be solely his, no way would he come near me now. This sordid arrangement would not allow for me to have his children either.

Anyway, I was probably just fooling myself that I could ever have had him. Ever since the time when Nonna had almost walked in on us kissing, he had taken a giant step back and away from me. And tonight, when I had met his gaze and wanted to run to him, he had clearly shaken his head to indicate I shouldn't give the game away.

For the most part, this was what broke my heart.

I really thought he cared for me. Well, maybe not a lot, but a little. Maybe this was how he'd been with all his sexual conquests. I had no experience with men and maybe I had read more into our relationship then there had been. Jesus, what a mess!

Tears started to burn my eyes. I let them flow freely.

I sobbed my heart out for the smile I'd had to plaster on my face all throughout the night. The countless thank yous I had said, and the endless embraces I had received. For the life everyone had planned out for me. For the fact Angelo was not prepared to fight for me. I knew I was being silly. Of course, he couldn't fight for me. Things like that only happened in silly Hollywood movies. In real life, mafia bosses like my father would hunt you down and kill you no matter where in the world you went if you took their daughter.

I realized now with a suffocating feeling, that from now on this would be my life. Outside - I would be smiling and people would be thinking how lucky and privileged I was, and inside - I would be a shriveling, embittered, lonely mess. As the years went by, I'd probably end up hooked on pain meds. I sniffed even harder when I thought about my future.

A small tap came on my door, and I startled. It could only be Angelo. I jumped to my feet, my heart thudding painfully in my chest. I wiped the moisture from my eyes and cheeks just as the tap came again, and then pulled the door open.

It wasn't him. It was Nonna bearing a small wooden tray with some pastries and a steaming mug of hot chocolate. There were even marshmallows in it.

I didn't have the appetite for any of it, but I knew she had fixed the tray for me herself. I felt touched and I wondered if she could *see* me, unlike everyone else, if she could understand the despair, slowly killing me inside. "Hi, Nonna," I whispered, my voice thick from sobbing. I bit my lower lip to stop it from trembling, but it wouldn't stop, so I turned away from her, walked to my bed and slipped under the duvet. It was a hot night, but I felt cold. The cold coming from deep inside me.

"Sit up, my child," she said, putting the tray on the bedside table and sitting next to me on the bed.

But I couldn't. The tears were just rolling out of my eyes.

She reached out a hand and wiped the tears away. "My poor, poor Sienna. You've had a rough evening, haven't you?"

I didn't know how to respond, so I just stared at her, doing all I could to choke back even more tears.

She lifted the mug of chocolate and offered it to me.

I shook my head and worked up some semblance of a smile. "No, Nonna, I'm not hungry or thirsty."

"I watched you all night," she said. "You barely ate anything."

"I did," I replied, "before Fabio's announcement."

She returned the mug back to the tray, then rubbed her hand up and down my arm. "I'm sorry, Sienna," she said. "When your parents discussed this marriage agreement with me, I didn't realize how much pain it was going to cause you. Sacrifices like this are a norm in our family, as little else matters beyond securing the safety and wellbeing of the next generation. I didn't even know who your grandfather was till the week before our wedding." She brushed my hair away from my face. "I want to ask you a question. Do you have someone else in your heart? Or is it that you just don't like Fabio?"

I wanted to respond truthfully and tell her about Angelo, but then I remembered she might under the guise of doing what was best for the family, attempt to harm him.

"Don't worry," she said, as if she had read my thoughts. "I won't do anything to hurt him. If I wanted to, I would have already, so don't lie to me."

I knew then she already knew about Angelo. Of course, she did. She had seen enough at the hospital to know. I sniffed. "Nonna, can I tell you a secret?"

"Of course."

I sat up and looked her in the eye. "You must promise never to tell anyone. If you do, I will never speak to you again."

"My, my, how dramatic you are," she said with a chuckle. "I promise I will never reveal your secret."

"Not even to mama or papa?"

"Not even to them," she confirmed solemnly.

"Fabio is gay," I blurted out.

Her eyes widened with shock. "A homosexual?"

I nodded. "He wants to have a pretend marriage, with both of us having lovers. He'll even get me my own apartment where I can go to have sex with whoever I want. He wants children of course, but he has given me the choice of having sex with him during the days I am most fertile, or he doesn't mind jerking off into a cup and having me artificially inseminated in a clinic."

She released a heavy sigh and shook her head. "The world today has changed so much."

"What would you do if you were me, Nonna?"

She sighed again. "I understand your parents and their desire to keep you safe, but I sure didn't give up the things I wanted and make all the sacrifices I have so far just so the generations after me would also be forced to do the same all over again. I was lucky, your grandfather was a good man, thankfully, but if he had not been …" She let the sentence trail away.

For a while neither of us spoke.

Then she placed her hand on the side of my face and cupped my cheek. "Don't be sad, my little pumpkin pie. I actually have a plan."

"What plan?" I asked hopefully.

A twinkle sparkled in her eyes. "I will tell you soon. In the meantime, behave as if you are still going to marry Fabio and tell no one we spoke today."

"Okay," I breathed the word out.

"Now, do you think your appetite might have come back?"

I smiled broadly at her. "I think so."

"Good. These pastries were brought from Sicily from a friend of mine today. They are delicious."

I lifted the mug of hot chocolate to my mouth. "Thanks for the marshmallows, Nonna."

"I hope the day never comes when you drink your hot chocolate without marshmallows in them."

"Nonna?"

"Yes?"

"You do know I love you, don't you?"

"Yes," she said softly.

I took a sip of the hot drink and felt the silky-smooth beverage warm my body up instantly. Then I spooned a melting marshmallow into my mouth. I was digging around for another marshmallow when she called me.

"Sienna?"

I looked up at her. "Yeah."

"You do know I love you too, don't you?"

I grinned at her. "Yeah. I do."

CHAPTER 45

SIENNA

*T*he next morning, I woke up in significantly brighter spirits.

After Nonna had left I had brushed my teeth and been so exhausted with all the crazy emotions that I had fallen asleep as soon as my head touched the pillow.

My phone rang and it was Christine. She wanted to set up a little get together. "Let's meet for brunch. I'm dying to eat some poached eggs that I haven't ruined," she said.

I just laughed. Christine was famous for her terrible poached eggs. Why she continued to attempt them was a mystery to Charlotte and me. We've both told her to give up, but she never gave up trying to make a good one with dogged determination.

Since Charlotte was no longer around for me to confide in or even just have a good gossip with, I figured a little catching up with some old friends, and some fresh air outside the house would do me some good.

I knew I was supposed to keep away from Christine until Angelo had finished his investigation into who was responsible for the attempted kidnapping or at least find the Judas in our midst. Which meant Christine and Mandy were still not cleared, but I knew he would find nothing on them. Hell, Mandy didn't even know I was coming till she got to Christine's apartment. As for Christine, I knew he would find nothing on her. Christine was like a sister to me. Both Charlotte and her were the sisters I never had.

I had another very important reason to agreeing to the meetup without a second thought. I needed to know if Angelo was still in my father's employ. What if he had quit last night? This would be a good way to confirm if he was still my bodyguard. I went downstairs and didn't see him around, which was worrying because he was always hanging around.

I had no choice but to tell Gemma I would be heading out for brunch. I gave her the address and the names of the people I was meeting, and told her to pass the information on to the security room. As I walked towards the elevator leading to the garage I thought I would die if some other man turned up.

I waited with bated breath inside my car in the underground garage. Nervously, I watched the doors of the service elevator until I spotted the light that showed the car was descending. It seemed a lifetime had passed while the car descended.

When the door slid open, a tall man with a baseball hat hanging low on his head, exited the car with a leisurely gait. The kind of relief and wild joy welling up in my body was indescribable. I started the engine, then leaned over to push the passenger door open.

Angelo made a gesture with his hand to indicate I should move into the passenger seat.

I felt too happy to see him to argue. Obediently, I shifted over and he got into the driver's seat. "Hey," I greeted, as he put the gears in motion, and drove up the ramp into the lovely morning sunshine.

To be honest, I even felt too shy to meet his eyes, and we rode in silence for a little while, but it was killing me that I was so nervous I couldn't even casually glance at him. I truly wanted to speak to him. I didn't know when we would get a chance like this again, to be alone together and not a prying eye in sight.

We were halfway to the restaurant when I decided to speak to him no matter what, and my first question was going to be why he hadn't spoken to me. I mean, it wasn't like we were strangers to each other.

We stopped at a red light and I turned to face him, but before I could open my mouth, he spoke instead. "Your eyes are swollen. You didn't get enough sleep last night?"

"Uh, I did," I replied, unable to work up a more coherent response. My throat had clamped up.

The light turned green and we continued on our way.

"You said you were going to quit?" I asked, the word quit actually sticking in my throat. "Did you decide not to?" I braved a glance at him then.

He looked mysterious and aloof.

I wished I could pull him to me and turn him back into that passionate man who burned kisses down my body.

His mouth twisted. "Why? Do you wish I had?"

I swallowed hard. "Of course not."

"Good."

It seemed clear he didn't want to talk so I decided to say no more until after I'd met Christine, Mandy and another acquaintance of ours, Natalie.

We walked into the restaurant together and found the girls were already seated at a table. Angelo walked towards a window table that gave him a good view of both entrances and the road car park.

Once we had all kissed and hugged, then placed our orders the conversation turned to the difficulties the girls were facing in the job market. I listened with a certain amount of sadness. This should have been me too. I wanted this struggle. It was part of the journey of life. Instead, I was being forced into a lie of a marriage with a man I actually couldn't stand.

"I thought you would invite me over for the celebration at the vineyard," Christine blurted out suddenly. "But the call never came."

"It was a private ceremony," I said quietly, unable to meet her eyes. "And my dad was the one who set it up. It was full of people connected with the establishment than anything else." I could feel her staring at me with hurt eyes. One day, I would tell her why and she would understand.

"No problem, but Charlotte was here for just a week and you never even once brought her to meet me. Not even an invitation for a visit to your house. She's my friend too, you know. I love her too."

I felt horribly guilty. I knew exactly how she felt. If Charlotte had come to see her and they had not invited me to join them even once, I would have been devastated. If Angelo hadn't said what he had about her, I would have invited her for more than one sleepover. In fact, the three of us would have gone everywhere together. "It was a flying visit, Christine. I thought we had loads of time, but before we knew it she was getting on the plane. But guess what? She's coming back next month and this time, why don't you come over and stay at my place for the whole time she is here?"

"Really?"

"Why not?" I said with a confident smile. By then, I hoped any suspicion about her would have been cleared up. Before she could ask more questions or get a firm conviction from me about it, I had to divert attention away from that topic. "By the way, I have news. I got engaged."

The entire table went silent, as the girls stared at me with dropped jaws.

"What?" Mandy exclaimed.

Christine seemed shocked. "To that guy? They still forced him on you?"

I nodded.

Her face fell and I knew then Angelo was wrong. She wasn't the Judas in my camp. She truly cared about me.

Natalie wasn't aware of anything, so Mandy quickly brought her up to speed.

"I didn't even know that arranged marriages were still a thing in this day and age," Natalie said, her voice full of wonder. "Can't you sue or something? Isn't there a law against this?"

"They're my family," I said, "I'm not going to sue family."

"Well, you can if they're being unreasonable. I would," Mandy said.

"Me too," Natalie concurred.

"He didn't give you a ring?" Christine asked, as she noted my empty hand.

I had the damn thing in my purse. "He did." I pulled out the massive oval-cut solitaire diamond, and tossed it carelessly across the table.

Their gasps made the other heads in the restaurant turn towards us.

"It's goooooooorgeous. Why the hell aren't you wearing it?" Mandy screamed.

"Whoa! Is that real?" Natalie asked, her eyes wide and shocked.

Christine reached out to pick it up and inspect it. "A hundred percent real," she announced confidently. "This should be at least 10 carats, but I would think more, right?" She looked at me expectantly.

I shrugged my shoulders. It honestly didn't matter to me. I wanted nothing to do with it.

"Okay," Natalie said, 'it's either you're so rich this ring means nothing to you, which by the way should be nothing less than a million dollars or—"

"It costs more than two million," Mandy interrupted. "I used to work at a top-notch jewelry store after I dropped out and that ring is at least two million and a half."

Natalie collapsed dramatically into the back of her chair. "Why don't you like this guy again?"

"He's a dick," Mandy reminded her.

She nodded, but remained unconvinced. "Still for that ring … phew."

The diamond was passed around before it was returned to me. I tossed it back into my purse and tried to change the topic, but that was like trying to put the cat back into the bag. The girls were utterly taken with the whole scenario.

"It's almost like an enemies-to-lovers romance. You never know, you could fall in love with him," Natalie said.

"Hell will freeze over first," I said.

Then Mandy began to narrate the ordeal we'd had when the men had tried to kidnap me. She turned to me. "Sienna, do you have any updates on the men that tried to kidnap you?"

I shook my head.

"That was so fucking scary. I was sick for a week after. Thank God, your bodyguard was able to catch up to them and rescue you."

"You sure do have an interesting life," Natalie observed, taking a sip of her orange juice.

"I wish it was completely uninteresting," I said as I lifted my mango and plum juice to my lips. "I wish I had a normal life where I was free to do what I wanted to do."

"But it all does seem peculiar, does it not," Natalie said. "How did the men know that you guys were going to take that exact route. You said that one of the vans was parked in front of your car, right? That means they were waiting for you. How could they have known you were headed that way?"

"A chill just went down my spine." Mandy shuddered. "I've been wondering about this exact thing. How the hell could they have known where we were going to be? Even we didn't know until we got there, unless your cell phone is tagged or something, Sienna."

"It's not," I replied. "They never had access to it ever. It was always in my possession."

"Then there's no other explanation," Natalie said. "And we can't conclude that they were just waiting randomly there, because they called your name, right?"

I was about to respond when Christine cut us off. "Ugh … it's morbid to talk about this before breakfast. Let's talk about something else."

Mandy laughed. "Christine's getting scared again. She was so shaken after the whole thing. I just made a joke that she must have been working with the kidnappers since she was the only one who knew that route. Hell, she almost bit my damn head off."

Christine shifted in her seat.

The other two girls laughed, but I saw something in Christine's eyes. Something I never thought I would see. My whole body felt cold and shocked. "Is it a joke though? I asked.

he other two girls stopped laughing suddenly, and an eerie silence fell upon our table.

Christine frowned as she met my gaze head on.

"Sienna, what are you saying? Surely, you don't …" Mandy whispered.

"Christine was the one driving and she took that route. She is literally the only one who knew where we were going."

Christine's eyelids began to flutter with shock. She made a scoffing sound and took her trembling hands off the table. "Are you accusing me of colluding with the people who tried to kidnap you? Have you lost your mind?"

I was suddenly tired of pretending. I grabbed my purse off the table and rose to my feet. "Christine," I said. "If I really wanted to accuse you, you would not be here right now. I'm sure you know exactly what I'm talking about and just what my father is capable of."

Her face fell.

"Why?" I asked.

"I'm not rich like you!" she snarled. "I don't have men giving me rings worth millions which I carelessly throw across restaurant tables. I have to work for every cent I get."

"Money? You did it for money?"

"I'm sorry, okay. I really didn't know they were going to kidnap you. All they wanted me to do was put a tracker into my purse. They said they just wanted to know where you were."

"And you believed *that*?" I asked incredulously.

Tears filled her eyes. "I'm sorry, Sienna. Really I am. You don't know how much I've regretted it since then. I just— they just didn't look rough. They were polite and they were nicely dressed. It was so much money for so little effort. And I promise you I didn't drive into that neighborhood on purpose. I really did get lost, but they had the tracker, so they knew which way I was heading."

"Have you got a tracker on you now?" I demanded fiercely.

She shook her head violently. "No, of course not."

Without a word, I stood, and turned to walk away.

She called to me, "Sienna." Her voice was full of desperation and fear.

I turned to look at her face with disbelief. Even though the truth had come from her own mouth, I still found it hard to believe she had betrayed me. I'd never believed Angelo and I never let his accusation stay even one second in my head. I'd been that confident of her loyalty and friendship. I thought because I would never do something like that to her, she wouldn't either.

Christine stared back at me with pleading eyes. "Are you going to tell your father?"

I shook my head … she was worried about … herself. "Unlike you, I don't want to see you hurt," I said, and stormed away.

I knew Angelo would catch up in no time. From the corner of my eye, I could see him throwing money on the table. Even before I had reached the entrance he was walking next to me. His cap sat low on his head, hiding his eyes from view. I saw his hand snake out and hit the button of the elevator. The doors switched open immediately. I walked in and waited stiffly for him. It was a small space, but he managed to keep a generous distance away from me, just as I had known he would. And I hated it.

A wave of loneliness suddenly overwhelmed me. At Christine's betrayal.

"You can stop investigating who gave my location away to the kidnapers," I said bitterly. "It was just like you said. Christine let herself be bought by some smooth-talking guys. They persuaded her to put a tracker in her purse."

"I'm sorry," he said softly.

"Yeah, so am I."

For a while, neither of us said anything as we crossed the deserted underground car park. Then I stopped and looked at him. "Are you going to tell my father?"

He shrugged. "She's young. She made a mistake. If you are not going to see her again or reveal important things about yourself to people who are friends with her, I guess it won't be necessary."

"Thank you," I said softly. "Thank you. I know it sounds like I'm being silly, but I know her parents. They are good people and it will break their hearts if anything bad happens to her. She is everything to them. They even sold their home to send her to the university in England and they live in rented accommodation in a horrible part of town now."

Angelo just shook his head. "That's a real shame."

"That's what I thought too. I was planning to buy them a nice house, because I thought it would eventually go to Christine, but now I'll just move them into a nice house and let them live out their days there."

His sharp gaze softened. "That would be a really nice thing to do."

"Can I drive?" I asked. "I don't want to stay still. I need something to distract me."

"Okay," he agreed, and passed the car key to me.

We walked to the car in silence.

Once in the driver's seat, I turned on the engine. Then I couldn't wait a second longer. I switched off the engine and turned to him. "Why are you still here? You said you couldn't protect me after being so intimate with me. So why are you still here?"

He folded his arms across his chest ... his gaze straight ahead. "I'll leave," he said, "when I can convince myself you'll be okay if I do."

My heart stumbled. I felt raw and I decided I didn't really care anymore for relationships that did not serve me. If someone was going to leave me anyway then let them go. It killed me to say it, but I did. "It'll hurt," I whispered, "but I won't die. I'll recover. You don't have to force yourself to stay just because you're worried about if I'll be able to take your absence or not."

"Okay," he said, turning his gaze towards me. "Then I'll put it this way then. I'll leave when I'm able to convince myself that I'll be okay if I do."

Shock reverberated through me. I returned my gaze to him, eyes round at what he had just said.

He released a shuddering breath. "I wanted to be sure you were the one. I wanted to give us some time. I had plans, but they needed time. After Fabio proposed to you last night though, I knew there was no need to wait a moment longer. You are the one. You always were. From the moment I saw you at the pool, you got into my brain, my blood. I'm going to fight for you, Sienna. Just be patient. As you know very well, I need your father's approval."

Tears fell from my eyes and splashed onto my cheeks. "He'll never give it. Not to you."

He took his hat off his head, placed it on his lap, and then curved his hand around the side of my face. "Will you trust me? I know what I am doing. I promise to be the man waiting for you at the altar."

I leaned into his warmth and his touch, my heart close to bursting. I nodded blindly, tears filling my eyes. I breathed in the warm, male scent of him and felt like I was in a beautiful dream I didn't want to wake up from. I wished I could remain inside my car in the car park forever. The rest of the world could go to hell. I would never have believed he would make such a promise. God, how I wanted to believe him. That we could actually have my father's blessing. A part of me knew it was a lie, but with the same stubborn determination I refused to believe Christine could have been the one even though it was clear she was the only one who could have done it, I clung to his promise.

"When that bastard proposed to you yesterday, the look on your face ... hurt me. I wanted to tear him apart with my bare hands. I hated him that much."

I remembered it as clearly as he recalled it. I also remembered the one person I had searched for in the midst of it all, was him. That the only thing I could believe right then was that as long as he was still around, that somehow things would be okay. I didn't understand when or why I had developed such a deep attachment and trust of him, but it had seen me through that incredibly dark moment. "Why did you shake your head at me?" I asked, more tears crawling down my cheeks.

"Because I saw you were at your limit, you were about to fall apart, and do something stupid like run to me. It would have ruined everything. Like I said before, I have plans. They have to be uncovered slowly. Your father's pride has to be kept at all costs. He puts a high price on it." He brushed my hair gently over my shoulders.

I felt my bones begin to melt. "Why can't we just run away to Europe? I'll get a job and you can open a gym while you carry on training to become a champion boxer. You can't be a bodyguard because I'd be worrying about you day and night. Once we have a few babies, my father will forgive us and we can come back."

His lips curved into a smile. "I ran away once, but it was the right thing to do, but running away is not the right thing to do now."

CHAPTER 47

SIENNA

https://www.youtube.com/watch?v=ZAfAud_M_mg

I moved away from the driver's seat and boldly went over to him. I positioned myself till I was sitting astride him and staring straight into his eyes. "So what do we do?"

With the edge of his finger, he stroked my nose. "That's where I come in. It might seem most of the time that the world is conspiring to hurt us and bring us down. But if we pay attention, we might see that what it's trying to do is to give us the answers to the questions we have been asking for a very long time."

I leaned even closer to him and slowly ran my hands down along his hair. "I truly wish that I could understand a single word of what you just said."

He burst out laughing.

The sound stunned me.

His eyes exploded with light and his chest rumbled with amusement.

I had never seen him laugh like this, and it was beautiful. He was laughing then he wasn't.

Suddenly, he grabbed the back of my head and took my mouth in his. His kiss was hard and fierce and through it, he conveyed his deep passion for me. "I'll fix this, Sienna," he swore, breaking the kiss. "I promise I will."

Right there and then, I actually lost it. I crushed my lips to his again and showed him with everything I had just how much he meant to me. I was trembling, tears pouring from my eyes as my entire heart completely opened up to this man.

No matter what happened between us from now onwards, I would never again love any man the way I loved him. To hear the words from him … *don't worry, I'll fix it*, was the answer to a prayer I didn't even realize I had. For someone to stand up for me, when I couldn't for myself. For someone to save me when I couldn't save myself.

I broke the kiss and gazed into his eyes. "I'm in love with you, Angelo," I told him. "I'm not asking for you to feel the same way, but I'm telling you now, so you will know that you can't leave anymore, not unless you want to make me fall out of love with you."

His grin almost blinded me. "Sorry, but I'm gonna make you fall even harder."

The words scrambled my brain. He couldn't be real. With one sentence, I had fallen even harder and it was a steep, brutal fall. It made me desperate. I gripped the edge of my blouse and pulled it over my head.

"Sienna," he muttered in surprise.

But nothing was going to stop me. "Pull us backwards," I ordered.

He didn't look convinced, but immediately, as if on autopilot, he obeyed. The chair slid backwards, and we moved smoothly together. "Sienna," he called again, his eyes quickly surveying the surroundings. "Not here."

On every side of us were rows and rows of parked cars, the only note of life filtering down was from the buzz of the street above.

"Right here, and now," I told him. "You can make it quick if you want to, but I'm not leaving here until I feel you inside me." I reached behind to unhook my bra and the moment my breasts spilled out of the fabric, I saw his gaze flare with wild excitement. His breathing came hard and fast, and it felt good to watch as lust completely took over his reasoning.

"Damn you," he swore as he cupped the heavy, mounds of flesh in his hands. With a groan, he covered my aching swollen nipple with his mouth.

The moment his hot mouth touched me, I was lost. I was wearing a short skirt, and I had never been so grateful for my decision. I suspected now that I might have even done it deliberately, with the distant expectation that perhaps something like this would happen between us.

I bit my lower lip, my eyes fluttering close as the sweet tension began to build inside me. I writhed my hips, my now soaked panties brushing against the hardened bulge straining through his jeans.

The sound of his low groans turned me on even further, as he tightened his arms around my body, crushing me to him as he feasted on my breasts, I felt my heart almost fail. I wanted him so bad then it felt as if I could never become sated.

"How the fuck did I let this happen? Your hold over me is dangerous, Sienna," he muttered.

A smile widened my lips as I leaned forward to cradle his face in my hands. I pulled him away from my breasts, impatient with my need to taste him. I slipped my tongue to his mouth, and when my tongue met the fervor of his, I felt my entire body begin to burn.

I was tingling all over with the heat and urgency, and the knowledge that we were in a public place. At any time, we could be seen by anyone passing by. But you know what? I didn't give a damn who saw us.

His hands moved underneath my skirt. He pushed it up till it bunched up around my waist. Then he found the strings of my thong and ripped the flimsy lace material off me. He pulled it from underneath me and flung it away. With one finger, he pushed me back so I was leaning against the dashboard. My throbbing pussy now completely exposed to him.

"Jesus, Sienna," he growled and he licked his lips in anticipation.

Without taking his eyes off me, he began to incline the chair even further backwards until he was almost horizontal underneath me. He gripped the sides of my thighs and lifted me completely off him.

I squealed with surprise.

"I want you over my mouth," he said.

He didn't even give me a chance to process his instruction. I was thrust forward and had to quickly figure out my balance. With both my hands against the backseat, I was lifted until my ass was over his face. His hands were occupied with releasing his cock from his jeans so I decided to tease him. I leaned down just enough for him to anticipate contact with my sex. As his mouth opened, I pulled my dripping sex away from his face.

His mouth closed around nothing. "What the hell?" he snarled, gazing at my opening hungrily.

I laughed out loud, but soon paid for the tease. His hands came over to ferociously seize my hips and I was slammed down onto his face. My clit so swollen with desire, I almost screamed with the sensations coursing through me.

But just like always, he worked his way expertly around my sex, his tongue lapping at my folds, in maddening strokes, and then licking the sensitive tip of my clit. I almost passed out from the delicious torment. My body jumped as his lips closed around the bud, and began milking me greedily of every ounce of pleasure.

He feasted on me until I was leaning weakly over him, unable to hold myself up anymore. I rode my hips to the feverish rhythm, aware a shattering orgasm was on its way.

But it seemed he was more in tune with my body than I was, and knew exactly how to punish me. Just as I came to the very edge, he lifted me off his face.

My sex was buzzing. I stared down at him confused. I felt disoriented, like someone awaking from a deep sleep. The mischievous look in his eyes told me all I needed to know. "You dick," I cursed.

Before I could complain too much, he lifted me down his body and brought my body towards his waiting cock. He settled me over the hard, protruding shaft. A shiver of excitement shot through me as an almost frantic urge to be filled and possessed by him overcame all else. I felt the silky-smooth, thick head at my entrance. My sex pulsing and throbbing uncontrollably in anticipation.

He sucked in his breath.

Then I felt myself being slowly impaled on that big, hard shaft. I relished the sound of his moan as my walls stretched to accommodate him.

Angelo hissed. "How can you be so fucking tight?" He never took his eyes off me as he slid deeper and deeper into me.

When I had completely swallowed his length, I was once again floored by the depths he could reach.

He splayed his hand across my belly, and positioned his thumb in place to torment my clit. "Move," he rasped out softly, his gaze still locked on me as the pad of his thumb made languid circles around my clit.

I began to lift off him.

At the luscious friction, his eyelids clenched shut, and his face looked ravaged by the delicious agony. I felt exactly the same way. It was simply stunning how just being joined with him in this way could evoke such crazed and overwhelming emotions throughout my body.

When the head of his cock reached my entrance, I slammed back onto him, his body bouncing in response. He growled out then.

In one swift move, he sat upright. His face came so close to mine I could see the faint hint of silver in his irises. I began to writhe my hips, riding his cock in a slow and sensual pace. He seemed to completely approve of what I was doing. He placed his hand on my face and his touch seared my skin. He didn't speak but I didn't need him to. The way he caressed me so gently and intimately as his eyes filled with wonder was everything I needed to know.

I felt his breath on my face become more and more urgent as I increased my pace. Then, all of sudden I couldn't hold his gaze anymore, the torrent of pleasure was rapidly taking over. It spread out from where we were joined, all the way from the top of my head to the tip of my toes. I was tingly, at the sweet torment, while his breath came hard and fast.

Unable to keep myself upright anymore, I threw my arms around him and buried my face in his neck. "Angelo," I gasped out and held on tightly, my knees on the seats on either side of him.

He grabbed my hips violently, and lifting my ass off him, slammed me back down onto him.

I stopped breathing but he wouldn't let me recover. He took complete control of the motion of my hips, and from then onwards, my brain took a backseat, while my body reveled in the sensation of being bounced wildly on his cock. We were both fueled by the sole need to relieve the maddening tension woven through our bodies.

I gasped out loud with every thrust, my body jerking and writhing— his name a constant cry from my lips.

He had never fucked me so hard before. Something just seemed so alarmingly carnal about the state we were in. The car was shaking, the windows and windscreen foggy, while our bodies were coated with sweat. Our entire existence seemed not to matter beyond the need to fuck each other so ruthlessly.

The sweet tension built and built until I shattered into a million pieces. As molten ecstasy ripped through me, I screamed.

"Sienna!" Angelo roared into my neck, as he exploded inside me.

I felt his seed, hot and thick cum shoot deep inside of me. His thrusts didn't stop. They came harder, and faster than ever before as he raced on to milk us both for every bit of the mind blowing orgasm.

Finally, when neither of us could move even an inch more, we collapsed onto the other. We were soaked and sticky around the most intimate parts of our bodies, the scent of our desire and lust filling the air around us.

I couldn't even form a single thought, but as I slowly recovered the only thought playing in my mind over and over again was just how unbelievably good the sex with him was. "Does everyone feel this way?" I asked, beyond amazed.

"No, it has never been like this for me with anyone else."

"Good, because every freaking time you touched me, Angelo, I transcend, as though I'm no longer in this world.

His chest rumbled with low laughter.

I found the strength to lift my head up to watch him. That same wild excitement remained in his eyes, and I loved more than anything seeing him so filled with life when he was usually otherwise quite mellow.

"That better be the case," he said, kissing my forehead. "Because I'm pretty sure that you've ruined me forever for anyone else."

CHAPTER 48

ANGELO

https://www.youtube.com/watch?v=bpOR_HuHRNs
-Without you-

*S*olitude had been my constant companion since I left home. I'd not only accepted her with open arms, but held her so tightly to me that no flesh and blood woman could ever get close. I had a dream. I saw myself with that golden belt. My hands raised high in the air. The crowd roaring. The undisputed champion of the world. Never had I imagined there would be a woman who would come in to change that. A woman, I had at first, naively dismissed as a beautiful, but spoilt brat. Someone I would come to despise the more familiar I became with her.

Boy, was I wrong.

The more familiar I became, the more I wanted her. She was no spoilt brat - she was the most intriguing, annoying, tempting, delicious, irresistible, brave, fun, strong, kind, independent, troubled, bundle of curves - I'd ever met in my life. I broke all my rules, and like a moth to a flame, I went to her.

Again and again.

She didn't burn me. Her taste was sweet, intoxicating. At night when I lay awake, staring at the ceiling, the sound of the fan whirling. She represented everything I had run away from. With every whirl of the fan the freedom I had long cherished was fading. My dream was becoming less and less attractive.

Then came the day when I didn't even want my dream anymore. The belt seemed garish, tarnished even, the crowds were still baying, but the noise was jarring. There was no loyalty there. No love. No permanence. They would roar for me until the day they no longer cared, replaced by another contender. In her arms, I was already the champion of the world. I thought of my family. I thought of my older brother. That twisted smile he wore. Once he wrote to me:

Chase your dream Angelo, but if you ever change your mind. There's a place for you here. Always.

I looked down at Sienna's head as she lay sprawled on top of me. I'd made pretty big promises. She moved slightly and I could feel my cock stirring restlessly. It just seemed incredible how insatiable she made me. I heard the sound of people walking towards their car, snatches of their conversation as they passed us by. The sound of their door closing, the engine starting and dying away as they drove away.

I sighed with contentment.

She moved her legs, and the rub of her heated thighs against my cock instantly sent all the blood rushing from my head. I tried my best to control myself but when the stroking and nudging from her thighs against my cock became too precise and frequent, I realized I was being toyed with.

"Are you sure that's the game you want to play?" I asked.

Her entire body jiggled with soft laughter. She lifted her head off my chest then, her hair falling in a dream-like cascade all over us. She met my gaze with a blinding smile.

I felt my breath catch.

"Why? Don't you want to?" she asked, her tone soft and silky.

I knew then, her voice was the only sound I ever wanted to listen to. "You're something special," I told her. "Unfathomable." I leaned forward and placed a soft kiss on her forehead.

She placed a butterfly kiss on my left eyelid. Then she began to trace her lips down the bridge of my nose. To the tip. From there to the edge of my jaw and all the way down my jaw bone before she slipped her tongue into my mouth and began to drink me in a long leisurely kiss.

I couldn't hold back anymore, so I squeezed her naked bottom, and slipped a finger into her open, wet pussy. She came up gasping for air, her squeal ringing into the air. All I could do was watch her, mesmerized at how one human being could have such a magical hold over me.

I let my finger slide in and out of her. For a long moment, she simply looked down at me, her eyes jewels of knowing ... Jezebel-like. Then she pulled my finger out of her, grabbed my cock, and positioned it at her entrance. I was rock hard and throbbing with the need to enter her wet heat again.

She pushed herself onto my cock until she completely sheathed me.

Pure wonder coursed through me.

I fucked her slowly, our pace less hurried than before, as we basked in the sheer joy and excitement of being so intimately joined together. She cried into my neck as she clenched and trembled above me.

It didn't take long for her to climax and me simultaneously with her, I was sure somewhere amidst the ecstasy I had pledged my life to her.

When we were done, I held her in my arms. "We have to head back now," I told her. "You've been gone for too long."

"No, we don't have to," she said as she wriggled around, sat up, and began to dress.

I felt like it was a shame when her bra went on. I instantly missed seeing her naked breasts.

"I told my mom I was probably going to spend the day with the girls so basically, I've got all day to spend with you." She brought out a box of tissues from the dashboard compartment and cleaned herself. "Don't look at me while I do this," she scolded.

I couldn't stop. It was just so fucking sexy.

"Stop gawking, I said," she begged.

"You have no underwear," I observed.

Sienna pulled down her skirt. "And whose fault is that?" she asked tartly.

"Mine," I said proudly. I loved it actually. I loved the thought of her being utterly bare. Anytime I wanted, I could slip my fingers into her, or my tongue, or my cock. I felt my cock harden.

She noticed it too. "Don't you start," she warned.

God, I instantly allowed to roam free what I knew for so long was true -I was so in love with her - my head was fucked. "Did I ever tell you, you're amazing."

"Wow," she said while laying her hand on her chest. "I can't even believe you're the same person who left me to drown in the pool. What the hell is going on?"

"You know exactly what is going on. You seduced me and now I've become a soppy, love-sick fool."

"Good," she said with a cheeky grin. "Because that's exactly how I like my men. Now, let's go back to your place."

She would get no argument from me there. I cleaned up and zipped up, while she put the car into motion.

As soon as we got through the door, I leaned against it and watched her. "Are you hungry?"

"I'm starving, but if I remember correctly, you have nothing in your fridge. If only you had a bit of salami."

My eyebrows flew upwards. "You want salami?"

"Or something similar to suck on …"

"I'll give you salami," I said, scooping her into my arms. I threw her over my shoulder and carried her to my bed while she shrieked and giggled like a child.

I threw her on the bed, put her on all fours, and gave her my cock to suck on. I loved watching my cock disappear into her pretty face. When she had filled her belly with my seed, I opened her legs and feasted on sliced salami. Once she had climaxed, I was ready for her again. And this time, I fucked her until she screamed.

Afterwards, she flopped face down on the bed. "You're a freaking beast," she whispered hoarsely.

For a long time, I didn't speak. I couldn't. My brain was like mush. Then I picked up my phone and called for some food from around the corner. Mehdi made the best chicken kebab and garlic sauce I'd ever tasted, and I knew Sienna would love it.

"Now that the food is ordered and I have you all to myself," she said, "I'm going to ask you at least a million questions. I want to know everything there is to know about you. Don't you dare hold back."

"I won't," I replied, for the first time my mind and heart were completely open and ready to let her in. "Fire away."

"Okay," she said, drawing circles on my chest. "Tell me about your dream of becoming a boxer. When did that start? What's next?"

I thought of how I would tell her I'd abandoned the shining dream because it had lost its luster.

She misread my silence as reluctance and rushed on to speak. "It's okay if you don't want to talk about it. I'm sorry, perhaps that's too personal?"

I turned to look into her beautiful eyes. "True, my natural disposition is to keep things to myself but with you, I don't want to do that. So push me when it seems like I don't want to say something. Chances are that I really want to, but I'm not used to opening up."

Sienna hid her smile and snuggled even more closely to me. "Alright, I demand you tell me."

"I was going to," I said. "I was just trying to find a way to tell you that it's not my big dream anymore."

She shot up in shock. "What do you mean?"

I shrugged. "I mean I don't want that dream anymore. It's lost its shine."

She licked her lips. "You're not doing this for me, are you? Because, I'm not standing in the way of your dream. I would hate you to give up anything for me. One day, you might start to hate me for it."

I put my finger over her lips. "Stop it. I'm giving it up because it was not my real dream. I realize now it was just an excuse to run away from my real responsibilities. I didn't want to work in the family business, so I poured myself into the first glamorous thing I could think of. I was nineteen when I decided I wanted to train to be a fighter. It was actually too old to start. Most fighters start when they're kids, but I was told by a trainer in the gym that I was a natural. After hearing that, I was prepared to put in the grueling hours. I was absolutely determined to make it. I guess I would have made it, but I don't want it anymore."

"What do you want?"

"I want you."

"We should run away," she whispered.

I shook my head. "We're not doing that. I know an easy way to bring your father around, but I would rather do it the hard way. I'd rather prove myself to him."

"What's the easy way?"

"I'm not telling you," I said, with a chuckle.

"Angelo?"

"Yeah."

"How did you meet my father? I mean how does a fighter come into contact with a man like my father? Also, I get the impression he really rates you as a bodyguard. You're not just an ordinary bodyguard, are you?"

I scratched my chin. "I was recommended to your father through a mutual friend and associate. The reason he rates me is because he knows the kind of training I've been through."

"What kind of training is that?" she asked curiously.

"I was trained by the Mossad in Israel for two years, and I spent a year with a Russian martial arts master. He lived next to a lake in the mountains between China and Russia. It was breathtakingly beautiful. From him, I learned the art of killing. I can kill a man with an envelope."

Just as I expected, I felt her shudder at my words, so I lowered my gaze to hers and waited until she found the courage to meet mine. I laid out my cards. "I have an extremely dark side, Sienna, and I hope it won't scare you off but this is me. You have to know the real me."

The corners of her lips twisted. "What do you take me for?" she scoffed. "When was the last time you killed a man with an envelope? I come from a brutal world and even though I was shielded from much of it, I'm not naïve. My father has more bodies weighed down with rocks at the bottom of the sea than you could imagine." She then threw her arms around me to crush me into a desperate hug. "So don't. Don't ever think you can scare me away with your bullshit stories about killing men."

When she pulled away, I had my own question for her, "What about you? How was life in London? Were you lonely? Being so far away from home?"

"At first, I was miserable," she responded. "I missed Gemma and Nonna all the time, but eventually, I made a few friends, learned to weed out the bad ones, or thought that I had until recently. I soon had a handful of people I cared about. I learned to stand on my own two feet. I wasn't 'the boss's daughter'. I was just Sienna. It was peaceful. I dream of going back."

"You want to leave me behind?"

"Well, until yesterday, you gave me the impression that you could barely look at me. So yeah, I've had to not include you in my plans … for my own sanity."

I planted a kiss on her temple. "Well, all that's going to change from now o—"

I was interrupted by a loud knocking on my front door.

CHAPTER 49

SIENNA

https://www.youtube.com/watch?v=a7SouU3ECpU
-we could be heroes-

I was so deeply involved in the world we had created for ourselves that I jumped when the banging on the door came.

We both looked towards the bedroom door. Then I returned my gaze to him. "Is that our kebabs?"

He frowned and got off the bed. "It's not. Mehdi doesn't bang like that."

The bangs came again and this time, they were even more aggressive.

"Boston!" someone yelled out, loud and angrily.

I too got out of bed. I dressed hurriedly, instinctively. Something was wrong.

Angelo had already pulled his pants on and was heading out of the room.

"Aren't you going to take your gun?" I whispered, glancing at his piece lying on the bedside table.

He faced me. "I'm better without it." He took a step away from me then, turned back again towards me. "Stay here. No matter what happens, don't come out," he instructed.

I stopped breathing. The warm passionate man was gone. In its place was the cold-eyed killing machine he'd told me about.

I went to the door and put my ear against it, so I could listen to what was happening outside. Angelo had obviously opened the door and there was muted conversation, but then the voices began to rise. And then there was a loud roar and an accompanying sound of pain.

"Let him go!" a shout roared.

What was going on? Was he in trouble? I almost burst out of the room then, but I knew going out empty handed would be a mistake. So I turned around, ran over to his side table and picked up his 9mm. I opened it. It was fully loaded. Gripping it tightly, I went to the door.

As I stepped out into the hallway, I heard the question that sent a cold chill through me. "Where is she?"

My hands began to tremble. What if these men weren't from the same rival family who tried to kidnap me, but were from my father?

I took several steps backwards. They called him Boston, which meant they knew him from the gym. If my father had somehow found out about me and Angelo and these men were here on a fishing expedition, then Angelo would be in more trouble if I showed myself.

The best thing then was for me to hide so they wouldn't find me.

I turned around and was about to do just that when I heard something else. "Our instructions were to bring you along with her, alive, but if we don't find her here then we are meant to blow your head off and bring it back."

"God-fucking-dammit, Boston!" another roared. "How could you do this? I knew you had guts, but the boss's fucking daughter. Did you lose your damn mind?"

"She's not here," Angelo said calmly.

Angelo's voice sent chills down my spine and I began to panic.

"Well then, it's a bullet through the head."

I sprinted towards the living room without a second thought. "Wait!" I screamed and walked in to see a gun held to the back of Angelo's head.

There were two other heavily armed men present. One seated on the sofa, a sawn-off shotgun in his hand, while another was leaning against the wall with a dark scowl on his face and his hands clutching an automatic against his chest.

All the men turned at my entrance. I could see the disappointment and anger on Angelo's face.

"What the hell are you doing?" he roared at me.

For a moment, everyone in the room was startled. It was most certain that none of us had ever heard his tone rise to such a pitch.

"Get out of here," he roared. "Right now!"

I couldn't leave. I stood frozen staring at the gun held so close to his head. Maybe he could take them. It was clear he thought he could, but I couldn't take the chance.

The man leaning against the wall straightened and began to point his gun in the air. "Look, we don't want to hurt anybody. Nobody needs to get hurt," he said. "Your father gave us instructions to bring you home. Please don't make things difficult for us."

I took a step towards Angelo and one of the guns suddenly went off. I screamed at the deafening blast and dropped to my knees, my hands going to my ears. Then I looked up and saw with horror that Angelo had been hit. He was crouched on the ground and blood was pouring out of his arm.

Enraged, I jumped to my feet, and fired the gun at the man who had pulled the trigger on him.

He was lucky. I was out of practice and the bullet lodged in the wall.

Wild curses rang out as the men scurried for cover away from me. I was just about to fire another shot when the gorilla who'd been behind Angelo pointed the gun at his head. His tone and the look in his eyes made my blood curl.

"If you dare fire another shot, I will put a bullet through his head. He has only been shot through his arm, but if you push our hand, he will be dead in a second."

"Sienna," Angelo called, the strain in his tone heartbreaking as he held his hand to the wound. "Put the gun down, I'll be fine."

I didn't believe him. "No you won't," I said. "They're going to kill you."

"Put it down!"

"No!" I refused.

"Look, please just calm down," the man who had been silent until now spoke up. "We're not here to harm anyone. Please don't let this get more complicated than it already is."

I turned the gun and pointed it directly on my head.

"Sienna!" Angelo roared.

"What the fuck!" one of the men exclaimed.

"If you hurt him," I said, "then consider yourself dead too. I'll pull this trigger and I don't need to tell you how dearly my father will make you pay for it. I'm prepared to die, are you? Throw your guns on the floor and move the fuck away from him. Right now."

They looked at each other, then dropped their guns to the floor.

"Put your hands up where I can see them and get into the bedroom," I said.

Nobody moved.

Angelo was staring at me, part admiration, part fury, part astonishment.

"Get into the bedroom before I splatter my brains all over these walls!" I screamed, my voice sounding satisfyingly hysterical.

The three men shuffled towards the bedroom, their hands held in the air.

CHAPTER 50

ANGELO

https://www.youtube.com/watch?v=1y6smkh6c-0
-Don't you worry child-

I couldn't believe her. She had held a gun to her own head. The risk she had taken against herself made me want to explode.

I'd watched her lock the men in my bedroom and then run to me. "Get to the car. Get to the car," she screamed in a panic.

It was a mess. If only she'd stayed in the bedroom, I'd have dealt with it in a completely different way. I followed her out to the car. Now, I needed a different plan. "Drive to your father's house," I said.

She turned towards me, her eyes wild. "No!" Hell no! My father wants you dead. They were going to kill you. Why can't you understand that?"

I took a deep breath, my hand pressing down on the injury in my arm to suppress the blood. It was only a flesh wound, but they always hurt the worst. "Sienna, your father can't intimidate me."

"Yeah, I know you can kill a man with an envelope and everything," she said, her voice trembling with fear, "but we're dealing with the Mafia here. They bury the bullets into your head while you're sleeping."

I sighed and kept my voice calm as I spoke, "I know how to deal with your father. My family is as deeply rooted in the mafia as yours is. So please, trust me. I know what I'm doing."

That made her still … for a second. "What? Your family is Mafia?"

I nodded. "Yes, so I know how it all works. You need to listen to me and trust me. I understand your father better than you do. He has been disrespected. His whole reputation is at stake. Not being made a fool of is more important to him than anything else. If there is any way at all for him to salvage this situation, he'll jump at the chance and take it. Right now, he'll still be willing to listen to me before his men cut off my dick and bury me alive, but if we run away like this, with me hiding behind your skirt, he will lose what little respect he has left for me. I will be hunted down like—"

"Is that what's important right now?" she yelled. "To hell with his respect. If your family is Mafia you should know the punishment for your crime is exactly that … having your dick cut off and stuffed into your mouth before you're buried alive."

If the situation wasn't so serious, I would have laughed. She was a cute little thing. "In all the years I've known your father, he has never taken a man's life without hearing him out first. I've built up a lot of goodwill with him. He doesn't know for sure we're together yet, so he'll be hoping I come back to deny it. That it's all a big mistake. But if we run away like this from him, he'll never care to listen to what I have to say. I'm not stupid. I know how to protect you and me, so for God's sake, have a little faith."

She stilled. "So are we going to lie?"

I shook my head, but softened my tone, "Sienna, trust me."

"We should treat your shoulder first," she muttered, eyeing the blood seeping out between my fingers.

"It's just a flesh wound. Tear a strip off my shirt, bandage it, and we're good to go."

WE RETURNED BACK to the estate with my left hand in a completely unnecessary make-shift sling. I wasn't nervous, and just as I'd expected, we were allowed into the house without any trouble.

Sienna seemed confused and panicky. "Why is there no one blocking our way? It has to be a trap."

"Your father has already heard what happened. He doesn't want any accidents with you, so he'll keep his men out of the way until we're separated," I explained.

I could tell my response didn't console her. She hung on to my unhurt arm tightly.

The look Gemma gave her was heartbreaking.

"I'm fine, Gemma," she said quickly.

Gemma turned her gaze on me and glared at me in fury. "If you dare hurt her," she threatened, "I'll kill you myself."

I didn't blame her. I appreciated her concern for Sienna, so I just nodded politely and carried on walking towards her father's study, but when we walked in it was filled with half a dozen men. To my surprise and annoyance, Fabio was also there, standing in a corner. Ah, I should have known—he was the one who told her father.

"You fucking bastard!" he roared in a highly dramatic, faked anger, the moment we walked in. Then he headed straight for me.

While I was debating whether to knock him out cold quickly before anyone else could react, or simply to evade him and allow his own momentum to send him crashing into the wall behind me, Sienna handled him.

She swung her legs with a brutal precision and kicked him right in the solar plexus. "Get the hell away from us!' she spat.

His eyes bulged, his mouth opened in a shocked, soundless cry, and his hands rushed forward to hug his stomach while he staggered backwards with the force of Sienna's attack.

I was impressed. Not a bad kick, as far as kicks go.

He reeled about for a few more seconds before he stumbled into a shelf. The items on it came crashing down on top of him as he collapsed to the ground. He looked too dazed to pick himself up.

Everyone in the room watched him silently, and I sensed satisfaction in the air. It was clear he was despised by almost everyone in the room.

I glanced at the seven guards, dressed in dark suits, and positioned all over the room. Impossible to take out quickly. In all their eyes, I saw the same veiled astonishment. They were my compatriots, and they couldn't believe what I had done. We all knew the rules. *Never touch the boss's daughter.* They gaped at me as if I'd lost my mind.

I turned my attention to the most important person present.

Her father sat behind the desk, his hands linked together, and his gaze on me.

I noted the glint in his eyes and knew he was livid. Based on my experiences in the past, rarely had anyone ever come away unhurt when he got into this state.

Sienna took a step sideways and stood in front of me, as if to shield me from him. "Dad," she said. "Please don't hurt him."

I stared her father straight in the eye.

He finally spoke, his tone extremely cold and low. "Is this your master plan? To hide behind my daughter."

"He's not hiding!" Sienna cried.

I turned to her. "Be calm," I told her.

She was struggling to even breathe properly. "Be calm? How can I be calm when my father wants to kill the man I love?"

Her father now turned his annoyance on her. "Love? What do you know about love? You are a silly little girl. I am so disappointed in you."

"I'm sorry," she said. "I'm incredibly sorry, but I won't let you hurt him."

"Get her out of my sight," her father ordered.

Two of his guards stepped forward.

"No!" she cried out while planting her feet further apart as she bent her knees. "Don't come anywhere near me, or I can't be held responsible for my actions."

The two men stopped in their tracks and looked over at her father for further directions.

"I'm not going anywhere, Papa." Sienna remained firm. "You need to listen to me. For once, would you just listen to what I have to say?"

He held up one hand and the men returned to their positions.

Sienna looked nervously at them, and released a deep breath. She swallowed the lump in her throat and turned to her father. "Papa, I'm not going to marry Fabio. I know you chose him with the best intentions but I'm in love with Angelo, and he is the only one for me. I understand you are concerned about our family and about our strength when you're no longer here. This is my family too, and whether you believe it or not I do care about our wellbeing, continuing your legacy, and ensuring every member of this household is safe. This is my duty, and I will not walk away from it, but the only way I will ever be able to do this is if I'm first of all, happy. I know you may not see any reason in what I'm saying now, but I need you to believe me when I say that if you cannot allow me to be happy, then I will not take on the obligation to keep this family safe. If you think that it can only be done with Fabio in the picture, then you don't need me. Pass it all on to him, I don't care. But if you want me to be involved and to put all of my heart into this family and this business, then please let me choose who I spend my life with. It would break my heart, but I would rather abandon this family than to be in any way attached to this pathetic human being."

A brief silence fell after she finished speaking, and then a sick, pained laughter pierced the air. I didn't need to turn her around to know whom it was from.

Holding his bruised stomach, Fabio struggled to his feet. He looked so furious he was almost frothing at the mouth. He had been knocked to the ground by a mere woman and now she had insulted him in front of his father. "You are a tragedy, Sienna. This is why they say that females are useless burdens to their families. You would rather abandon this family than be attached to me? Who the hell do you think you are, you cheap whore?"

My brain couldn't catch up with my body. I whirled around and before anyone realized what was happening, I was on him. My fist struck his face and the impact lifted him clean off the ground and once again, he crashed back into the shelf, but before he could even recover, I lifted my leg and kicked him in the ribs.

He screamed out loudly at the pain.

The fire in me was still raging. How dare the dog insult Sienna. I wanted to kick him to a pulp, but I forced myself to stop right there. Out of respect for Sienna and her father. I'd cracked at least two of his ribs and they should hurt him for a good few weeks.

Sienna's hand curled around my arm.

Now it was time for me to talk, but before I could say a word, the door to his study was pushed open.

Everyone turned around in surprise and wonder at who would have the audacity to come in without knocking or waiting for permission to be granted first.

Only one person in the entire household could do that.

Her grandmother walked in. Her face completely expressionless. Her dark, intelligent eyes scanned the room quickly. The first person she focused on wasn't any of us, but on the bastard on the floor groaning from the severity of his pain. She gave him a look of distaste, and then turned to Sienna's father. "Is this who you want to give your only child to?"

Her father scowled and didn't respond.

"Everyone else except you two." She pointed to Sienna and me. "Leave! And take that piece of human trash with you."

Her father nodded slightly and everyone moved to obey her command.

In seconds, the room emptied out and it was just the four of us.

She turned to look at me and Sienna. "You two are quite the spectacle, aren't you?" she commented, then turned her complete attention to her son.

CHAPTER 51

SIENNA

*T*he last person I had expected to join in on this argument was Nonna.

Throughout all the years I had known her, she had steered clear of interfering in any of the family's major matters unless my father explicitly requested her guidance.

But here she was, and the importance of her presence was not lost to me. She was the only one who could change my father's mind, or give a contradictory response to any instructions he had given out. She had indeed made me a little promise that she would help me and I whispered a small prayer that she was here to help us win.

"Nonna," I began.

She held up her hand for me to be quiet as she addressed my father. "I've told you from the very beginning not to force this proposal on Sienna. When you found out that she wanted absolutely nothing to do with that man, you should have listened to her and respected her will."

My dad frowned. It was obvious he didn't appreciate being scolded and especially not in front of me and Angelo. "I'm going to handle things my own way," he said stubbornly. "Please wait outside."

Totally ignoring him, she moved closer to us. "Young man, what's your name?" she asked.

At first, it seemed like a trick question because I knew she already knew what his name was. Nonna was astute and well informed, although she usually kept what she knew to herself until it was absolutely necessary to reveal it.

Angelo respond politely. "Angelo Barone."

A slight impatience flashed in her eyes.

Under more normal circumstances, I would have been amused to see I was right about her. She wasn't asking because she didn't know, but because she wanted to confirm something.

"Yes, Barone." Her eyes narrowed at him. "It means free man, but before you changed it. What was your name then?"

I turned to look up at Angelo. Although to most people he would seem to be expressionless and unmoved, I could tell Nonna had hit a nerve he wasn't particularly pleased about.

"Messana," he replied. "Angelo Messana."

"Ah, Messana. A name that harks back to the old city of Sicily." She turned to my father. "That doesn't strike a bell for you?"

My father's eyes changed from being irritated and filled with suspicion, to realization, then widened with shock. His gaze left Nonna and darted to Angelo. "Messana? Messana from Boston?" my father muttered hoarsely.

The few seconds of silence that followed his question infuriated my father. He shot to his feet. "Answer me!" he roared.

Angelo met my father's angry, confused eyes head on. "Yes, sir. That's right."

Then I watched in wonder as Angelo's spine straightened. He appeared to grow in stature, as if he had purposely made himself small at this time. It was like watching an angel unfurl its wings.

"How did you find out?" my father asked Nonna. He kept watching Angelo with part disbelief and part horror.

Involuntarily I moved even closer to Angelo, partially standing in front of him to protect him from whatever was about to unravel. I felt so confused. I turned to Nonna. "What's going on?"

"Your lover here is no ordinary man," she replied. Then she turned to my father. "I became curious about him after I saw the little one falling in love with him, so I requested his background check. One far more thorough than the one conducted by your men."

My father shook his head. "When he first came to work for this family and before I put him on to the role protecting Sienna, I did a very thorough check or I would never have put him in charge of protecting Sienna. This connection did not come up. He was clean."

"Well," Nonna went on, "being the son of the renowned and most powerful mafia boss in Boston is not exactly a crime, now is it? And he is clean. He left the family when he was nineteen."

My brain scrambled to a halt. *What?*

"Let this be a lesson to you," Nonna continued. "You're too impatient and too quick to come to conclusions, which I've warned you about. Also, whoever did the check for you probably wasn't capable enough to make the connection. Anyway, there you have it. He's not just a bodyguard. You've had the direct offspring of the *capo del capo* of the Messana house under your roof for the last two years, and you didn't even realize it."

"Loosen up on the criticism mother," my father said, starting to recover from his shock. "This was one mistake. "

"Well, it could have been a deadly one if this young man's intentions over here had been evil."

My father turned and glared at Angelo. "And what makes you think they aren't? He's hid himself too well over the years has he not?"

"Is he acting like he's guilty of anything?" she asked.

"Well, with this moron daughter of mine standing right next to him and fighting all his battles for him what has he got to worry about when he could use her as a shield? Get the hell away from him!" My father pulled out a gun from his drawer and in a flash pointed it directly at Angelo.

"Papa!" I screamed and moved to stand directly in front of Angelo.

"Marco, what are you doing?" Nonna asked tiredly.

"Sienna, step away from him," my father ordered.

"Are you seriously considering hurting Messana's youngest son?" Nonna asked him. "I believe he is the apple of his mother's eye. You want a war on your head?"

"Well, I have a damn good excuse. He invaded my turf. Do you know how much information about us he has been able to obtain over the last two years? Such behavior is unacceptable."

Nonna's sigh was heavy. "Young man, why aren't you saying anything?"

Angelo turned to my grandmother and bowed his head slightly at her. "Sienna," he said "Go to your grandmother's side."

"No!" I refused, and turned around to face him, but at the sternness in his gaze, my mouth sealed shut. I understood that he meant what he was saying. Earlier, he had implored me several times to trust him ... to have a little faith and yet, I had defied him at every turn. Now, it was time for me to trust him. I conceded and begrudgingly went over to my grandmother's side.

"Wow," she said. "He can obtain your daughter's obedience with just a stare? Marco, don't you usually have to nearly threaten Sienna with her life for her to even pay attention to you?"

"Don't you think you're enjoying yourself a bit too much?" my papa asked, his pride hurt, and he looked clearly irritated. He was starting to look less and less dangerous even with the gun in his hand.

She laughed softly. "I am enjoying myself immensely. Now, let the young man talk."

We all turned to Angelo.

He wore the same stoic, and fearless expression he usually wore. "My father or my brother do not need your secrets. They are very successful on their own, perhaps even more successful than you. I am not a plant. I didn't come here to steal your secrets. It was one of your associates who connected us, and as strange as it sounds, I came to work for you because you had a pool I could use in the middle of the night and plenty of time to perfect my fighting skills."

"So why did you hide the fact that you are a Messana?"

"I changed my name because I did not want to be connected to that name. I wanted to make my own way in the world. When I became a champion fighter. I didn't want anyone to say my opponents threw the fights and let me win because of who I was. Even now, I would have preferred to have won Sienna's hand on my own merit not because of whose son I was, but now that you know, you will understand I am more than capable of taking care of Sienna. I have a vast fortune put away in offshore banks for me and I can, at a moment's notice, call upon an army of protection for your daughter. In fact, just knowing who I am will instantly keep your daughter safe. I will give my life for her."

Nonna clapped. "Nicely said, young man. You're great for my Sienna. I approve of you, but you better not make the mistake of hurting her, I don't give a rat's ass whose son you are, I will put out the order to send you to the grave myself."

My eyes widened with shock. I had never heard Nonna speak like that.

Angelo's response was to bow his head. "Her skin is my skin," he said simply.

Nonna rose to her feet. "Anyway, I have some chamomile tea waiting for me, so I better get to it." She went over to my father. Her hand reached out and touched his face.

I had never seen her act so loving in public before.

My father still held the gun, limply, all the fight gone out of him.

"Once you stop being angry, you will realize that this arrangement is a dream come true. I couldn't have hoped for a better future for this family or Sienna." Then she turned around and exited the room.

Angelo spoke. "I am deeply sorry you had to find out about me and Sienna this way. If I could turn back the clock that is the only thing I would change. I would come into your study and tell you everything and make my intentions clear. I promise to cherish her to the best of my ability and to remain loyal to you to the day I die."

My father fell back heavily into his seat. Suddenly, he looked old, frail and alone. "I'm tired. Go now, both of you, but come for dinner later and we'll talk some more."

I felt almost sorry for him as I ran to my father's side and knelt next to him. "Papa?"

He looked at me and seemed to search my eyes.

"I love him with all my heart, papa."

He nodded slowly. "Yes, yes, I can see that."

"I love you, Papa."

"Hmmm … yes. Go now."

I placed a light kiss on his cheek. His skin felt a little cold and I felt a sight frisson of alarm. "Are you okay, Papa?"

"Yes, I'm just a little tired." He smiled. "Looks like I was wrong, little one."

"It's the price of being human," I consoled.

"Quite." He paused. The words seemed to get stuck in his throat, but he got them out, "I'm sorry."

I threw my arms around him in a big bear hug. "Oh, Papa. You never need to say sorry to me ever. I owe everything to you. I know you were just trying to do the best you could for me. It's just that I found a better solution for me."

"Yes, it looks like you did. Run along now."

I rushed to Angelo, took his hand and we went out of the study. "Wait here for me," I said to him at the foot of the stairs and I ran up the stairs to my mother's room. I knocked once and she called enter.

When I went in, she was lying on her daybed and doing something on her iPad. "Hello dear," she greeted with a big smile. It was astounding how completely my father kept her away from any kind of unpleasantness … his way of showing his love.

I knelt beside her. "Mama, papa needs you."

She frowned. "Why? What has happened?"

"Don't worry. Nothing bad has happened, but papa just needs you. He's in his study."

She scrambled off the daybed and hurried downstairs with me. She gave Angelo a distracted smile and hurried towards my father's study.

I turned to look up at Angelo.

He winked at me. "I told you we shouldn't run."

"Don't you even dare gloat," I said. "We could have ended up dead. If Nonna hadn't stepped in who knew how things would have gone?"

"I had a plan, Sienna. A solid plan that included bringing together our two families. I already called my brother and started discussing it. If your grandmother hadn't walked in I would have revealed exactly what I had in mind to your father. As it happens I will do so at a more appropriate time."

I put my hands on my hips. "Yeah, that reminds me. I have a bone to pick with you. When were you planning to tell me you were a Messana?"

"I told you I was from a mafia family."

I made a scoffing sound. "Was from a Mafia family? There are hundreds of tiny Mafia families. It's a far cry from being the youngest son of the head of Messana house, isn't it?"

He grinned. "I didn't want you to love me for my money."

"Wow," I said, pretending to be sarcastic, even as scorching joy rushed into my chest. "You're even more insane than I am."

"I have become a bit insane ever since you dove into the pool to catch my attention."

My eyes nearly popped out of my head. "Excuse me? I didn't dive into the pool to catch your attention. I fell in. Accidentally."

He bowed his head mockingly. "I believe you."

"You really know how to sweep a girl right off her feet, don't you?"

"Not any girl. Just you."

"So ... what now?" I asked.

"Now, I have to return home and make my peace with my family. Then I will come for you." He stared into my eyes.

The look in his eyes filled me with wonder and love. I felt my bones begin to melt. "You don't really believe I dove into the pool to catch your attention, do you?"

"It'll be a nice story to tell our grandchildren, won't it? Especially, how you followed me into the shower."

"They won't believe you," I huffed.

Angelo leaned forward and caught my lips in a searing kiss.

EPILOGUE

SIENNA

Six months Later

https://www.youtube.com/watch?v=09R8_2nJtjg

*J*couldn't remember ever feeling so nervous. It was easy for Charlotte to say, "Relax, they'll love you. What's there not to love?" She was miles away, probably eating ice cream right now.

Me, I was waiting with the rest of my family in the vast foyer, flutes of champagne in hand, and light laughter in the air. I kept glancing at the front door. Today was the day that Angelo would be returning from Boston, as he had so many times in the past six months. The only thing was this time around, he wasn't coming alone.

My hands tightened nervously around the stem of my full glass without realizing it until Gemma came up to me.

"You're going to break the glass," she said.

I turned to her and exhaled in relief as she handed me an identical glass, but filled with darker colored liquid. "Thank you, Gemma," I said as we swiftly switched glasses.

All around me were the closest members of my family. My parents, a few aunts and uncles, and close cousins. We were a party of twelve awaiting the arrival of my soon to be in-laws from Boston. It would be my first meeting with Angelo's family members and I was on the verge of pooping my pants.

I lifted the glass of apple juice to my lips and instantly drained it.

Gemma took a sip out of the champagne flute she had taken from me, her expression one of amusement. "Relax," she coaxed. "They will love you."

"Well, they have to now. It's too late otherwise."

We gazed at each other knowingly, the reminder of the pregnancy test she had found in my room two days earlier coming to mind. She pulled me into a hug and kissed me lightly on my cheek. "I'll get you a refill."

"Thank you."

"They're here, Boss," one of the guards suddenly announced.

The other family members immediately rose to their feet from the adjoining foyer living room.

My mom glided over to me. Dressed in a baby pink Chanel suit, her slender neck lined with pearls, and her hair arranged into a low chignon at the back of her head. She looked absolutely exquisite. She held my hands, a smile on her face, and light in her eyes. "Don't be nervous," she said.

I nodded, as I allowed her to fix my outfit and dust away imaginary specks of dirt from my crisp, white blouse. I had teamed it with tight black pants. A pair of shoes I had designed and made myself graced my feet, and around my neck was the gorgeous emerald necklace Angelo had given me for my birthday.

I lifted my hand as the simple but beautiful champagne and cognac 11 carat diamond engagement ring sparkled on a split shank band. I loved everything about it.

The massive front doors were finally pulled open, and beyond was an entourage of shiny black town cars. A few men, all large, and all dressed in identical black suits, quickly got out of the first car, and in no time they were pulling the back doors open for the passengers in the cars that followed.

In the one in the middle was the one person I most wanted to see.

Angelo got out of the car and instantly found my gaze. He smiled at me, his grin almost blinding, then he went and added a wink.

It made my tummy flutter. All my apprehension and tension melted away.

"Don't faint," my mom said.

I even found myself laughing. "I think I'll be fine," I said out loud, but completed the rest of the statement in my mind. *The moment that man gets over here and stands by my side.* His presence was all the support I needed.

He opened the passenger door and a tall, older man, much older even than my father, stepped out. All the hair on his head was white, but there could be no doubt he was Angelo's father.

They walked in through the door and I immediately stepped forward to greet him.

The moment his gaze settled on me, I felt a chill go down my spine. He had the coldest eyes I had ever seen on a man. But then Angelo placed his hand on the small of my back, and warmth immediately filled me once again.

I gave the old man my brightest smile.

Angelo introduced me to him, "Dad, this is Sienna."

"It's such a pleasure to meet you, Sir," I said.

He regarded me without expression. "So you're the one who finally sent my son back home."

I laughed nervously in response.

He nodded at me. "Thank you." Then he went on to meet my parents.

Angelo went with him to make the introductions with my parents.

I focused on the rest of his party. His mother had come down with a migraine last night and been unable to make it today, but there was a standing promise I would head over to Boston in two weeks to personally pay her a visit.

His older brother, Luca, who ran the family also did not come. He had to fly to Geneva. I saw a photo of him, wearing a dark suit and he looked more like a movie star than a Mafia don. You could only tell when you looked closely at his eyes to see how cold-eyed and dangerous he was.

On this trip, only his nieces, a pair of twins, his sister's daughter, and a few extended family members had arrived.

The two teenage girls giggled excitedly and I was instantly charmed by them.

Angelo soon came to rescue me and he remained by my side until it was time for lunch. It looked like a banquet fit for a king, one I savored every moment of. It was everything I'd ever dreamed of. My parents happy, Angelo by my side, his father approving of me.

Once we were done, everyone retired to their rooms to rest before dinner while I returned to mine with my fiancé.

The moment we got in, I collapsed on the bed. I hadn't spent time with the love of my life for two whole weeks and I was desperate to taste him again. I stared up at him as he shrugged his jacket off and with my forefinger, beckoned him over. He quickly took off his shirt, a wide smile across his face as he joined me on the bed.

With his weight on his forearms, he poised himself just above me. His torso was bare, his flawless skin glistening with life and his rock-hard muscles bulging.

I lifted myself up and slipped my tongue into his mouth for a long, sensual kiss. My arms tightened around his shoulders and he collapsed on top of me. We both burst out laughing. I reached down to kick my heels off, when he said. "Don't take them off."

I grinned cheekily at him and rolled with him till I was on top of him. Then I sat up and looked down on him. He was beautiful. So beautiful, I just wanted to sit here and watch him all night long.

My hands cradled his face while he brushed my hair to the side. "I missed you, Sienna. God, how I missed you. I can't wait until everything is sorted out and we can be together again."

I nibbled lightly on his chin. "I missed you more." And I meant it too. He'd been busy sorting things out, but all I had to do was make a few shoes and wait for him to come back. I missed him with every fiber of my being.

"Did you enjoy lunch?" he asked.

"I did, but I couldn't stop feeling a bit tense," I replied.

"Why? You knew my father liked you."

"Yes, I kinda got that impression, but I was afraid someone would pull out a gun on someone else."

His chest rumbled with low laughter at my comment. "What? Why would anyone pull out their gun?"

"Well, two powerful mafia families in the same room? A lot could go wrong."

"You, my love, have been watching too many Hollywood mafia movies," he teased.

"When I was eight, my mom pulled out a gun on my father during my birthday lunch. Apparently, she thought he'd been cheating on her and she had kept silent about it. That afternoon, she just snapped. Gemma immediately carried me away and I never saw how it ended, but I'll never forget that. So yeah, the dining table can be a battleground."

"It's always the *sweet, butter wouldn't melt in my mouth* ones you have to watch out for," he said.

I narrowed my eyes at him. "What? If you ever cheat on me, I'll do the same!"

He smiled. "If I ever cheat on you, you're permitted to pull a gun out on me. I'll even help you put the bullet through my head."

I shuddered slightly at his response. "You're too serious, Angelo. I was just teasing you."

"Speaking of the dining table, I watched you tonight. Do you have anything you want to tell me?"

"It's good when you can't take your eyes off me," I teased.

"Yes, very good, but this time I couldn't stop watching you because you weren't drinking. Everyone at the table was enjoying the best champagne from your father's vineyard, but you kept rejecting it. You didn't even take a single sip. Is everything all right?"

My heart felt as if it had stopped beating inside my chest. I splayed a hand gently across my stomach, and could have sworn I heard his breath hitch.

His gaze went to my stomach and remained on it.

It became almost too excruciating to breathe.

"You do know that inside, I'm slowly crumbling into pieces, right?" he asked softly.

"What?"

His blue eyes were sparkling. He rolled me to my side on the bed. Then he vaulted off the bed.

I stared at him in shock as he started pacing the floor. Then he strode over to me and picked me up twirling me around and around the room while I squealed. "I love you, Sienna," he said. "I love you. I love you. I love you. And you've made me the happiest man in the universe!"

"So, you're happy?"

"What do you think?"

"I think you're happy."

"Right now, I feel as if I could cross a sea, jump a mountain, reach out and touch the stars. I would get the moon for you if I could. I think I'd do absolutely anything for you."

"I see. Hmmm … Did I fall in the water, or did I dive in?"

He looked at me with mock solemnity. "You dove in."

I hit him then.

And he laughed.

The sound filled my soul. Pure joy filled me. Inside my body, even the minute growing life must have known how happy it had made us.

As time went on, I'd probably start to believe I dove in after him too, because I wouldn't be able to remember a time when I didn't want him.

He was my life, my love, my everything.

The End

COMING SOON...

BEAUTY & THE BEAST

Luca

It was a beautiful night, but I didn't notice. I never noticed things like that anymore. I had no time for it. Lately, I'd even lost interest in women. Sure, I slept with them, but I kept it as anonymous as possible. They were bodies I pumped into and discarded in hotel rooms after I'd satisfied my needs. Every one of them was picked for her beauty and nothing more. Sometimes when they began to talk I had to bite back the desire to tell them to shut the fuck up.

Sometimes I looked in the mirror and I couldn't recognize the cold, heartless monster I saw. His eyes were like morgues filled with the frozen bodies of all the men he'd put to death.

I had become my father.

He was a great dad to my brother and I, but you couldn't run a business like ours and be anything else. It was a ruthless business. You have to be prepared at all times to kill or be killed.

From where I was sitting in the summer house, I could hear the sounds of the party floating from the big house. It was a boring gathering of low-lives and their broads. I didn't even know why I came. This had stopped being my scene a long time ago. After this cigarette, I planned on leaving through a garden gate I'd noticed on my way out here.

I put out the cigarette under my heel, and as I lifted my head I saw a woman in a white, short dress heading towards the summerhouse. Something about the way she moved made me watch her. Even in the darkness I could tell she was very young. Early twenties, perhaps. Her hair was blonde and she had incredible legs. Long and shapely. As she opened the door of the summerhouse I caught a glimpse of her mouth. It was the sexiest thing I'd ever seen.

My cock stirred. It wanted to be in that mouth.

She closed the door and leaned against it. Quickly, she pulled a phone out of her purse.

"Mariam," she said urgently. "Is Dad okay?"

She listened to the reply and almost sagged with relief.

"Thank God. It was just a false alarm, then."

In the darkness, I could make out her head nodding to whatever was being said to her.

"Me? I'm fine. Of course, I'm fine. Is it okay if I come around to see him tomorrow?"

There was quiet as she listened, then she said. "Yes, five o'clock is fine. Please tell him I love him very much."

She ended the call suddenly, just as a small, choking sob escaped out of her. She pressed her hand to her mouth as if to stop more from coming out. With great interest I watched her take deep breaths to calm herself down.

"It's going to be okay," she whispered to herself. "Everything is going to be just fine."

From far away a man's voice called out and she froze. Her whole body went still. The man's voice came closer still. From my position by the window I could see him coming towards us. It was too dark to make him out properly, but I thought I recognized his voice.

"Skye," he called.

She opened the door and went out. "I'm here."

"What are you doing there?" he asked.

"Nothing. Just wanted to take a break from the noise."

"Come back to the party. I'm missing you."

She didn't answer.

They started walking towards the house together. He had his arm around her waist. As I watched he let it drop down to her butt, then grabbed it roughly. She did nothing.

Inside me something came alive. Like a reptile that had been slumbering for many, many years. It opened its eyes, scented prey nearby, and began to move its cold-blooded body towards the warm, breathing thing. It remembered it had eaten for a long time. And it was hungry. Very, very hungry.

I uncoiled myself from the rattan chair I was sitting on, and sauntering towards the party.

I was no hurry.

I knew exactly who the man was and exactly how to handle a man like him.

Pre-order here:
Beauty & The Beast

ABOUT THE AUTHOR

Thank you so much for reading my book. Might you be
thinking of leaving a review? :-)
Please do it here:

Bodyguard Beast

Please click on this link to receive news of my latest releases
and great giveaways.
http://bit.ly/10e9WdE

and remember
I **LOVE** hearing from readers so by all means come and say
hello here:

A Kiss Stolen

Can't Let Her Go

Highest Bidder

Saving Della Ray

Nice Day For A White Wedding

With This Ring

With This Secret

Saint & Sinner

Printed in Great Britain
by Amazon

26469693R00191